VULGARITY
FOR THE MASSES

J.S. Lawhead

Burning Bulb
PUBLISHING

Vulgarity for the Masses
By **J.S. Lawhead**

Burning Bulb Publishing
P.O. Box 4721
Bridgeport, WV 26330-4721
www.BurningBulbPublishing.com

PUBLISHER'S NOTE: This book is a work of fiction. Names, characters, places, and incidents are either the product of the author's imagination or are used fictitiously, and any resemblance to actual persons, living or dead, events, or locales is purely coincidental.

First printing.

Edition ISBN

   Paperback 978-0615529547

First edition.
Printed in the United States of America.

Library of Congress Control Number: 2011937186

Dedicated to Jessica Arnold.

Introduction

J.S. Lawhead is a child of the mystic Smoky Mountains in East Tennessee; where magick and logick often collide behind shadows left by the Einherjar, ghosts rise above the waters and mists to further dull the grey air, and the fabric that separates life and death between dreams is camouflaged as the seasonal mountain canopy of nature. It is an excellent environment to foster the concepts in this book and is recommended to all.

He is a practicing Lutheran, lives with a wife and a moderately extended family, dives off the deep end to get shit done and occasionally releases music under the name 12 Followers/Meteo Xavier. Born in 1984 and completely ignorant of his blood type. Is currently confident the reader has all the information he or she needs to know on the subject of J.S. Lawhead.

The Whale Story

Oh, God, no...

Meteo Xavier.

A man whom God had cast out of heaven and hell onto Earth.

A man whose very name inspires fear and mortal bedwetting across the Texas Panhandle.

A man who turns slack-jawed ignorance into atomic genocide.

A man whose very image inspires face-palm in every culture across the divided world.

A man for whom no level of tolerance could ever be held.

A man who has been rotting away at mankind's will to live with bountiful, bouncy dementia since the days of Eisenhower.

A man who has balanced both life and death atop his Macedonian genitals.

A man who was once classified as prime rib striplets by the FDSA as part of a failed peace treaty with Hizbul Mujahedeen.

A man whose thought processes enter space and destroy entire worlds that haven't even been born yet.

A man for whom the laws of nature are simply shitting themselves in fear trying to accommodate.

A man that, for all intents and purposes, *should have been killed hundreds of times by now,* has been released *once again* into polite society to start a new adventure!

Today he is going to accomplish something no mentally capable human being would ever try to do.

Ride the rare *Blue Whale*!

The blue whale, spotted several months ago by scientists of the *Northern Pacific Oceanography Consult* of Seattle, is the Marlon Brando of the ocean blue - it is elusive, weighs thirty-four tons and has sex with anything in its immediate vicinity. All of the ecosystem below the waves bow down to their king; even the Kraken knows its place in the presence of its sovereign - usually bent over a coral reef with its tentacles pulled back and learning through its rectum why he's called a "sperm" whale. The beast has never been tamed by God or man. In the olden days of yore, the Blue Whale could ingest a full supply ship on its way to Rome and whatever it regurgitated washed up on shore and became cheap housing for beach-dwelling gypsies in southern France and Italy. It could create giant vacuums or hurricanes with its flow of breath and when it would come up to breathe, its lust for life was so great that it would jump hundreds of yards into the air and create tidal waves that would end an entire civilization. It is, after all, historical fact that many of our greatest cities, histories, accomplishments and technologies have all become ocean floor clusterfuck thanks to the mighty prowess of the rare Blue Whale.

The Blue Whale symbolizes all the majesty and horror of the natural world. It is the greatest evolution of existence on the planet. *The Darwin Icon*. The mightiest beast in all of God's creation!

This is going to be a challenge, but Meteo is an idiot. He is far too ignorant to understand fear or common sense and, thus, the obstacles that would prevent any other man on Earth, even serial killers lost in fantasy, flat-earth society members and 9/11 conspiracy theorists, will have no effect on him in his pursuit to ride the rare Blue Whale!

He took his fastest boat - a downed helicopter with an oil leak through the windshield, carrying anchors for some God-forsaken reason, and scoured the seas to find the beast.

Days went by. Meteo searched miles and miles for hours into weeks only to come up with nothing. Neither a scratch nor a clue, neither a sliver nor hair, nothing even halfway resembling the largest mammal in the galaxy throughout all the ocean. Meteo searched for days still, through heartbreaking nothingness of the sea, through storms and epic god battles with Poseidon himself, through pirates and pilots and Pontius Pilate doing Pilates in a pickle pie pink parka off the Pacific Rim, but nothing brought him closer to his goal. Meteo survived on a steady diet of himself and slept in the spacious four bedroom condominium and mountaintop resort center that was kept in the back of the helicopter for emergencies. He did well enough, but how long could a man survive on self-cannibalism in a four bedroom condo?

Finally, at the crack of dawn one day, after wasting years of taxpayers' money, he spotted the mighty Blue Whale circling the Queen Elizabeth Islands of Antarctica and basking in the glow of its own filth. Meteo took the helm and piloted his vessel slowly and carefully around the backside of the creature so as not to startle it. He crept up close to the beast's starboard abdomen and tossed a hook high into the cavernous blowhole.

Success!

Meteo reared back and ducked down as he prepared for a thrashing reprisal, but there was no reaction from the beast at all. He jerked the rope once. No reaction still... Meteo put both hands on the rope now and strongly jerked it several times with great strain and endless, thankless effort. It was not unlike the hand job he had to give Roger Waters to stop him from making solo albums in a bid to save Montreal (now there's a story with no winner). Still there was no reaction. Perhaps all was well here? Was it resisting fighting back?

Meteo climbed the rope until he reached the top of the beast and made such a clamor that no living thing could possibly ignore. The whale moaned low for a solid minute before pitching its multiple-voice higher up to indicate a playful mood and the positive acceptance of its new guest. The beast was game for a ride! What luck! A mammoth figure with as much hunger for adventure as the great Meteo Xavier! The great and hungry adventurer gracefully removed the hook from his newfound playmate and the two dashed off across the seas! To ride like the wind! To stop for nothing - not even land!

The two came ashore and swam through thick farms and bounced across busy highways parallel to major roads like ping-pong balls all across the continental states of united America. From that inhuman carnage, they crashed through the urban jungles of Boston, Atlanta, Georgia, Los Angeles, Philadelphia, Knoxville, Grand Rapids, Dallas, Milwaukee, Munich, Detroit and Chicago. Meteo saddled the whale and threw his hat into the air like a crazed midnight cowboy as he and a large aquatic animal plowed right through the middle of the Sears Tower and brought the entire borough of Chicago down to the flaming caverns of hell underneath it. Not a single survivor had a full cecum or a home to go back to that day, it must be said, and soon it was back to destruction on the high seas as they laid waste to Portland, Oregon, having literally caused them to drown in a shit-storm.

Meteo and his new friend rode for days into weeks. This grand adventure was just what Meteo needed to quit his obsession with Jodie Foster's concave boobs. Ah, he had never felt so free, so happy and so jubilant - especially with such a unique new playmate! Never once in the history of man has the union of beast and blubber been so perfect; the bond between them idyllic and blessed by the living Lord who smiled on them from on high. They shared stories of action, adventure, sexual misconduct and minorities from every generation of contemporary history. They traded recipes and nodes of immediate wisdom brought on by laughter and tears. They both opened up to one another about their joys, beliefs, concerns and fears; as though they were both doctors knowing full well they were just patients. Both shared a mutual respect for the guru Peter Gabriel and love for the Christ Jesus. Immaculate. Some people would say such a relationship could never happen in this modern, go-go world of industry, entertainment and hysterical pregnancy; but, then again, these are the sort of people that touch themselves at night with poison cattle prods watching illegal videos of lizard-tailed, bifurcated Siamese Asian orphans giving Martin Luther King Jr. a lap dance during his assassination. No, these wild mammals were the perfect match for each other. Soul mates, *Moiré Te deis* (which is poor French for a pregnant nun) and, thus, buddies.

But after a week of bonding and illegal medical practitioning, the beast stopped very short and very, very suddenly; throwing Meteo off into the deep blue like Meteo thrown off a blue whale into the deep blue like Meteo thrown off a deep blue whale into the blue. He hit head first with a viewtiful splash into the arctic sea of ice and, while getting only mildly damp, he cursed the beast with words not suited for this world. As the beast was stunned and seemingly shocked by something, whatever loose and random synapses formed the makeshift central nervous system in Meteo Xavier's dick compiled and concluded that something was wrong. He apologized to his new best friend in the entire world and decided to find out why the beast had stopped so abruptly.

Meteo sunk down into the cold, dry waters under the whale until he came to the source of the beast's sudden vexation and, to his disgust, discovered the problem.

The whale had, at some point as they drew near to the area, been immediately sexually assaulted... *with a chainsaw.*

So the beast *is* female, Meteo thought. That would explain why she just wouldn't shut the fuck up about tampons already. Hoarding blood-soaked cunt sponges was one thing, but this was no time to think about breakfast. The very idea of a whale mating with an inexplicably placed and rusted chainsaw sent shivers down an already frozen spine - suppose this item carried with it some sort of genetic code meant to spawn repercussions of itself inside the doomed womb of the innocent?

Imagine... a cross-breed of *chainsaw whales*... destroying the aquatic atmosphere without prejudice; making the swordfish look like an impotent bitch; uprooting and devouring harbors with the simple erection; penis torpedoes raining havoc on Pearl Harbor; evaporating the vampire race as we know it! Ending the golden age of Web 2.0 and ushering in the dark age of Web 3.0! Good God! The Blue Whale was a dangerous fellow already, but this would be an eldritch apocalypse - a satyr play written by the masturbating chimerical fusion of John Waters, Richard Elfman, Ingrid Newkirk, David Murray Brockie, Lily Braun, Georg Christoph Licthenberg, Leroy Jenkins, King Ludwig II of Bavaria, Bugs Bunny and Justin Bieber. The image the human mind would associate with that *alone* is enough to earn humanity the righteous, fatal ass-pounding it is now dangerously close to receiving. Sweet Judas, this must stop immediately!

Meteo took it upon himself to remove the device and save mankind from another potential disaster showcasing a dumb animal mating with a power tool. With the frozen waters solidifying vaginal lips (thank you, Jonathan), Meteo put both hands on the offending industrial effigy and pulled with all his might. He pulled and pulled - until Hercules wept in pain just watching the daffy do-gooder pop every muscle in his body in competition with the laws of nature and coital engineering logistics. This is was not unlike the hand job Meteo had to perform on Roger Waters (so many babies died... yet he unfortunately survived). He would not let that happen again! Meteo pulled like fourteen horses in heat and slowly the chainsaw was exiting its self-invited party. More and more... c'mon, Meteo, you can do it!

Success!

The foul instrument was removed safely and securely. What an enormous relief! The people of the world could exhale their bated breath knowing apocalypse had been delayed once again thanks to the mindless, indescribable efforts of young Meteo Xavier! He took the chainsaw in hand and surfaced to continue the ride...

Until he caught in his sight three hundred Coast Guard agents who had appeared, seemingly out of the blue and armed with guns, knives and launchers of all kinds, surrounding him for arrest.

Surfacing with chainsaw in hand left little to their imaginations as to what he could be guilty of, and, well, no bible verse he could throw at them could stop them from hauling his ass to jail straight from the ocean. There he would spend the night in a cell with a transsexual hooker of whose original gender and subsequent transformation were impossible to ascertain.

The next morning, after an uncomfortable scenario generously referred to as *The Crying Game Parts II and III,* Meteo was rolled up and packaged into a tube of toothpaste and transported across the desert to *District Court.*

The most feared of all courts.

Meteo heard stories of this place; often with ejaculatory endings and bridges and all of them could curl a man's teeth into fingernails and paint those fingernails with a pasty concoction of blood, feces, and cholesterol. This was a place where Murphy's Law was a living being of fangs and skin and blood so hot it could freeze molten lava in our sensitive plane of existence. It was a monster beyond all monsters and its jaws sweated at the savory image of clamping down on Meteo Xavier's private parts until the end of time. Meteo's fate was in jeopardy; not for the first time, but almost definitely for the last.

Despite all that, Meteo was not going to give in to bizarre circumstantial occurrences. He was going to fight the system tooth and nail, like a ten-foot-long Bruce Lee, until the system, in his words, "[...] got down on its knees and gave me a *Missouri rim job...*" and by that, he means the system will beg for forgiveness.

Armed with a stunning, sharp blue suit that was passed down to every man in the family, starting with the patriarch, Abraham, the man who fathered many nations despite constant promises that those nations were on the pill, a cunning sadistic attitude (Abraham again), and the kind of animal magnetism that make men infertile and women explode into pregnancy by the mere twitching of his lustful brow (from his mother), he was ready to take on his next greatest challenge:

The District Judge.

The Honorable *Marshall Anus.*

A being of unfathomable girth and evil, Anus would have had the power to condemn the devil himself if the devil wasn't the Judge's personal au pair and German-bred sex slave. He was a fearsome demon; a godless blob of rotting flesh that made Jabba the Hut look like Tim Burton. No man, woman or God had ever crossed Marshall Anus and lived to tell about it. The Honorable Judge, rumored to be the hell spawn from the world's only sodomic pregnancy (another inadvertent reference to Roger Waters), does not kill his victims; preferring them instead to live and spend each of their wretched, crestfallen hours wishing for sweet, disfiguring, horrible all-purpose death; rendering mortality infinitely soaked in woe. The Honorable Judge sends people to the darkest depths of their souls the way most men expel a bodily fluid into the pretty face of the prom queen. He takes his razor-sharp fingers, grabs both sides of your penis (or *mangina*, as it were) and tears it open like a slice of bread to turn you inside out so that your inner darkness would scald the sewn flesh of your body while the sinews would burn and flap against what's left of your skin like flaming whips on a helicopter rotation piloted by Satan's yeast infection.

Amen.

Ordinary criminals, when confronted with the task of judicial appraisal with this megalithic crone, often take their own lives knowing the alternative is far, far worse. The honorable, almighty, everlasting blight of the Judge has butchered, slaughtered, and processed criminals of royal and commoner blood into food for the denizens of Hell for thousands of years... and now the legendary Meteo Xavier was next. What cruelty is the cumstain of fate!

But Meteo Xavier is no ordinary man; he is, as was stated before, an idiot, and unable to be restricted by fear, apprehension, or any kind of cumbersome thought producing mentality ever recorded in psychological science. Meteo had conflicted with incredible evil before and every single time had come out on top; from the *Pygmy Yetis* to the *Electrophile Pigeons*; from the possessed *Hitler Cow* to the bowel hungry *Rasputin Worm*; Roger Waters, Elton John, Bob Geldof, Chet Atkins, Garth Brooks and his pansy alterna-clone Chris Gaines, Trent Reznor, Jerry Lewis, Jackie Gleason, Horatio Sanz, whoever the hell that guy is that plays the drums for U2... *no* evil has ever been too great for Meteo Xavier to overcome. If he could take out Freddie Mercury and convince the world he was not assassinated for secretly using his rock personality to fund communist terrorism in China and the U.S.S.R[2], then certainly this was possible to get through.

This was going to be a clash of the *Titans* and who would win?

Playboy protagonist or antichrist antagonist?

****

When the sun rose the next morning... it actually didn't. It was 10:00 AM the next morning when Meteo was escorted via Aquafresh to the courtroom and it was still night outside. This was not a good sign, but Meteo stayed vigilant. As the trial to end all trials began, he waited patiently in the tiny little defendant box while millions watched from the stands of the district court room. Millions more observed from the supposed safety of their television as camera crews from every corner of the world, including Uganda which had just now discovered the concept of "video", set up innumerate press tables and coverage space to capture every moment of what would very well be the last moments of recorded time. The press was releasing up to minute news for the controversy-hungry public who, by this point, had stayed up late at night masturbating to the dream of Meteo Xavier being removed from the *Book of Life* once and for all. A lifetime of eternal darkness was an easy choice compared to a world full of Meteo Xavier. This was the day they had waited for for years and years. It was finally going to happen.

Meteo stood tall, defiant and confident, but even he still felt the sting of fear and sexual repression.

Clang!

Meteo's pants were soaked upon that disturbance. It was the funeral bell and it was the announcing sound that the District Court Judge had arrived.

Just then, a cloud of black smoke filled the air and the foulest smell to ever pervade the senses overwhelmed the audience. The stench made an outline and soon filled with color, or whatever one could call it, until a form could be reached. This form then expanded outward into the third dimension the same way the Huns expanded their reach from Germany to the Ural River and the Baltic Sea, with eerily similar consequences, and gave rueful shape to deeply unpleasant form. Marshall Anus was here and he was going to begin.

The two combatants were now ready to square off.

"Meteo Xavier!" The judge shouted with all his might; commanding him and the entire audience to stand up in his reverence. The Judge also stood up and towered over even the building itself like the forgotten prototype of Cthulu he was. "Today is the last day of your miserable life! Today, the people of the Earth sleep soundly knowing that the disease that plagues and destroys society will be brought to justice. Today, everything that there ever was about you comes to a screeching halt over your sun-baked carcass! You are a profane individual, Meteo Xavier; a filthy heathen of gastronomical proportions that the stars themselves refuse to align in their recognition of you! Your contributions to the suffering and demise of humanity will not be tolerated any further and I will see to it, sir, that you never receive positive stimulus as long as you exist; which I will *additionally* see to will forever be. Have you anything to say in your defense before we begin?"

Meteo stood up; his sharp blue suit cutting through the spectrum of light like a hot jizz laser on some old woman's hot dog.

"Strange as it may sound, you bastard son of a goat," He said slowly, surely and confidently, "but you said every word in perfect sequence of what it was I was going to say to you, you intumescent sack of shit. As far as my defense is concerned..." Meteo then turned around, pulled down his pants, bent over so all the world could see inside his alveolated posterior and mooned the judge while whistling "God Bless America" through his tone-deaf rectum.

"Care to sing along, Judge?"

He would not. The Judge was furious and the audience was beyond astounded at the incredible display of defiance. Anus quickly tried to regain himself and continue the trial.

"*Where is your defense attorney!?*" screamed the Judge Anus, as though he were preaching to deaf sinners.

Meteo responded without fear, "I will represent my own defense."

The judge erupted in laughter and the scared flock of sheep that represented an audience followed suit. "They say a man who represents himself has a fool for a client!"

Meteo spat in the judge's general direction; hitting the cute lady who does the typing and thus impregnating her. That was his response.

The Judge grimaced and shouted with all his might: "*Where is the prosecutor!?*"

"M'lud....." started Meteo; raising an eyebrow to the aging fart. "I shall also act as my own prosecutor!"

The courtroom exploded into activity upon those words. Women fainted and went right into labor as flames burst from their birth canals into the streets for all to swallow unto their journeys through the river Styx. The scorching placentas that leaked out from there formed a political party near the jury box and marched on the streets of Washington confusing and then converting hundreds of people. The Judge himself looked like he was about to have a baby right there on the courtroom floor.

"Are you *serious?*" the words crept out of the Judge's lips.

Meteo nodded. "Read me my charges, impotent pedophile!"

While the audience moaned and winced collectively in pain, the judge smiled, farted gasoline, and prepared to do exactly that.

"*Very well!* Let it be known, Meteo Xavier, that you are charged with the following heinous acts:

* Illegal activity involving endangered animals.
* Use of an illegal and dangerous device.
* Blatant disregard for safety; your safety and the safety of the whale.
* Obstruction of justice.
* Satire of justice.
* Harassment of justice.
* Harassment towards inanimate objects.
* Petty larceny.
* Petty homicide.
* Pretty homicide.
* Ugly homicide.
* Impersonating a police officer.
* Impersonating a prostitute and *then* impersonating the two involved in public sexual activity with a senior official.
* Impersonating inanimate objects.
* Petty prostitution.
* Pretty prostitution.
* Ugly prostitution.
* Assaulting a police officer..."

Meteo interrupted, "Your Honor, if you can even be called that, the police officer I assaulted was in fact me as I was impersonating a police officer, as I impersonated the prostitute, and then proceeded to impersonate both figures at the same time as we were sexually involved with the senior official; of whom I was also impersonating."

The courtroom groaned in unison and the judge continued on secretly hoping God would interfere and strike Meteo down.

*...assaulting a district prostitute.
* Driving a commercial airplane without a license.
* Assaulting a commercial airplane.

* Assaulting a commercial airplane with a district prostitute.
* Possession of underage firearms.
* Possession of mind-altering documents.
* Abusing your right to incriminate yourself at every single fucking opportunity.
* Illegal U-turns on the roof of the Parthenon.
* $34,509 in traffic violations.
* Reckless jogging.

"You don't own a single valid I.D. or proof of American citizenship *and* we found what you keep in your sock drawer...!" He removed his glasses and spit a black substance from his mouth, "How you kept from spontaneously exploding by the heat of your sins is a question mankind will never answer."

"Well, we don't know why a fat fucker like you won't just give up and die in the face of someone as gorgeous and suave as I am... so let's keep it at that!"

Again the courtroom groaned at Meteo's insane defiance of forces no man could comprehend and many died in shame.

So the trial went on; Meteo defending and prosecuting himself for weeks and weeks on end while spectators wept in sorrow. He produced and refuted evidential item after evidential item - including those that would have solved other cases which he then destroyed inside the crotch of his pants. He acted as his own witness which lead him to badger said witness and forced him to cry before he invited himself for drinks and sex after the proceedings for the day; of which Meteo then threatened to sue and used the entire court as a witness who he then forced to sign witness testimony papers and waivers for future car insurance purchases. The jury was so confused they didn't know what to think and many left sighting uncontrollable bowel movements and generative death resulting directly from Meteo Xavier - which was nothing compared to the effects the trial and his behavior were having on the world at large as people left and right were breaking their mouths like fine porcelain china from their jaws hitting the floor every hour of every day. For every idiotic, naked pelvic gesture Meteo Xavier thrust onto the cameras to illustrate his innocence, stock prices fell through the roof, gas prices tripled instantaneously and people drove themselves off bridges. Levees broke and the flood waters came in to drown the cities of America for his irreverence. For every stupid, fake Spanish sentence that came out of the defendant's mouth, an angel lost its wings, shaved a kitten with scissors, and stuck it up the butt of a passerby. The rate of people in the world who suffered from rectal feline molestation jumped from 1% to 88% overnight. Whole kingdoms fell in the wake of Meteo Xavier's defensive-prosecutive process.

The Judge was livid as hell and tried every vile thing known to God to annihilate every atom of his annoying, annoying, *annoying* defendant and all to no avail. Finally, as things looked grim for Meteo, he was able to bring up the *Killer Whale Preservation Act* of 1984 and threw the courtroom into a mad circus of stupor fury.

"*Enough of this!*" screamed the judge as fountains of human waste poured from his mouth, "What the fuck is the *meaning* of this!? What do you hope to accomplish with this unending wormhole coda of absurdity!?"

"I am going to prove myself innocent, you whore!"

Meteo's brash attitude had sent Marshall Anus over the edge.

"*Who are you to be so bold!?*" screamed a frantic District Judge.

Meteo stamped his foot on the ground and looked the Judge square in the eye. "I am Meteo Xavier!" he shouted back. "I wear bold like a *condom!*"

And with those words, the most defiant words a man could ever scream in the face of such evil, Meteo Xavier had done that which even now was still unthinkable.

That was it.

That was the final straw.

The earth cracked open and released that which is unspeakable from the flames of Hell onto the living Earth and every man, woman and child who dared to be born. The Judge's head turned black and started screaming and screaming until it levitated off his neck and began spinning wildly with the sonic disturbance of his voice eradicating solid material objects and people for miles around. The lights illuminating the structure began flickering wildly and forming vague silhouettes of spirits and damned souls on the ceiling. Rivers of blood poured from the walls of the courtroom while the desperate audience sacrificed themselves to God in hopes of escaping the cataclysmic horror. No such luck. It was supernal martial law now. Panic-stricken citizens filled the streets engaging in mass love-making and oily, droopy orgy with whoever and whatever warm body they were lying on top of and running for their lives as chaos reigned high. Whole cities disintegrated in the flash of unholy light, and when the eye blinked, there was nothing left.

There it was, Meteo. The end of the rainbow. The death of the Mana Tree. It was the death of civilization as we knew it.

At the brief pause in time before the events recorded above and the events described below, Meteo was able to rekindle his youth in great melancholy detail. He remembered, as a boy, wondering how he was going to die; always hoping it would be while saving the world from evil or something heroic just as his father and grandfather did before him... It was Meteo's dream to fall with the paladin lineage that his family always lived by. He was never going to die as long as there was evil in the world.

That was his dream.

But Meteo had to face the music now. His paladin lineage was about to be cut short due to an Anus. It was a sad way to go... and he could do nothing but his best and pray to God for forgiveness. Meteo was a *man* and he had to face death like one.

"*Meteo Xavier!*" said the Judge, literally fucking with rage. "I am ready to pass judgment! In the thousands of years I have put stained individuals like yourself away, never have I seen anything like you. You have plagued, ridiculed and sexually molested the things that build a good, proper society for *much, much, much, much too long!* You are the decay of mankind, Meteo; a senseless dung beetle that wallows in filth while you destroy the backbone of the things holding humanity together: ethics, morals... common sense! Nothing is safe from your corruption and now you will be *punished!* Hell is not good enough for you, but it's all we can hope for! You are looking into a *saaaaaaaaaaaaaaad* future, you little bastard!"

Meteo hung his head in defeat and waited for the sentence to be read.

"For the good of people everywhere; for need to heal society; for the command of God to rid the evil of this world... Meteo Xavier, I hereby sentence you to....."

And just then, the walls of the courtroom burst down and the few remaining survivors watched in horrific disbelief as the Blue Whale herself broke through the courtroom walls in its ultimate triumph of nature against man. Despite being thousands of miles from a body of water that can sustain the largest animal on Earth, she was enraged at the sight of her friend being tortured by the system... and now there would be *blood to pay!*

"Kill that whale!" screamed the Judge, but then the beast rushed forward and no guard, after the horrors they experienced in this court, would dare tempt their luck fighting a whale. The Blue Whale stood up, a half-mile tall into the air, and now it was the judge that was being towered over. As she glowered down at the foul Judge, it became clear that no matter how girthsome and loathsome he was, no beast of Earth or Hell was a match for the Blue Whale. Marshall Anus had been killing people for hundreds of years... the Blue Whale had been eradicating man for *thousands.* She was a fucking force of nature and even evil was subject to nature!

As the crumbling, crumpled world watched on TV or right in front of them, as it were, they gasped as they watched the Blue Whale's vaginal canal open wide like the doors of doom colliding with stars across the galaxy and devoured the subjected beast in an unprecedented carnivorous carnality. The District Judge Marshall Anus screamed his last as the behemoth of the ocean came down on him and absorbed him like a human tampon. *Moiré Te Deis.* Ashes to ashes... Anus to dust.

Immaculate.

The Blue Whale jumped off toward the ocean with Meteo Xavier waving goodbye in the increasing distance to the new horizon appearing from the former penumbra of darkness that was lifting with Marshall Anus' influence leaving the world. "Farewell, my good friend!" Meteo called as he dropped his arm and looked around him in the carnage that was once a planet he called home. He picked up the jacket part of his sharp blue suit, smiled at the shared victory between two best friends across borders and headed toward the door - which was now understood to be a giant gaping hole in what used to be a wall caked with blood and marrow.

"That was pretty bold, Meteo..." said one of the bodies just before it died.

"Yep..." Meteo smiled at him. "Bold like a condom, baby..."

The body smiled back and passed shortly after that. Meteo made the sign of the cross on his forehead, said a short a prayer, and continued on his way back home.

On a Sunday Afternoon - This Happened

It was 1:32 PM on a Sunday afternoon, in the Summer of 1987, in the year of our Lord, 2009 *Anno Domini*, when professional elementary school dropout and teacher Mr. A. F. Packard McDonough walked toward the *First United Methodist Bank* on Asstits Avenue with a brown leather-bound briefcase in both hands and dressed in the finest threads that a meth-addict on speed could find in the middle of the road. His name was something he invented on the ride over; his real name having been sold for drug money the week before. The week before that he had run into trouble with an old friend and mentor who ran the drug cartels of the Northern Hemisphere - having blown through enough blow to literally shit bricks of cocaine that were *supposed* to be headed to the inner circles and distributions of Thailand did not sit well with said mentor. "A colon with a street value of $874,000..." he explained, "...is worth quite a bit more than that on the black market, I can assure you. So if you don't get me the money you owe me, motherfucker, I'll be taking that instead. Whatever's left over will be used to pay my boy Jules here to beat your colon-less, bloodied ass all over your daddy's grave. Now quit humping that reindeer and get your fucking ass out on the street! Now!"

A colon-less ass is never any man's destiny, and the two weeks the recently affirmed A. F. Packard had to come up with the money was spent tripping to the sounds of Timothy Leary singing *Dark Side of the Moon* to a congregation of headless children on a field trip to the Stretch Armstrong Nazi Museum of Shangri-La,

North Dakota. There were all kinds of colors and lights and music and fun and talking double-insects and naked proselytizing, but unfortunately all the money he won in the Smurf lottery during a bender inside a psilocybin lab at John Hopkins was immaterial because of his tax status and because none of it was really real. Sunday was the last day to recover *real* money. Sunday was going to be a seismic event in his history; sharply dividing everything that came before and everything that will come after with a jagged, black, colon-shaped scar.

This had to work, dammit!

"*I'm not pooping through a machine!*" he screamed until he realized all the people he was talking to were just acid flashbacks that had nothing to offer him in the real world.

The stairs were the first issue for this opiate-addict on crack. "Why were there so many damn steps!? What kind of a bank is this!?" he thought he screamed but actually never made the sounds to produce words, "There's one... two... three... four... five... *six!?* Who the hell builds six steps in America!? No wonder the stock market's plugging up the toilets, there's too many fuckin' steps everywhere! *God Bless America*, how are people supposed to *get* anywhere with their money when there's just so many damn steps everywhere!? Oh, sweet Lord, I think I saw a seventh step! Shit! I'm in over my head! I'm drowning! Help!" He tried in vain to accomplish the pernicious spire of the seventh step, but instead his knees turned to sand and he fell down, down, down... deep into the desert that was born of his crumbled knee cap.

And from there he wandered for forty years through the silent desert of eternal death. The Hebrews that had followed him all perished cursing his name and now it was his turn to do the same. "Water..." he choked out. "Water! Water!" and he collapsed in the desert dune with a buzzard nipping at his ass. The sun bore down hard on him and only the cactus would be able to mourn this poor boy and mark his grave. The rest would soon be collected by the buzzards and the sand leeches if the coming hurricanes didn't erode his miserable corpse first.

"Waterrrrrrrrrrrr..." he choked out once more before he passed out forever in the Sahara.

Wendy, the loan officer, whose desk was facing the glass door, motioned for her boss to come forward.

"Keith, there's an alcoholic on the rag outside who just dove headfirst into the koi pond. Should I call the police?"

The man who called himself Keith, but was actually an assumed identity to hide his multiple sex offender status, rubbed his hairless chin and threaded his beard for a minute before answering her. He was actually just undressing her with his eyes and dreaming about making an erotic, body-sized club sandwich out of her zooming, buxom figure, but eventually just said, "Nah, it's Sunday, the police station isn't open. Just let me handle this," so he'd have a reason to leave before she noticed his boner. Keith, a boy in his mid-50s with silver hair and a fair brown suit that all executives with his confidence and swagger obtain at gold-level management with the parent company at *Our Savior Lutheran Savings and Loan LLC*, strode proud as a toad to take this young dipshit's money on such a fine day. Sunday business he could write off in this district's financial regulations and could therefore easily embezzle into secret grocery bills filled with mysterious giant, human-sized sandwich items. He opened the door gingerly, as he was a ginger, and prepared to coach the man to save himself from self-drowning.

"Y'alright there, young man?"

And the boy with the briefcase splashed up from the depths of oblivion.

"He's alive! Yay!" Keith clapped.

"Ohhh, I'm sorry man... I dreamt I was lost in the tundra... and I was visiting Santa Claus... in the North Pole... He was going to sell me a dime bag of *red ochre corridor* and *green leaf ganja* that's put together for a Christmas motif... and you... you... smoke it through a candy-cane..."

"That's perfectly fine. Is there something I can help you with?"

"Yeah, man, I need to get to the bank... can you give me a ride?"

Keith's smile did not diminish; he simply cocked his head to the right, used the minimal requirement of motions to open the door and swung his free hand to make the ushering sign of "go on it."

"Here we are!"

"Ahh, thanks man!" the dumb fuck actually walked forward and somehow fell back into the koi pond again. "Blah! Hey, I appreciate that, man. Hey, I never forget a favor, man. If you ever want to hang out some time; smoke some bud or shit, just call me up man." He continued to struggle with his feet underwater. "I don't have a phone right now, but just call me up. They know me down there, man. They'll tell you how to get a hold of me... arggh!"

Somewhere in the neighborhood of five minutes later, the soaking boy that was now more water than man splashed his way through the door and to the cashier's table, which he mistook as the world's biggest brownie, and started to eat it. Blood and teeth and woodchips flew like the Kentucky County Fair, and when he was done he stood up on his hind legs and let out a fiendish howl to the moon. He had a blank stare in his eyes; so much so that the cashier, Kristin, wondered if he was blind... at least until he opened his mouth again.

"...you got *booooobbbbbbssssss*..."

"Thank you, sir, I agree. What can we help you with today?" she said with a chirpy voice.

"Uhhh... My name is *Skibby-Z*. I'm O.G., yo. I got boys all over the city and hoes all over the world. I'm up east from the *wess-cy-yeed.* I used to be with the Bloods and I once gave a man a *buck-fifty* because he wouldn't give me a buck-fifty. I'm street, yo. Hardcore motherfucker. I got so many baby mamas, I'm a baby grand pappy. Yea. I'm so good-looking, I got arrested in Wisconsin... for being sexy! Unh~! Yeah, you let me work my business, baby. I'll be riding you like John Wayne into the sunset, bitch. I'm wiggity-wiggity wack like that. Word..." and then he threw up a collection of bent fingers which was supposed to be a gang sign but looked more like he was making arthritis shadow puppet kitty cats.

"I believe you. What can I do for you today?" she said; completely ignoring his soliloquy.

Skibby-Z continued to move his mouth like he was talking, but nothing came out except for a vaporous form that smelled like the inside of a car crash. Then he stopped moving his mouth thanks to pharmaceutically-inclined partial paralysis and hung over the cashier's desk with an immobile stare. He was like a wind-up doll that needed some additional twisting.

He didn't move for three whole minutes.

"Did you want to make a deposit?"

"...huh? Oh... uhhh... uhh... no."

"Ok, did you want to withdraw some cash?"

"...yeah."

"Good. Do you have an account with us?"

"...*noooooooooooooooooooooooooooooooooooooooooooo ooooo...*" and some drool, which was at least 89% rubbing alcohol and baby laxative, poured out of his mouth like syrup on pancakes; except syrup doesn't usually drag one or two molars with it on the way down.

"Ok. Would you like to start an account with us?"

"I... I want to take some money out."

"Ok. Do you have an account with us?"

"Yeah... no, wait, I mean no..."

"Ok, Mr. Z. So what can I do for you?" she smiled and flashed her pearly, white teeth as all bank tellers are trained to do under penalty of federal indictment.

"Uhhh..." he thought for a second and nothing came to mind. All his knowledge and mastery of the English language that he had pieced together over the last few months went right out the door. Then he pulled out some paper and started jotting something with the pen. When finished, he stuck it out in her face with a huge sweaty palm soaking it into a transparent mess.

"Just do this..."

Kristin took the yellow scratch paper, which simply was scrawled *"gimme some money"*, and examined it thoroughly.

"...I see. Mr. Z, are you trying to rob us?"

"No... wait... no, I mean, yes."

"Ok, well, we don't do that at this bank." She said and sat back in her chair, smiling those bright, pearly whites and flashing her eyes like an epileptic chipmunk.

"You don't?"

"No sir, we just handle checking deposits and withdrawals, mortgage lending, savings, CDs, retirement accounts - that kinda stuff, we don't do anything like that."

"Oh really? Shit, I'm sorry. Ummm... you know any banks in town that will?"

"Oohhh... umm... today's Sunday... umm... tsssssss... nope, I don't think anyone around does that. You might want to go to *Christ Baptist National Bank*, that's over in Sylvan on I-39."

"Ok, are they open today, do you think?"

"They should be. It's Sunday."

"Ok, cool, thanks, tits." and he reached over the counter to stick his tongue in her mouth. He fell flat on his damn face because his swollen depth perception forgot he was actually twenty feet away from her. After that, he dashed out the door and completely broke his nose as it was not yet opened to allow passage. He then survived another death-defying trip into the koi pond. When Skibby was able to dry himself off, he grabbed and assembled his nuts to get ready to take on Christ Baptist National Bank on I-39.

"But how would I get there?" he asked. He had no car. He had gotten a ride in a car with a stranger who had no face, no legs, and no car. He said his name was the inverse square root of *like I give a fuck* and he was a Scientologist from Utah. He is likely not coming back.

"Oh, great Djinn, master of time and space... come to me in my time of aid!"

The great Djinn of the *Eastern Sphere* materialized instantly. He was a tall Persian of the utmost rotund facilities; a quadrilateral head crowned with a turban made from the skin of King Kamehameha V, a vest that pretty much invented every Middle-Eastern stereotype throughout history, pointed shoes that no conventional feet could possibly taper off to, and slacks from Dockers - brand new and still pressed.

"What is it, son of Man? Has mortal life finally quenched thy thirst to turn on this planet? Art thou prepared to vex thy sting in favor of eternal respite?"

"I need a ride to Sylvan on I-39..."

The Djinn was most displeased. Being the immortal zenith of power for this solar system, his power, as he constantly reminded young Skibby, was not to be used for trifles. Rides across town, tickets to Cypress Hill, and unpregnating women from his venomous seed were *not* acceptable uses of his unending influence on the universe.

"...son of Man, I am immortality incarnate and even I grow deathly ill of thy shenanigans. If thou seekest to impugn the course of fate on this planet so as to tread on the hallowed grounds of I-39, I shall decree the course set before thou though I fear it will lead to an earnest and ignorant death. A point of space may be folded or, more accurately, bent to thy will if the universe

recognizes your power and influence of being. By super-exceeding the kinetic energy of your life force, space may to thy will be bent or likely crush you if your intent is ill. The universe has no forgiveness for beings manipulating its force to selfish quests of glory. Well, son of Man? What say you? Canst thou accomplish this foolish crusade?"

"Psssh..." said the irreverent Skibby and, before the mighty Djinn could respond, the boy lifted his sleeves and shoes and hair follicles and skin folds and nostrils until, there in the midst of the immortal's infinite vision, eyes widened in terror for the first time as an entire Persian desert of cocaine fell in a googolplex of flakes upon the pavement. The Djinn's immaculate vocabulary, for the first time, failed to draw up words as he watched this man snort the entire desert in mere minutes.

The mortal stood up high, elevated off the ground, with sparks shooting from his cocaine-infused white aura. The "light" cresting from his nuclear fusion of life and death tore the universe a new asshole and Skibby, now the youngest god in creation, climbed right up in there as all gods eventually do. *C'est la vie.*

The Djinn stood motionless as the events before him shook his very foundation; the same foundation that the world sits on.

"*...the universe has gone mad...*" he said silently and faded back to his realm.

Elsewhere, the once divine Skibby Z, having traded his godhood in betwixt dimensions to arrive at this point (and a six-pack of acid) at the Christ Baptist National Bank, fell dick-first onto the hard, sun-scorched asphalt of their parking lot. With his suitcase in hand, he charged inside and demanded attention.

"Everybody listen the fuck up!" He screamed at the top of his lungs; waving his briefcase like a madman. "Everybody down on the ground! Get your hands over your head..."

And he stopped. Everyone was already down on the ground; cowering in fear with hands exactly where he instructed them to be. Skibby looked around and saw many bodies flattened to tile and holding their heads as their tear ducts and bowels could no longer contain themselves and painted the floors a brand new and thoroughly unnecessary series of colors. There was only one person standing and it was a figure all in black, holding a gun, and looking at him in bewildered confusion.

It didn't take a stoned fucking idiot to read between the lines on this one...

"Oh shit..." and he ducked for cover as the man opened fire on him. There were six gunshots fired as Skibby scrambled for cover under a series of mahogany desks. After two more shots barely dented the thick, heavy desk, Skibby dashed for a smaller desk of thinner wood. The gunman fired four more shots, some of which dented the desk heavily but still failed to penetrate. Still, bank employees watched, baffled, as the grown man squealed like a tiny piglet feasting on its afterbirth and zipped to an even smaller desk made of imitation wood that did not cover him completely or protect him at all from the gunman's three additional shots. Finally he dashed again, dragging his butt like a dog and came to a good old-fashioned card table made of good old-fashioned thin plastic and called it good from there.

"Stay back!" Skibby shouted. "I gotta bomb in the briefcase!"

"What!?" shouted the gunman.

"I gotta bomb in the briefcase so back the fuck up!" he held the briefcase closer; preparing to use it. Also, for no decent, conceivable reason whatsoever, he took all six tablets of acid in one shot.

"A bomb? Man, what the fuck are you doing?" He fired three more shots into the table. "There're innocent people in here! They're scared out of their minds! You don't bring *a bomb* to the bank - you could get arrested!" And he fired several more rounds into the card table; many of which penetrated the table and bounced off the floor to hit people in the leg or the eye. "People could get hurt! *It's not safe*." And he fired his final bullet which came dangerously close to Skibby's spine.

The boy was in trouble. The gunman was reloading and he needed to focus and come up with a plan, but he was too busy watching his body melt into a puddle of crap and form itself into a candle with all the colors of the rainbow puking on him. Then they took the vomit and turned them into stairs so they could build a stairway to heaven.

"Stairs... why is it always stairs...?" he mumbled.

"What did you say, *muthafucka*?" he fired twice more after quickly reloading. "Something about stairs?" *Bang, bang.* "Bitch, you better not be disrespecting stairs. My father builds stairs!" *Bang. bang.* "He's a volunteer building contractor for victims of land mines! Stairs are what America is all about!" *Bang, bang, bang.*

"What should I do?" Skibby asked.

"Hang on, brotha, I got an idea." said the oil painting, tie-dyed land shark with sunglasses swimming at his feet. "Just stay here and you'll know when it's safe to come out." And the land shark submerged itself under the tile floor.

Skibby had no idea what to expect; the last time a land shark had promised him help, he found himself in a jar of pickled pigs feet sharing a bed with Stanley Milligram. Milligram swore revenge against Skibby - is this what was going to happen? What to do now? Would Milligram exact his reprisal for being tricked into intercourse with the Hadron Collider?

"Where'd you go, fuckface?" screamed the gunman as he prepared a rocket-propelled satellite missile. "You still dissin' stairs? Boy, when I get my hands on you, I'm going to stomp your ass with my steel-toed boots and then you and I are going to be walkin' *up and down the stairs!* I'm going to teach you respect for America! We're going to go to my dad's house; a whole fucking house of stairs! There'll be one... two... three... four... five... six stairs! Six sta..."

Then there was silence. Seconds later, there was a sudden explosion of sounds where screaming, gnashing of teeth, guns going off, chomping and mariachi music all combined for a sickening symphony sting of noise. Skibby slowly came up from behind the table to find the gunman replaced by 120 sq. ft. of miscellaneous entrails and some bloodied shoes.

The herd slowly rising to their positions, but still spooked, Skibby jumped up and ran to the cashier counter; which took several tries because, as far as his body knew, he was swimming in a silver lake of feeling overlooking a gnome village while the moon was trying to suck itself off.

And just for fun, he fell into another koi pond...

"Alright, give me all the money in the bank! I gotta bomb in the briefcase and I'm not afraid to use it!" and he quickly undid all the snaps to the briefcase to showcase his weapon of choice.

The teller's eyes, cautious and scared, slowly made the motions to peer inside, and instead of crisis and further urination of her grandmother's antique pantaloons, her eyes went from terrified to that same look of bewilderment that pretty much everyone Skibby has ever met has given him.

"Sir, this isn't a bomb... it's a *bong*..."

Skibby looked inside and sure enough, it was old *Chongo Bongo* lying in the case; soaked in the residuum of brain-eating sludge and green leafy shit with dusty fingerprints adorning the proud neck of the bottle and threatening no one.

"Oh, hey, Chongo Bongo! I've looking for this! Holy shit..."

"Can I help you with something, sir?"

"Yeah, gimme my money. Now."

"Ok, do you have an account with us?"

"*Fuck!* We're *not* doing this again!" he raised his arm with a drawn weapon. "Gimme all the money in the bank or I'll blow your fucking head off!"

"Sir, that's not a gun, that's a *carrot.*"

"*Open the fucking vault!*" he shouted at the top of his lungs, cocking his carrot to accentuate that he means business. "This is your last warning!"

"Sir, this bank doesn't do that. We just handle checking deposits and withdrawals, mortgage lending, savings, CDs, retirement accounts - that kinda stuff. If you want, there's First United Methodist Bank on Asstits Avenue, they might be..."

Skibby squeezed the trigger on the carrot and *boom* - her head exploded upon impact and rained on the other bank employees who, at this point, were replaced with drop-jaw mannequins staring in anaphylactic shock as they questioned with themselves silently everything they believed in about the natural world. As the body of the last living heir to King Herod's fortune slumped to the ground, Skibby leapt over the counter and the headless rag doll of a torso into the vault. The vault had no further safeguard to circumvent.

Minus, of course, the Sphinxtor.

"*Son of Man!*" screamed the mighty portal muscle that guarded the money, "*I am the mighty Sphinxtor - guardian of the gold; protector of the principle; savior of the savings account! No mortal child born of the screaming woman's womb may enter here without submitting to my riddle! If thou hast courage of the heart and fire in thy belly, entrance may be granted. However, if thou failst to solve the riddle of the mighty Sphinxtor, consider life as you once knew it a brief dream in the face of everlasting nightmare! Prepare thyself, mortal!*"

Skibby overdosed and died through most of that, but was prepared all the same.

"Once there was a man who thought he was a tree. He grew as tall as a man could be. He filled his gardens full of seeds, and soon they were eaten by the bees. He built his house of brick and stone, but not was it a house that he could own. He used a pot to cook his meat, but the pot refused to let him eat. All his life, the sun was his might, and finally one day, he died in the night. Who was this man?"

"Hey, I got one for you."

"...what?"

"What walks on four legs in the morning, two legs in the midday, and three legs at night?"

The Sphinxtor was dumbfounded. No one has ever ignored his riddle and had the gall to ask one of his own - especially the very riddle the family of the Sphinxtor was well known for. What manner of man-matter was this humanapod? Who dares speak to a god with such self-centered interest!

"...son of man, perhaps thou art mistaken and afflicted with illusions of understanding. The responsibility of the riddle falls on thy shoulders, not mine. My role in this supernal facade is to disperse and question; not absorb and answer."

"Hey, I didn't ask for your life story there, hombre, I asked you a question. What walks on four legs in the morning, two legs in the midday, and three legs at night?"

"...man. The answer is man."

"Nope! It's two octopuses fucking!"

There was a silence while the heavens shook under the weight of this newfound insanity. This bold creature was trying to use childish manipulation to get his way in the face of true heavenly royalty.

"Son of Man, I revisit my previous latter question with compounded interest: What!?"

"Two octopuses... having sex... at a rodeo. You're wrong, now get the fuck out of the way!"

"Foolish mortal, I would know the answer to that question. My father first asked it thousands of years ago and it has been riddled to fools like you ever since! It has been told throughout the world!"

"Shut up, asshole! You lose; I win! Get the fuck out of the way!"

"Art thou fucked in the head!? Dost thou not have the sense the good Lord gave the common pretzel? I submit that thou art a multi-volumous compendium of incompetence! I posit that thou..."

Then there was silence. Seconds later, there was a sudden explosion of sounds where screaming, gnashing of teeth, guns going off, chomping and zydeco music all combined for a puerile orchestra of orgy noise. Skibby slowly opened his eyes to watch the land shark gorge his way through 120 sq. feet of muscles and sinew and crap. Skibby thanked the land shark for turning this Sunday bank into a bloodbath unexplainable by conventional language standards and dashed inside to collect the money he was indebted to his boss who made his lair deep in the Northern glaciers and the magnetic tundra of everlasting ice. He grabbed two sacks filled with cash and one filled with meat just to be ironic (though no one had bothered to check his definition of irony). When he finished his coffee, Skibby took his load and dashed outside.

"Great and mighty Djinn, I am ready to leave! Come and pick me up!"

But this time, the great and mighty Djinn did not appear. Skibby called twice more for the aging deity, but there was nothing.

Instead, his cell phone went off...

"Hello? Hey, is this Keith? Hey man, sorry I haven't been able to hit you up, I haven't had a phone until just recently..."

"What? The fuck are you talking about? It's me, Santa Claus!"

"Oh, hey man!"

"Where the fuck are you at? You owe me some money and I fucking better get it today, motherfucker."

"I'm at the bank on I-39 and I got your money. I need a ride; so if you need to get it, you better pick me up."

"You better be there when I get there, *nigga,* if I have to chase you down..."

"Shut the fuck up and get here and you won't have to."

"...alright, be there in a minute."

Minutes later, Skibby was picked up in Santa Claus's new pimped out sleigh that he stole from a rival drug lord who was a Christmas icon in Japan. They flew up, up, and away... doing 156 MPH down the wrong side of the highway. Skibby handed over the money he owed Santa Claus and all was well.

"Hey man, look what I found." Skibby said as he opened the briefcase.

"Fuck yeah - Chongo Bongo!" and he took a hit of some red ochre corridor. "Yeah, this is good shit... but wait 'til we get home. I got a new shipment from Colombia."

"Oh sweet, dude!"

"Fuck yeah. You think Rudolf's nose is red now, just wait until we open that fucker up! Haha!"

And they disappeared over the horizon - toward the North Pole.

And just above them, hovering high over the world with a glare that was melting the ice cap they were heading towards - was the Djinn. Fiercely, murderously indignant only began to describe his contempt for the events he had just witnessed.

"Son of man, thou hast been warned what would happen if thy ill-intent abused powers that the children of Adam were never heir to wield. Thou hast demonstrated an ironclad boldness to defy me, but the road to Hell is paved with boldness and thy blood will seal the cracks for thy crimes against creation. This is the law of

nature. The universe does not forgive egregious fools cowering in thy skin... and I? Even less so..."

He watched them over an ancient monastery high up in the mystic mountains of southern Asia.

"...and now thou hast given me a great opportunity to strike two birds with one stone. Thou wilt not need that money where thou art going - let us share that wealth, shall we?"

Just then, a lightning bolt of divine wrath struck the sleigh and everyone in it. The flaming sin-wagon spiraled out of course and soon drove into the prehistoric rock of the mountains above the monastery. A wild combustion of chemicals and pieces of ash that used be alive, drunk, stoned and tweaked all to hell now fell like black and white snow over the innocent lands below.

At that point, two dozen monks and nuns in the service of the Lord came out to witness the beginning of what would be a turning point for their ministry - the day they could financially save their church. Money of all kinds rained from the sky with the snow... and their prayers were answered.

"How did this happen, father?" asked one of the nuns.

"We have faith, sister. The eyes that watch the world looked down on us this Sabbath and decided it truly was a day that the Lord should make. We should be ever mindful of the forces that be and the good that comes from everything. Gather the money and then gather our people. We must thank the Lord for this day."

Happy Mother's Day everyone!

Aurora Terminus

Inspired by *Selling England by the Pound*

It took some time, but the tea was ready.

And when it was, it was served in the customary china from the china cabinet in the corner near the cabin door. Usually the bone porcelain was reserved for special occasions such as Christmas and Easter, or even the *Royal Coronation* which was rare in these days, but as was the state of the country these days, and because a certain someone forgot to bring dishware from the townhouse, it was deemed *acceptable by gentlemen* to be able to use them for their game tonight. This was an attractive set of china too - the Maltese Pig's favorite set; so it must be told. It was handed down to him by his father, a chamberlain in Sussex, who received it from a long line of previous sires. It was rumored to be a prototype set from the Royal Worcester company, before even they merged to become the Worcester Royal Porcelain company, that was going to be designed and marketed strictly to the aristocracy, but was never used and thus donated to the family as a substitute for a real gift during Christmas.

It was also the favorite set of a Mr. Graham Anthony Cheffield, an accountant on the payroll of *Her Royal Majesty,* and a close personal friend to both guests occupying the country chalet this very night. His presence this evening would mean more than a welcome participant; so far as to say that he was very much *needed* for their joviality in these late, dark, winter hours; for Mr. Graham, it could be truly said, was the last true patriot of the *Union Jack,* one of the last truly chivalrous knights for Her Majesty, The Queen, and by far the most cheerfully optimistic person in any regard to the British Empire. His radiance for *King and Country* would undoubtedly part the dark clouds surrounding them; at least for the night.

"An eye for an eye..." said the Peregrine Falcon between puffs on his gold-rimmed *Don Carlos Lancero*.

"At a boy, old chap." said the Maltese Pig in admiration. He squeaked clean his monocle with the addendum, "We need more of that around here. The *British Empire's* falling apart these days..." and he turned his pig's head, dusted with the finest top hat in Christendom, towards the window with the black, deep forest permanently painted over it, "...and you never know when you can turn your back..." he said slowly as he watched the window apprehensively; as though an evil wight come loft from one of the many scorched cornfields was expected to intrude.

"You're getting suspicious, my friend." The Peregrine Falcon said with a swagger of the cards. "Hard times are no excuse for superstition."

"Rot. I have every reason in the world to be superstitious..." he turned his head again to the ghastly window behind him for a final glance. He wasn't quite sure, but he could swear he just saw something flash across the window. It was pure white with a feminine figure that just barely escaped his vision in time... "Oh, but... come! Let's play our game!" and the Maltese Pig turned back and straightened his fancy jacket with his fat front hooves. He trotted back and sat across the card table with his Royal Worcester half-filled with the last known ounces of tea Catherine of Braganza had ever owned in her tea collection.

And the chalet roared with laughter; the only sounds of life arguably present in the death that was Corfingham Forest this black night. In truth, there was much, much more laughter erupting across the accursed wood - in tiny holes and little nooks; between roots and in tiny fairy villages that were all but empty thanks to chronic genocide and rape by these dark forces. They were all erupting through frequencies that God above was generous enough not to let us hear.

As the moon ducked down below *Aurora Terminus*, the last fragment of horizon in the northern sky, the tree lines grew taller and more menacing through the ancient and now almost impenetrably dark wood. At this hour, every lollygagging spirit, every evil, drunken dwarf, every wisp in Satan's command, every witch with a cunt bleeding hymns of dark service and every misguided *fatae* this side of *Toad Hall* feasted and gorged on the tender, innocent lifeblood of the unseen populations of the old island of Angles. The fish no longer swim the streams for fear of what mutation of piranha pike or poisonous serpent may lie in wait for them. The birds no longer settle in the trees for every tree was possessed either inwardly or completely by some unholy predator with long, scratchy limbs that separated, very violently, the flesh and feathers from their bones and beak with touch alone. - and God help you if you were a fairy trying to walk a path at night; for, by the break of dawn, that path would be strewn with your shredded, molested body scattered around; your bones and tiny, separated arms snapping like tiny twigs under foot of the day traveler.

There was not one glen that wasn't haunted by a demonic remnant of the old Germanic tribes; not one glade that wasn't watched by thousands of eyes illuminating nightmares; not one field that the daughters of Merlin, once revered guardians and now pathetic shams in the *goat's* service just like the rest of them, did not menstruate their tainted fluid all over. There were hundreds, maybe thousands, of these earthen urchins dancing in grim fantasies; conjured by no particular host in hand. These shapes, if shapes they may be called, laughed with the winds that howled and the bombs that dropped from above.

But on this night, the gentlemen of the chalet did their best to drown out their gypsy voices with the sounds of genuine life and joy that only proud gentlemen of the empire could boast.

"Gin!" cried the Peregrine Falcon.

"Soddit!" cried the Maltese Pig as he wiped clean his eyes and monocle with a hearty laugh.

"Tigermoth chances, my friend..." whispered confidently the good Falcon tycoon.

Suddenly, for no reason at all, the music box chimed in for a silly tune.

Ding-da-ding-ding-dinnnngggggg. Dinnngggggg-din-din-din-ding-ding.

Dun-ding-da-dung-dung-dunnnn.... Ding. Ding. Ding-din-da-ding-din-dinngggg...

The Falcon cocked his eye and finished his cigar. "That sounded like *William Sterndale Bennett*... did you do that?" He asked.

"I did not..." whispered the Maltese Pig as he arranged the cards for a new game, the smile fading from his eyes and his eyes dropping downward. He complemented this change with a heart-heavy sigh.

"...it doesn't *mean* anything, old boy..." The Falcon lied.

Bollocks - as a school boy from Yorkshire might say. In fact, they both knew what it meant.

****

About a mile away, just near the river banks, he was lost in the thick thickening thicket where the branches were curling and extending out to fragments of things they used to be. Mr. Graham, regardless of the unnatural *abattoir* of the atmosphere around him, remained upbeat as he endeavored to join his friends for tea; dark night or no.

But now there was a very queer notion that tickled his brain wrinkles and made his soul shiver. He realized he was not lost; the forest was changing. There never once was this immaterial mist that fogged not only sight, but heart, mind, soul, spirit, blood, and even shit so thick the vapors could not be penetrated by even an A9 Cruiser MK1 driven by *Winston Churchill* - and his shit was pretty thick already even by Scotsmen's standards. Mr. Graham had to remind himself he was not lost, but the evil spirits saw it fit that, like his father before him, he would be molested at a relatively young age for his riches in money and humanity...

"Fear is nothing," he told himself. "Even if things change, the *Knights of the Green Shield* stamp and shout." He picked up his pace.

He wandered through the misty Celtic labyrinth of the dark mire; keeping up his pace but stumbling every now and again over blatantly gnarled roots and rocks that tempted to take his life. "Feet that were all thumbs"... that's what the lads used to say about him. He whistled his favorite tune, *Heart of Oak* and its piercing melody perturbed one of the daughters of Merlin who was haunting the area and preferred it *dead fucking silent!*

Now there were eyes on him; hundreds of eyes that studied him for any weakness of tread so that they may cut swift and chew his meat with a sharp, thick chutney sauce.

Snap!

A sickening sound dissonated his melody from underfoot and it broke his trance of positive British reinforcement. He paused, looked down and stepped back to see what it was.

"Oh my God..." he said and he picked up the poor creature by its shattered wing. It was a fairy' or at least the bitter half of one. The left arm and everything beneath the waistline was ripped asunder with a tiny little fragment of ribcage providing the only anchor. The right arm was twisted in many places and hair was ripped from the scalp. The flesh of this poor former creature, along with the right eyeball and socket, were also torn... one should not even wonder why its blood was still dripping and fresh...

"Protect me, Lord..." he whispered and now dashed for the path; forgetting his melody and forgoing his optimism, but the path was not clear though many eyes could see. The course laid down long before was now long gone. He rode majestic through graves of men who dare not gaze with joy at this once mighty country.

He drifted down a hill that was not a hill before until he smashed into a silken, velvet pie of mud. The forces that lived in that mud rolled him slowly off the ground and into the river.

Splash!

They laughed silently as they watched him float in the freezing vein.

He gained control to say the *Lord's Prayer* and exorcised the spirits from his vessel. He regained first his arms from their ghostly grips. He regained second his legs from the spiders that entangled him. He pulled the Piranha Pikes from his groin and mashed them with his fingers until they were no more. Then he regained most importantly his feet from the twisting serpentine devils that masturbated poison between his toes and crushed their evil heads with his Staffordshire heel.

"B'gone, *Auld Nick!*" he screamed as he splashed in the river; fighting the dark forces and tearing them limb from limb. "'Lest you find my feet swelling in your backside until Christmas!"

And with that, the *Evil One* faded out of the water and appeared on a bridge above him. Auld Nick ejaculated into his eyes and laughed blood for every Son of Christ to tremble.

Graham drifted further before he could finally get that unspeakable gunk out of his eyes. When all was clear, he came to a cave and struggled to find ground for which to remain stable. He could still hear the specters and demons laughing at him from the distance. Their laughter echoed in the caves and threatened to erode his skull from the ears inside and out.

But that was not all... as he floated even further into the anus that was this dark cavern, he also heard the melodies of William Sterndale Bennett slowly seep in through the cracks of the rocks. It was another melody; a slow and diminutive dirge that was completely counter to the tune he had whistled earlier on...

"I say, now!" he shouted at the pitch black casket that was no longer a simple cavern, "What is the meaning of this!?"

Then there was a sudden flash in his eyes, and he knew it was all over...

The blade twisted into his back until it snapped one thousand nerves and veins and made love to his vertebrae. He could not even turn around, but he could already guess who it was who had betrayed him...

"*Lady Britannia...*" he choked between gurgles of gore filling his lungs and throat. "You betrayed me....?"

"I could never be your woman..." she whispered as she turned the blade like a key further into his back. Her pure, white feminine figure soaked in the dark color of the waters and she began to transform into something else - something far more frightening.

"I could never be your *dildo*, woman." He seethed defiantly through bleeding teeth and decomposing gums and she plunged her sword right through his gullet. She called him a bold fool and slowly brought the blade towards the ceiling; separating his chest and shoulders, bisecting his neck and throat, obscuring his screams in pain, and further up until it broke through the jaw and he could taste the blade for a full second before it cut his tongue in twain. The skull was a bit harder to break, but it just took a little more effort until finally the brain erupted in a geyser of blood and pons.

His gambit, sadly, had failed. Lady Britannia slowly consumed his flesh through unnatural means. Her cold lips, once the lips that kissed and embraced every son and citizen of *Arthur Pendragon*, now attached via squid sucker to his neck and slurped his skin right off his pathetic, scrawny, pasty-white English body. There was gnashing of the teeth. There was stripping of the skin layers through iron tongues and the razor wind that was her breath filled his body and cut everything inside him.

He was nothing more now than a muscular skeleton, but even that did not last. Her jaws unhinged at the prospect of snapping whole his articulate forearm. She slurped the pink, pillowy fabric from his bones, sucked his eyes out through vacuums in her nostrils and crunched his rods and cones with teeth hidden in her stomach. He was expelled as most foods are, but unlike most expelled foods was soon consumed again and chomped and savored and lustfully absorbed in her whorish body in conjunction with all the new bits and pieces of him that are only passing through the first time.

And still she was not done consuming him.

William Sterndale Bennett played louder now, and he could hear her vulgarity in full chorus volume with it as she chewed deep into his pectoris like a common lad eating chicken. The knife was still in his back and it was now a luxury compared to what was happening up front.

"God made you a man," she whispered as she laid the pieces down in ritualistic ceremony. "And so, with Gods and Men, your sheep remain inside your pen. No longer chased; forever chastened. *The Knights of the Green Shield* are all dead - such is the fate of those born in my sight. A shepherd's malady - tale as old as time..." and she tore into his face.

****

"He's late..." instructed the Peregrine Falcon

"He knows the way..." reminded the Maltese Pig as he shuffled the cards.

And then suddenly, the musical box stopped its horrendous echo twain melody. It had died.

"Oh dear..." whispered the Peregrine Falcon as he covered his beak with his feathers.

"...a shepherd's malady..." started the Maltese Pig, "...tale as old as time..." and he glanced back toward the window where the dark shadows were still dancing and laughing.

"To err is human, after all..."

****

The next morning, his bones were discovered in the river by the Constable General. His trusted hound-dog spotted beavers making a dam out of them. In the surrounding areas were all forms of burnt grass and enough wreckage that smoke was the visible signal that this was the area they needed to find.

Fourteen villages of fairies and of gnomes and dwarves and pixies and elves - all destroyed in a massive holocaust. The stench of the rotting pieces was overwhelming even for their small size. Men, women, children and homunculi... one couldn't even tell them apart. Many were flayed and burned alive. Others were raped and dissected in far more creative ways. Not one survivor, *not one survivor!* This was beyond ethnic cleansing - this was blitz extermination. This was the end for them, and it succeeded.

Lord Balkus took one look at the mess and declared he'd never been so sick in all his life.

Joseph Merrick observed the pile, "Those poor bastards..."

James Anderton came by, dropped his trousers, and took an enormous shit on everything.

****

The next Sunday was the service for Graham Cheffield. It was disappointing. The Peregrine Falcon, dressed in his church best, followed by his good friend, the Maltese Pig, visited the gravesite, which was quickly established since there wasn't enough body to bury, and poured his share of the tea Catherine of Braganza acquired after she gave the Lord Chamberlain a *dirty-sanchez* in Parliament from the Royal Worcester. It was his personal favorite.

Graham Anthony Cheffield, III
September 7th 1940 - May 10th, 1941
For King and Country

"God rest his merry soul." said the Ham.

"He was a beacon in these dark times." said the Bird. "I miss him so."

There was a great and somber silence dating from their mouths and drifting slowly above the trees that were falling dead leaves and dirty ash. His burial ground, which had been dry throughout the summer, was now sopping wet in a deluge from their tears. Sad little posies popped up from the ground from all the water they had been getting and James Anderton came over to take a shit on them.

"This isn't what was supposed to happen." said the Ham. "What's become of us? What's happened to the Empire?"

"There is no more Great Britain, my friend. We're done for. Albion's a lost cause. Wales is next, I hear. This is not the Mother England my father fought for in the war, old boy. We're the citizens of hope and glory! *You're damned right* this isn't what was supposed to happen!"

They were silent for some moments. They both gazed at the empty, polished marble that was his headstone with nothing but images of the failed afterlife where Graham Cheffield was truly dead for all time.

"The Empire... our country... has fallen. We've been betrayed. God save Her Majesty... because now no one else will...!"

There was another solemn moment that was meant for remembering but sullied with thoughts of pain, depression and betrayal. The Maltese Pig closed his eyes but could not stop shaking. He winced and he whined; slow at first but then louder. The Royal Worcester saucer and cup shook violently in his hands until he burst forth a cry of anguish.

"*Gaahhhhh!*" he roared, and he grasped the cup and saucer and smashed them on the headstone.

Then he grabbed another set from the Royal Worcester.

Then another.

Then another.

"Take it! Take all of it!" he screamed until the final teacup shattered on his death date. The poor ham dropped to his knees and convulsed with the tears of his father; the tears of every father who fought in the war, who fought the invaders from the Vikings to the Normans, from the Dark Ages to the Renaissance, to the Union of the Crowns and to the establishment of the United Kingdom. How could a history go so far just to be stopped so short?

There was no answer for that question. Just tears...

...tears that inspired a burning resolve for empyrean justice.

They opened their eyes and looked at each other with the same inevitability painted across the faces.

"An eye for an eye..."

"You said it, old chap."

That night, a sheep was sheared in Graham's honor.

****

The Maltese Pig ran through the forest path with the Peregrine Falcon holding up the other end; trying very hard to catch up. The dark forces, overfed at last from their genocide, were still devouring the spoils of their conquest and made no notice of any other presence in their kingdom.

Over the hill, they spotted a cabin that shown with a diseased light as reflected by Aurora Terminus.

"There she is..." The Peregrine Falcon gritted and they scurried to the side of the building. "Shh..." said the Bird as he slowly crept inside the bedroom window holding the sheep's quilt.

"Right behind you, lad..." whispered the Pig as he put one truffled hoof over the other and lifted his heavy body with difficulty through the window in desperate silence.

In the bed sleeping was Lady Britannia; the real Lady Britannia; without sword or shield; once the warrior symbol of greatest kingdom on Earth; now just a common peasant living in poverty in a cabin.

A thief.

A murderer.

A whore.

A seditionist.

A traitor.

She didn't even have the power to be aware of their presence within her walls. The Maltese Pig went to one side of the bed carrying the sheep's quilt while the Peregrine Falcon took the other side. They looked at each other, smiled their last smile of sanity, and looked down at the last image of Lady Britain.

"...and so, with Gods and Men..." and he tossed one side of the sheep's quilt to the Falcon.

"...the sheep escaped the shepherd's pen..."

"...and on through Albion they will go..."

"...until the glory of Britain starts to glow..."

"...and live forever without fear or doubt..."

And they raised the sheep's quilt up high, their eyes lit up like Christmas when the Queen herself paraded through their streets. Their mouths twisted into barbs as they finished the battle cry they waited their entire lives to cry.

"Knights of the Green Shield Stamp and Shout!"

And they dropped the quilt onto her body. It exploded into conflagration without the slightest hint of delay. The flames shot out of her and the cabin like wings of a great phoenix and the two jumped out of the way to avoid being cremated themselves. Lady Britannia screamed, but her voice was choked by smoke and the sounds of her cries muted under the loud sizzle of her skin. Ashes to ashes, dust to dust. The aristocratic pair dashed out of the burning house with their lives. The walls tumbled under the flames and her body writhed in the bliss of agony. The fiery serpents of Auld Nick himself kissed her vaginal lips and caressed her bosom with the heat of the sun.

The Peregrine Falcon and the Maltese Pig came to a hillside and watched that same smoke fill the skies and get sucked into the cresting eye of Aurora Terminus. The cosmic gate swelled and contracted and the light of heaven absorbed the darkness from the still land. They cheered and they cheered and then they cheered some more as the vacuum consumed and sealed their resolution for justice once and for all!

"Yes! Yes! Burn, you motherfucker, burn!"

"Ha ha! Ha ha!"

Finally, the house collapsed under its own weight and there was nothing left. The sheep's quilt had done its job well. The smoke was drained from the northern sky by Aurora Terminus. When there was no more, Aurora Terminus quietly imploded and disappeared into some quiet galaxy yet to be discovered. It would not be seen under British rule for another five hundred years...

"An eye for an eye..." said the Peregrine Falcon as they walked down the dark hill.

"To err is human..." responded the Maltese Pig."What was it she used to say?"

"*I could never be your woman...*"

"Ha! Not anymore! She belongs to *him* now..."

"Indeed, old boy... indeed..."

They walked down the path until they came to the clearing they had planned on since the beginning. The moonlight shone on this bald spot and there was some apprehension between the pair.

"You know what we have to do now, right?" Asked the Maltese Pig.

"I know. It doesn't make it any easier, but I know what we have to do... we must be bold. This is a time for us to be bold..." he said fighting back tears.

"It has to be done. Our generation is finished whether we win or lose. When my father and your father died, this was all that was left for them to preserve their dignities and prove with their lives how proud they were to fly the British flag. We've become our fathers now, lad, and we must do what they did, and sacrifice what they sacrificed for the good of the common people."

They stared at each other and both slowly advanced until there was no space between them.

"For King and Country, old boy?"

"For Great Britain... and for Graham..." 'twas his last words before they had to accomplish the age old final sacrifice as their ancestors, the knights and lords of the land, had done before them.

In that calm moonlight beneath British skies, they stripped off their clothes and began to devour each other. The Ham started low and bit hard into the Bird's gizzard. The Bird pecked and stabbed into the Ham's head and pulled out chewy bits of brain peppered with skullcap. The Ham tore into the Bird's flesh and his blood splashed forth as feathered skin sludged down his throat. The Bird cracked open the Ham's shoulder and crunched, respectfully, his bones and tissue. A fresh coat of blood also splattered him in the face; and another as he tore open the whole backside of the Pig. They continued this until they were missing whole limbs and vital organs. The Bird was as bald as the curve of the Earth and just a mish-mash of avian entrails and snapping cartilage at that point. The Ham's ribs were poking out from the great crater in his abdomen and blood and pus were pouring out of his backside like a cascading waterfall.

And they continued this, all through the night, until the morning came and there was nothing left for either to eat.

The Peregrine Falcon died first just before dawn. His friend, the Maltese Pig would follow soon after.

When the Bird fell first, the Ham watched his friend until he saw his eyes close forevermore. He choked on his last breath and smiled for all of England to see.

"An eye for an eye, old boy... we did it..." he coughed."*Long live Britannia!*"

And he closed his eyes and listened as William Sterndale Bennett himself played for him a sweet lullaby that would echo in his floppy ears for all eternity. It was none other than *Heart of Oak.*

It was the same melody every British citizen who had ever lived wished they could hear on their deathbeds...

The Wisdom of My Father

My dad was a real trip growing up. He had this way about him that really stood out even in a huge audience. He was like a lighthouse in many ways; if you saw in him a large audience from really high up, you could still pick him out easily because he just had a certain look to him and a swagger that was unique. No one else looked or acted like him and for very good reason. He was the life of the party, not the face in the crowd, and he always liked to make sure you knew that.

He was the kinda guy who went to a restaurant for dinner and when the waiter asked him what he wanted, he would always yell, "Surprise Me!" Then he would take his car to the mechanic, and when the mechanic would ask him what work he needed done, he would always yell, "Surprise Me!"

That was old dad all right - never owned a car that worked and always vomited his meals up all over the waiters. He was definitely a character. A real card they would say.

Learning from him and looking up to him taught me a lot; even when I was a really little boy and very naughty. One year he caught me smoking behind the house and he grabbed my arm and pulled me inside and sat me down at the kitchen table. He looked at me square in the eye, and I'll never forget this look, with a straight, locked jaw and even great flaring nostrils. When he finally moved his strong, iron jaw, he said to me, "So you like smoking, do you, boy? Well, I got *two whole damn cartons* of Marlboro Heavies and you're going to smoke them all before dinner. We'll see how you like smoking then!"

Then a week later, he caught me fighting some kid in the street so he grabbed my arm, sat me down at the kitchen table with that same fixated glare and authoritative voice that used to make me quiver, and that same tone quivered me as he said to me, "So you like fighting kids in the neighborhood, do you, bitch? Well, I made some calls and there are *seventy-five kids in the backyard* that I shot up full of steroids and crack that you're going to fight before dinner. We'll see how you like fighting then!"

Dad always had that kind of strictness to him, and even though I can never close my eyes or feel anything but pain since that summer, I could always see the wisdom in his methods. Dad was used to the old-school way of discipline; straight from the drill sergeant mold of tough love, hard-knock lessons and brutal metaphors of random sentences and lead pipes. One thing he would never tolerate was back talk. "My way or the highway!" he would say and he meant it. One time he literally left me out on the highway smeared with honey. That was the day, the circus bears of the United States of America all got together to rampage through the highway and maim everyone they could find to cure cancer.

He would never tolerate cowardice either; like when I finally got home from the hospital that day covered in bear bites and ursine feces. "Be a man or wear a dress!" he would always say - until one year after graduating college when he made me do both at his Elk's Club Lodge; chained by the neck and bare-assed to a post with my hips screwed to a wall that had a glory hole.

Dad was always popular with the guys, and I was popular with them too (for reasons that are now obvious), and he'd always figure out fun ways to entertain them and embarrass me like all dads do. He'd get a real kick out of really kicking me in front of his friends and they'd all get a kick too (some even kicked twice). It was cute to dad's friends - all these funny little moments of our lives. One time, he came up with a song called "Hair in My

Underwear" and sang it constantly - then when I hit puberty; he started singing it at my school.

But I always forgave him, because dad was from a different time and place where being tough mattered a lot more than being outwardly loving or couth. Again, his job was to be tough. His job was to show me what being a man was all about and how much you had to take to get anywhere in life. There was no room for girly frou-frou stuff at our house. He didn't want to watch cartoons, thinking that was "pussy shit" (an item he actually adored during sex; we were sad to stumble upon one day) and didn't want me watching any of it either. One day, he came into the living room, saw me watching cartoons and shouted "Teenage Mutant Ninja Turtles my *ass!*" To this day, we still don't know what he was talking about, we just know every month since then, he repeated it over and over and over as he whipped me with the power cord to the TV until the red turned white and I couldn't move or shit for a week.

My dad was from a different time, like I said before... and even that didn't explain why he was so angry with black baby boomers. He treated them with the same level of paranoia and ridicule usually reserved for homosexuals; which he ironically loved, respected and more than once tried to become since gender-reassignment surgery was always too expensive. I had no idea how bad this was until he walked into an upscale restaurant in Atlanta during a summer vacation.

I thought it was a really neat place, but Dad, as usual, had other ideas. He took a look around the room, completely unaware there were African-Americans in urban Georgia, and he resolved from there to try his damndest to "put things in perspective to these people", as he called it. What he did next became part of Atlanta local legend, as I've heard, but it was, in fact, very real that he stripped off all his clothes, covered himself in hot sauce and jumped on a table singing an off-key "Amazing Grace". He felt a dented can of orange soda being spilled and some fried chicken tossed out the window would, in further fact, put things in perspective to these people. He called them "blinkies", accused them of starting the Civil War and killing Abraham Lincoln and still no avail.

Finally, he stuck some sunglasses on, shouted, "Hey, where'd everybody go!?" about a thousand times and eventually wandered his way into the expansive bosom of an eight hundred pound black woman. Whereas some people would've tried to apologize and step away, my dad tried swimming her like a river stream until he exploded all over her. When her nearby father, the Reverend *Jesse Jackson*, got up and condemned my dad very rudely, going so far as to pull a silver revolver out of his bible and cock it, dad then put his clothes back on, sprayed the crowd with a super soaker filled with urine (some of which was his) and ran out the door, locking me inside to take the heat.

Once I woke up from the coma and emptied my bank account to cover the damages, my Dad and I really bonded that trip in Atlanta. On the way back home, as we hid under a pregnant cow in the back of a cattle truck going cross-country and finally off the edge of the Grand Canyon, he turned to me and said, "I'm proud of you, son... you got whupped a dozen times over and you cried like a bitch. And then when that big black guy got down on you and raped you right there for everyone to see and grabbed your head back and told you to squeal like a pig - you did it and you cried some more. I could never do anything like that myself... I'm too much of a fucking *man* to do that."

If my dad liked anything more than watching his grown, adult son get beaten and molested by his actions and having to use him as a cushion when we free-fell a mile in Colorado, it was music. He loved classic rock bands like Grand Funk Railroad, Sly and Family Stone, The Byrds, and The Allman Brothers - so one could probably imagine my surprise to his reaction when I said I wanted a bass for my birthday. Being closely informed on music terminology, I thought that would've been enough to reasonably imply to him I wanted to own a bass guitar.

Instead, he came home that day with a fish. A fish. A fish some 25 in. long and weighing 6.4 lbs. I explained to him that the bass I was looking for is electric, plugs into an amp, and plays music.

Rather than get me a guitar, I watched in horror as he gutted the poor living creature, throwing bones into my eyes and raw meat up my nose, ran an electric current through him, stuck a 3 ft. fret board up its ass and plugged him into an amp. Then he gave it to me, aimed a loaded gun at my face, and threatened to shoot if I didn't play "More Than a Feeling" perfectly, on a bass-fish unguitar, the first time trying. Well, I did and he shot me in the face anyway.

It was just dad's way, you know? All dads have their eccentricities and no father can be *Father Knows Best*. It just comes with the job. It was technically my fault for the way I worded my request for a bass, but I still wet my bed constantly because of it.

Dad was also a big fan of television. He didn't take to it at first; thinking the broadcast signals coming from the TV would interfere with the magnetic brain waves he was sending to the aliens to power the nuclear core of their spaceship, but once he got one from old man Chester Frump down the hall (or stole it just before he was found dead under "mysterious" circumstances, whoever you choose to believe) he became a huge fan and watched it everyday. I'll never forget the wisdom he used to share with me on the couch there. He'd say, "Son, life is like an apple in an apple tree... now, shut the fuck up, Ann of the Airlanes is on!" Which was really interesting because it was a radio show, not TV, hadn't been broadcast in decades and dad was completely deaf.

Dad was always more concerned with the big picture knowledge than being practical though. It was just his way. He had many ideas and theories for how things should go and work and it always pleased him far more than matters here on Earth. He didn't believe in God - instead he used to tell me the universe was designed by a three-legged, three-headed transsexual prostitute from Myanmar who gave birth to me in an oxygen tank and sold me to dad when he was looking for exhibits to display at Ripley's Believe it or Not. After six years of being on display in The Dells, dad figured I was mature enough to know the *facts of life* and how the universe truly worked. He said to me, "Son, there is no God. There are no angels; there is no heaven; there is only Hell which I command. When your pitiful life is over, I will shellac your body and run burning preservatives through your veins so you will be awake forever while I bury you in cement with all the other rejects I've bought and dumped. Your corpse will explode with gases and bugs and grave robbers will eat what's left of you for ten thousand years. Finally, when I sick get of you, I'll kill you for real and there will be no afterlife to look forward to; just a painful blackness that erases you from being like you were never there at all. These are the *facts of life,* son, now get your three-legged ass back in that cage; we got customers waiting!"

So dad was pretty spiritual at heart even if he was never religious. He was, however, a fiercely political man who always strove to teach me how politics in this country works. He used to sum it up in one small paragraph; never failing to remind me that, "Son, one day I'm going to be President of the United States of America, the greatest country on Earth... and if you don't know your shit by then, I'll fucking hang you for treason and deliver your body to *General Hutu* in return for the blood diamonds of Africa."

It always made me feel good that I could be useful to my dad like that. He knew that and he always looked for ways for me to be useful to him; whether he wanted my face to soak up the beer he spilled in the commode; or he needed a new liver to replace the one that was dying in his system from years of alcohol abuse; or a lookout for when he would panty-raid the women's shelters in Sacramento. Dad knew he could count on me. He would always have me help him on anything; especially cars - not ours, usually other peoples' - but even though we were never very good at it (every car we worked on seemed to blow up near government buildings), dad would always laugh on the way home so I knew he always had a good time with me around. Then he'd laugh some more, and more, and then some more... and more... and even more; until his throat filled with blood and he'd spit it out at me as he cursed the infidels of the American government. He wanted me to learn that, "Son, sometimes in life... you really don't need a reason to do things..." and then he'd grab a jagged piece of stone sidewalk and beat me up and down the river bank, leave me for dead in a ravine, and then walk off to go fishing.

I never always appreciated dad's examples of generosity and selflessness and commitment to never paying taxes as long as he lived. I could be a real handful when I was a child and I regret to say I was even bratty to my biggest hero, but dad always knew the right way to handle it. Some of the most defining moments of my life came from when I childishly tried to defy dad and he would always say something that would stop me in my tracks and really make me think. One time, when I was about ten years old, I made up a little sack and a stick and I told dad I was running away. He looked at me square in the eye and said, "Doesn't bother me, I got another one just like you out in the garage."

And I stopped in my tracks...

...I had a brother...

That's the day I learned to always appreciate what dad was, because everything he said always had something amazing behind it. When dad spoke, you listened and you believed.

One man unfortunately did not heed this advice and boy did he have a lesson to learn. Some years ago, dad got into an argument with a man when he claimed dad "impregnated his son", as it were. They argued for hours and I'll never forget when the man insulted dad saying, "*God bless*, were you born in a barn, mister!?" to which dad replied, "I was born in a manger, motherfucker!" and to prove it, he killed the man and tried to bring him back to life. He failed and consumed the body to eliminate the evidence, but he got his point across.

It's always heartbreaking to a boy to see some ignorant man go against his biggest hero, but dad never knew defeat and that's why he was my biggest hero. No matter how bad things got, dad would always win. Whether he was fighting drunk bikers in a bar, drug addicts on the street, criminals that would break into our house, pedophiles that were friends of dad, angry neighbors, assassins from Morocco the neighbors had hired, the Girl Scouts of America, completely defenseless old ladies in the middle of the night, child protective services or the *Klingon Visigoths*... he would always win.

And I was always there, by his side... his little "human shield" as he called me...

Dad, as all dads eventually do, started to get older and had to slow down some of his wild man antics. He traded his cigarettes for carrots, his beer for a glass of red wine a day and his favorite hypodermic needle for insulin shots. He took to painting - which is what he called chasing farmhands around their property naked and bleeding with buckets of shit on his head, and it really seemed to relax him. He had his good days and his bad. Some days he couldn't remember my name - which didn't bother me too much as he never gave me one, and other days he found it difficult to drive to my cellar in an abandoned well outside of town to have dinner with me and watch the football game and beat me with the coffin he built for me just like in the old days. It was too much of a strain on his poor, arthritic hands to make a fist and just hammer away at my exposed kidneys anymore, so I had to move from my damp little hole in the rotting Earth back to his place and the damp little hole in the rotting Earth he had set aside for me to live and be his nurse for the next forty years he was expected to live.

It was sad to watch such an incredible character slow down, but being together again gave me the opportunity to finally get into the family business and follow in his inspirational footsteps.

I was going to be part of the *Mexican Drug Cartel!*

Dad got me an interview with Joaquin Guzman, one the main men in charge of the *Sinaloa Cartel* pharmaceutical company where dad's been going to work all these years. Dad even got me a suit for the interview which he said used to belong to the "famous" Miguel Ángel Félix Gallardo, who I've never heard of but I guess used to be a big rainmaker at the firm before he retired. The interview didn't take long at all and all I had to do was agree to drug testing (which meant I'd actually be testing drugs) and several major non-disclosure agreements with the media (and "Interpol", whatever that is) and I was well on my way to following in my daddy's footsteps!

I was hired to be a mule!

The job was actually a lot different than I expected it to be (though I did get fitted with horse shoes and branded once or twice) but I didn't let that bother me. As long as my dad was proud of me, they could cram as many tiny balloons of powdered sugar into every orifice of my living body as they wanted - and they did! In fact, they even made some new holes to hide balloons in!

And, no joke, not six hours later, I was on a private jet! My first job was to meet with a high-powered client in the desert just north of Ohio. I was talking business with the big boys now! I had awesome hip hop celebrities sitting next to me, I was eating roasted lamb, I was sipping champagne and something else that they didn't tell me what it was, but insisted I drink it anyway. I must have gotten drunk because the next thing I knew I was waking up in a hotel bed after having crazy nightmares that dad tossed me out of the plane into the desert and I broke my penis off on a cactus. It was quite a hangover headache, and the last image I saw was part of the nightmare where I was standing on a mountain of bloodied, dead bodies with flames roaring around me and I had a giant machinegun in my hands because I dreamt the business deal with the client I was supposed to meet went sour and I ended up killing him, which led to a police chase, which led to a manhunt, which led to the crucifixion of the President of the United States, etc. etc. It was pretty heavy stuff, though I didn't feel like I had to pee real bad, which was kind of weird.

So I got out of bed and got ready to meet the client when the bellboy came in with my newspaper and showed me something awful.

My client had died yesterday.

"Wow, what are the odds?" I said to the bellboy. "I was supposed to meet him today to deliver a shipment."

"Is that right, sir?" said the bellboy, who was fidgeting with his jacket for some reason.

"Yeah, I had a big meeting with him today. This is so weird. How did he die?"

"Well sir..." and the bellboy became very serious and looked me straight in the eye, "...you murdered him."

"I murdered him?"

"Got it!" he shouted into his jacket "*Go go go go go!*"

And so, somehow, I winded up in jail where I am today. It was so surreal but I remember it like it was yesterday; even though more than thirty years had passed. A literal army of SWAT team members descended on me as they broke through the doors and walls and bathroom fixtures and my bed to subdue me by force. I was shot a few times, but I was used to that with dad, so it didn't bother me too much.

When I got to court a year later, I was told the bellboy had my confession on tape and no legal defense team could represent me. I learned that they also had evidence that I really did kill over a thousand people with a machinegun and stood on their bodies claiming to be "Tony Montana." Its true Tony Montana was my favorite football player, but I argued back that all of it was nonsense.

And to make things worse, after I got a twenty-five year sentence with no possibility of parole for my crime, I was sued by Al Pacino, Oliver Stone, and Brian De Palma for infringing on their intellectual property. When I couldn't pay them the amount settled (a number that I'm told is still too high to mathematically exist) my sentence was extended to twenty-five years *squared* without the possibility of parole and I was expected to survive my term to completion before I could legally be allowed to die.

But the worst part was seeing my dad disappointed in me. His only son now a jailbird with the highest level sentencing any criminal has ever faced. I was truly heartbroken that I let my greatest hero in the world down after he did so much for me in my life - punched me in the mouth every time I opened it; slept and sodomized with every girlfriend I ever had; sold my genome map to buy smokes... who else has a dad that does that for you? I watched him take the witness stand time after time, testifying against me, even the stuff he actually did that I had no part of - I can't say I blame him. When your son shames you in such a way as I have and the police are paying you a quarter of a billion dollars for your testimony, it only makes sense. I had no right to ask for his forgiveness after I had wasted all the wisdom he taught me over the years and boldly tried to follow in his footsteps anyway. It just wasn't right at all. The only consolation was that I got to see him smile after he walked out of the courtroom with all that money.

That was the last time I ever saw him.

Actually, I lied. That wasn't the worse part. The worse part was the interview with NBC Dateline, which I only took part of as a plea deal to get back my bathroom and virginity privileges as I carried out my prison term, when that smarmy son-of-a-gun asked me why I didn't ever stand up to my father. "You said, earlier, that you wanted to follow "boldly" in his footsteps. Didn't it ever occur to you what he was doing to you? That he was conditioning you to be... someone who takes the fall?"

"No, it never did and it never will." I said back with a straight face.

"How can that be? How can you sit there and tell me it never occurred to you he was hurting you? You wouldn't have ever boldly walked in his footsteps; God would've fried you in a flaming meteor shower before that could happen. The bold thing to do would've been to stand up to him. Why didn't you ever stand up to your father?"

I refused to answer the question. Instead, I emptied the entirety of my bowels right then and there (which, in all honesty, I hadn't planned to do). My pants exploded and a typhoon of waste deluged the stage; washing both the defamating interviewer in defecation and his silly clown college full of tech crew right out of the building and deep into the maw of the Bermuda Triangle. Sure, some of the more creative sound engineers fashioned a make-shift Noah's Ark out of the log-like stool (and stool chairs, as it were) that I shot at the speed of light, but, in the end, they were cleansed from the world like the filthy diseases they were. All that was left was me, butt-naked, swimming in pools of my own boiling excrement, live on national TV.

I hope Dad was proud of me...

****

Dad died not long ago. When he finally passed, the whole family from around the country, except me of course, gathered together to witness his funeral.

And to make sure he was really dead this time.

Mom drove a stake through his heart.

Grandma cut off the head and stuffed his mouth with garlic and rosaries.

Auntie Bishop set the corpse on fire.

Uncle Bishop then torched the ashes.

Grandpa took the ashes, put it in a soiled bedpan, and stuck a grenade inside before he wrapped it up.

Grandma then summoned *Balphomet* to seal the ground we buried him in and cursed it onto eternity.

Auntie Bishop then salted the earth.

And Uncle Bishop called the authorities to have that plot of land removed from every official geographical and geological record ever made. It no longer legally exists.

I wish I could've been there to see dad given a proper burial. I miss him so, but the words and wisdoms and bold actions still resound in our beings, and still make me think of him. To some, he still lives in their hearts.

To me, he lives in my body as a talking, infected hemorrhoid.

Not one year after we did everything to abolish him from creation, he managed to come back as a possessed, swollen blob that blocked everything from the duodenal down until my intestines ruptured. I almost died of septic complications. Now he talks and wiggles all day, screams at me at night, makes cat calls to the other prisoners, and gracefully accepts them as visitors when they make good on them in the shower and laughs at me for hours on end.

And though, for many, their fathers would live on inside

them through their hearts, for those who really knew what my relationship to my father was really like, this isn't that surprising.

Some of his wisdom makes more sense this way too.

The White Screamer
(Three Incidents)

The deep and twisting dark glades of Tennessee have provided strange spirits reluctant but effective refuge from the arrogant logic of man for untold eons. Although hard to judge whether this land is different than any other southern land with rich forests and abundant mountain life, Tennessee truly becomes a different place at night, and the effects of the moon casting glances of our world to the world hereafter (and every perversion that lies within) have had bizarre, macabre consequences on the living.

If you've never lived in Tennessee, you wouldn't understand. In the summer, the trees swell and rupture with thick, lush greenery that becomes black canopy at night where no light can escape from; giving the devil all the shelter he needs from the fluorescent essence of man. In the fall, the leaves wither and die and the colors that shower the mountains remind us of the fragility of life. This pagan season where the ghosts and geists and demons and such parade down our streets mock the living as the forerunners of fate. They hide in the shadows and in Tennessee there are a lot of them. In the winter, the last leaf falls and death freezes over the mountains. The ones who have lived long enough finally join these disfigured hosts in the season where life is simply shuts off, and the forests and dark, mystic pockets and solid lakes and ponds fill with these undead abominations until spring when life begins anew.

Time, as time so often does, turns a meaningful phrase into a babble of nonsense. How can the world operate in cycles and have its effects be permanent at the same time? If memories are forgotten, where do they go? Time answers neither question and instead chooses to corrupt our recorded history with circular logic. The dark paths that twist behind the veils of Tennessee are no place for time to flow, so, instead, it breaks everything up and plants seeds in the rich, fertile soil to give the corrupted voices of our recorded history a chance to scream back.

The White Screamer is one of these corruptions.

Tales of this inbred phantasm have permeated from White Bluff, Tennessee, and no doubt from other areas surrounding, with an obscurity and somehow a longevity. Anyone who might've known what creature this is has long since become a corrupted spirit too - crushed by fate and then enslaved to this beast's will as it ravages innocent people for vengeance. The victims of The White Screamer are cut down in the dead of night long before they were meant to go, isolated from help and somehow expected to fight a white, sometimes even shapeless force of malevolent intent. Their sorrowful sewage of being joins and feeds The White Screamer simultaneously; a rare and ever vigilant reminder that life is not fair.

What sins of the South could account for this monster? Was it Tennessee's response to the Civil War and the hundreds of thousands of dead souls who roam her land like beggars never to be free? Was it a transcendental act of justice for Southern slaves and every dark-headed child who was born into a cursed land; living in bondage and whose only consolation in life was death? Was it summoned by any of the Native American tribes who knew fate would always side with the white man throughout history? It could be neither and it could easily be all three...

And as such - three incidents of The White Screamer left their mark in the pages of Tennessee's obscure and unnatural history. Many more likely exist, be they true or false, but it could take years before the picture is fully painted for this odd footnote in Tennessee's local lore. With our world so deadlocked into a false sense of *logic*, interest remains lost for any hope of real spiritual evolution.

Whoever or whatever is trying to send us a message here is clearly not pleased with the way history has entitled us to such arrogance.

* 1923 *

In the winter of this year, Garrett McCormack, a young man from Kentucky, had picked up everything he had and moved to White Bluff to marry a widowed woman he had corresponded for several years after he met her in passing in Kentucky. The woman who soon came to be known as Mary McCormack received him into her house and bed and aspired to use what little was left of the family fortune handed down to her for him to build a general store and smithy in town.

Not long after he arrived, though, he found the living arrangements unbearable. Mary had seven children of her own by way of her former husband and this small shack with the leaking roof and rotting wood was not going to do as a family house. During the construction of his general store and smithy, as the workers worked, he set out in search for someone selling a property that would meet his needs.

After a day of searching around, he found a man who was willing to sell a good-sized property for cheap. He met what was a small, nervous elder in the local public house that held a wrinkled deed in his hands. He looked to Garrett like he was going to have a stroke any minute, so he moved quickly throughout the transaction process before the nervous tick keeled over and died.

"Is there *anything* you can tell me about this property before I agree to sign the contract? The price you're asking for is lower than most down payments for a property this size."

"Is that a problem?" asked the nervous man; mumbling slightly.

"Sir, I have seven children now. This house could even more dilapidated than what we have now for all you've told me so far. I can't risk their safety out in the country where no one could get to us."

The nervous man replied with a sharp laugh. The staccato outburst surprised Garrett and many around him. He moved quickly to explain himself.

"What I mean is... the house..." he stopped for a minute, as if he was struggling with the words."The house itself is quite safe, I give you legal word of that, in fact its right here in the contract. *This house has been deemed safe by local authorities.*"

"I know. I'm trying not to take up a lot of your time because it looks like you're itching to get somewhere, but would we have time to go see it?"

The nervous man paused and there was a quick look of panic on his face before it twisted up to a smile.

"Well, sir, the thing is... I'm... *forbidden* to be on the property."

"*Forbidden?* How do you have legal authority to sign the property away then?"

"Perhaps forbidden was the wrong word. You see, the property belonged to my family who ran a plantation on it. The property used to be a plantation, you see, and my family's house is all that remains on the property currently. It was shut down by state authorities many years ago because they were still... using slaves, and out of respect I don't want to step foot on those grounds at all."

"What? Wait a minute, stranger. If you don't want a slave property, why would I? If you haven't been there to check it and it's been closed down for years, how can you guarantee the house is safe?"

"I'll tell you what," said the nervous man who was now shaking in the chair he was sitting on and shaking the chair itself. "I'll take half off the price if the next thing you do is sign the contract. I'll do it right now if you stop prying and trying to make me look like a bad man here."

The offer was odd, but Garrett, having experience with contracts and finding nothing else to question, agreed to do so. He could fix anything on the property with the money he just saved after all. The bargain was made and the man ran into the streets dancing like a fool and squealing like a girl. Garrett would've easily paid full price to not experience the deep foreboding that that action suddenly bestowed upon him.

The next night, the family of nine was fully moved into their new country house. The house needed minor repairs, but fulfilled its contractual obligations surprisingly well. The wife and the kids seemed to like it; so how would such a goofy little troll like the former owner come to own it and be so glad to get rid of it? It was a daunting puzzle to work over in the back of his head and it had played on his mind all day, so when night finally came, he put the children to their beds and sat out on the rocking chair on the porch for some relaxation. It had been an unusually warm day and night for winter from the minute he walked on the property earlier that morning.

Garrett had nearly dozed off in the chair when he heard moaning floating from the forest off to the east.

Soon he spotted something far off in the distance. It was bright white and moving between the trees in a very fluid motion like some sort of serpent glowing in the moonlight. It was impossible to see it clearly, but impossible not to hear it as the moaning soon gave way to screaming. And that screaming turned into loud screaming screeching away into the night. It sounded like a dying child at first and then dropped its voice down to a man's dying cry, and then it wasn't just one man crying of death deep into the night from this iniquitous source - now it was a chorus! That chorus breathed down low and swung its unholy song high up until its shrieking cluster of voices sliced through the clouds hovering under the moonlight. Every time it burst into shrieking, a strong gale would cut through the forest and shake the trees. This gale was deathly cold; the cold of all of winter in one breath and the foundation of the house rocked against it.

Then he saw it. It had a form, though that form could not easily be described with his limited vocabulary. It stood nearly ten feet tall with great human paws attached to an unholy body of flesh that was crowned with the head of none other than *Abraham Lincoln himself.*

Garrett was awestruck. His wildest nightmares could not have produced anything close to this - yet it was very real - and heading this way.

But when Garrett returned with his gun, he found the creature was gone. The beast had vanished but his loathsome screaming still tore the night sky away - ribbons of the starry atmosphere were sheered like bacon off a pig and fell to the ground in the terrible, sensational assault until it was morning. The tortured chorus soon fell back to moaning and finally faded into the sunlight.

It happened this way every night for a week. Garrett came to town one day, shocking the locals with his disheveled look and wanting to buy shotgun ammunition. When pressed, he would tell a crazy story about how he and his family were being stalked by a giant ghoul with a famous human head on it (he chose for very good reasons not to tell anyone who it was) and tonight, this night, he was going to find *The White Screamer* and kill it once and for all.

"The White Screamer? What the hell is that?" they asked themselves before he left; never to be seen again.

That night he sat in the tall grass field near the house with his shotgun and waited. He knew he wouldn't have to wait long; what he didn't know was where to shoot it because the creature's material quality was impossible to ascertain. What if it was a ghost or a demon and not a monster? What if it became mist again on contact with the shell loads?

It was too late to decide - it was already here with its screeching chorus line of castrated men that tore everything down around it followed by a sickeningly impure white aura and then the head... the abominable head of Abraham Lincoln. It went about the circuit it had taken, but just as it was turning to leave, Garrett took a defiant step out and shot the creature.

It seemed to be taken aback as the shell load hit. Its scream was interrupted and it turned its head to Garrett; melting its face into a grim grimace and wild eye stare that made itself somehow twice the monster it was already. Garrett pumped and fired twice more; again at the torso and this time at the head. When he hit the head, The White Screamer twisted his elongated tube of a neck further to meet Garrett eye to eye - except now it was no longer the face of Abraham Lincoln, it was a mask of Abraham Lincoln crunched up as the mouth had expanded far beyond the capacity to keep a face. Thousands of mirror-white daggers were smiling at Garrett in response and the eyes of the President turned red to pierce his soul and break his spirit. It evaporated back into mist and headed back towards the woods.

Foolishly, Garrett chased after it. He splashed through the darkness and waded through the trees to catch up to the phantom light. He tripped over many a branch and root and nearly shot himself more than once. The beast was moving quickly but still he chased as fast as he could. Finally, after an hour of running, he could no longer hear the weak moaning he had been following. It was gone. Frustrated, Garett took his gun into the cradle of his arm and made his way back home.

It was then that the screaming returned - it was the intense deathly screaming that kept him up every night this week - coming from the charred remains of his house.

When he got there, it was everything he had feared. His wife and children, his new family, his new reason for being... gone, and where they were, there were ashen doppelgangers left in their stead. When he tried to touch them, and hold them one last time, they collapsed under his skin and became the *black smoke* that filled his trachea with death and his body with anger. "Why my family? Why didn't he go after me?" he asked himself whenever he had enough strength for a voice. He vomited in the kitchen and lost the last shred of his being with it.

From the kitchen window, which was facing the accursed wood from which evil springs, he could see the abomination floating away like a wisp of light, but following him were these little silhouettes of people that resembled the family he had just lost. He dropped the gun and a compulsion-like hypnotism came over him. He opened the door and slowly followed.

He walked, entranced, through the woods until he came to a rusted box of a shack that was smeared with blood, chains and a filth only a human corpse could make; staining a spot in the accursed wood. Inside were the slave's quarters and on each bed was a glowing silhouette, smiling the same smile with eyes glowing the dark.

"*Do you understand?*" queried a voice from the darkness. The head of Abraham Lincoln popped out of the shadows attached to its rubbery tube of a neck, and snaked around the silent, shaking Garrett. "*We simply wish that you understand the gravity of your atrociously arrant sin; you and everyone like you.*"

"Why not me?" he asked finally, tears streaming down his face, "Why did you take them and not me!?"

"*We have poured over this question ourselves to no justifiable end. We have not received solace for the questions we have asked. What have you done to earn your answer where we could not? We have watched our mothers and fathers give their lives away under the unforgiving sun. We have watched our brothers and sisters die by the whip's crack and we have seen our children and their children starve all of life's promises even after the end of their bondage."*

Garrett felt his heart close off. His eyes starting filling with light and his ears were saturated with the noise of The White Screamer.

"You and your people live lives of delusion. You have taken this world from us with this same entitlement. What you are experiencing as the end of the world is only the beginning. This land and everything on it belongs to us, yourself included, and we are taking everything back. If your people had an ounce of the wisdom we have, you would have stayed in the stinking hole you crawled out of to conquer the Earth. Hope has been dead since your ships arrived on our shores. Your only hope, then, is to join us."

Garrett, with his last shred of humanity, stood his ground.

"I refuse. You murdered my family. They have suffered and I am suffering..."

"Your suffering is insignificant compared to ours!" The White Screamer snarled. *"You have a long way to go before you can understand what true suffering is. If it is any consolation, you will not make this journey alone."*

The light that filled Garrett's eyes exploded and he started to drown in the darkness. The beings on the bed held his body as the head of Abraham Lincoln unhinged its jaw and wrapped its lips around his head. The monstrous crop slipped down over his face and began sucking up the sorrowful body. The children followed soon after until The White Screamer was alone in the quarters.

"Welcome, Garrett. Good of you to join us." they said.

"Thank you for having me." Garrett said in return. And both vanished into the shadows.

* 1953 *

The snow was falling the day Amanda Whitfield had moved her simple possessions to the cabin on the edge of the woods. This cabin had her late father's name on the deed, just as it had his father's name on it before his, and now it was adorned with hers. There was initial reluctance to claim the cabin for a few years prior, but Amanda reached her retirement age before she knew it and with three grown children out in the world, she was nothing more than an old mountain woman now.

"Well, dammit," she resolved, "if I'm going to be an old mountain woman now, I better live the part!" Soon, she bought two old hound dogs to stay with her to enjoy some company and to go out hunting with as she did when she was much, much younger at her father's side. It brought a wry smile to her face knowing in a single month she could go from teaching in school to shooting deer and rabbits better than most of her students; just the way her daddy taught her.

In the backyard of the cabin, the day she moved in, she found a bunch of old junk that her ancestors had left beforehand. She spent a cold day arranging and fixing them up to be a place to skin and prepare whatever she could take home from a hunt. An entire bathtub was recovered from the junk and would make an excellent place to keep remainders and entrails.

The next day, with her two old hound dogs, she was able to shoot and take home a deer. It was a beautiful, clean shot right through the torso; right through the heart. Its legs twisted as it struggled to stay up and run, but fate had other plans for this nameless buck. It lingered as its heart absorbed more and more shock from the bullet until it finally gave out. Other organs soon, but not too soon, gave out until it fell in slow motion to the snowy ground below. It felt intense pain for only a few minutes more until it was blessed with sweet death.

"Come to mama..." she said, and she took the buck for her own. It gave one final jerk and she bashed it with the gun barrel to keep it dead.

Much later, after all the work to prepare it, she had plenty of raw deer meat to last a while in this cold winter. She placed the entrails in the bathtub and went inside to further work on the meat. After that and a scrumptious meal of deer for her and her two hounds, she changed into lighter clothes and picked up a guitar to play outside on the porch. This was another old favorite she picked up in her retirement and every night she sat outside on the porch playing the guitar to the night sounds of critters.

Except tonight there were no critters out... in fact, and she hadn't noticed until she sat down, but the snow had all melted. It warm outside. "Must have one powerful thunderstorm coming over the hills out yonder..." she said as she looked East, "Ain't no critters out neither... somethin's coming, I can feel it."

Then there was a noise and it came as sharply as a knife to the senses. Her two hounds immediately began yelping and running away from the house. She stood up immediately and turned to go back inside for her gun, but then she felt a sudden blast of cold air; like death itself breathing on the back of her neck from afar. She turned to face the darkness of the forest before her. Everything was still and nothing was moving - but it was there, she could feel it.

"Come on out!" she called to the darkness. "You devils 'r' witches! You haints 'r' haunts! You wretched remnants of a time long gone by! You sinful spirits and dancing wraiths! Come on out and show yourself! In the name of the *Father*, and the *Son*, and the *Holy Spirit*, I command you to come out!"

And just then, the thick, strangling silence of the night was broken by a childish moan that swung low. It was a sad and woeful melody at first, but soon broke from its drone to a massive orchestra of painful, soaring, shrieking and screaming. It sounded like hundreds of thousands of people screeching all around her.

Then she saw it. A white figure standing at the edge of the woods. It had to be at least ten feet tall, with giant human hands and the head of *Franklin Delano Roosevelt*, wrapped in an ill emanation of pure hatred and antipathy. And from his smooth-shaven head and chiseled jaw broke out a high-pitched baby scream that just about gave Amanda a heart attack. The trees surrounding the beast ignited and exploded in fire with sound alone, and then it looked straight into her eyes; her doe-like eyes frozen in the bright lights contrasting the darkness choking her heart. The minute she saw the daggers in his mouth, she immediately retreated to the cabin and barricaded every opening. The dogs barked as the screaming figure loomed closer, and they were soon drowned out by the noise.

Amanda nearly dropped her gun when an earth-shattering collision crashed against the cabin wall three times. It was already outside the door and trying to get in. Its giant hands slapped the door and crushed the windows around it. It wouldn't be long before it got in. During a random flash of synaptic confluence, she remembered the stories about this creature; her daddy called it *The White Screamer*. Amanda didn't believe any of the rumors about this monster and now that she's seeing its strength in real life, she still couldn't believe it. The White Screamer squealed in frustration and pounded against the door harder. Amanda was a tough old woman who rushed to the door and held it with everything she had, but she was losing it to that awful high pitched scream. She dropped to her knees whenever that insane cry pierced through the cabin and vibrated the blood in her veins. That world-colliding scream was aging her a hundred times over. She struggled to hold it together and thought and prayed. She thought about her hounds and her children, and she used them to keep her strength as she held the door.

The struggle lasted nearly fifteen minutes before the pounding stopped. Her legs nearly broke at the knees trying to keep this demon out and her ears were most definitely bleeding from excessive force. What little left she could hear was one of her hound dogs barking at the creature and running around to the side where the screamer was following. One of the hounds was trying to lead it away from the cabin to the back. It was working. She scrambled for her gun and tried to recover.

Amanda crawled to the kitchen. One of the other hounds was trying to get in from the side door and she quickly but quietly opened the door to let it in. It broke her heart, but she couldn't leave it open for the other dog. As she scraped up to the sink, she could hear it slurping away at something outside. A quick glance went grotesque as she saw it sucking up the remains of the deer she killed with its weird mouth unhinged and its neck quivering like a snake.

"How fast is this creature?" she wondered. Her legs could still run. If she bolted from the front end, could she outrun it? Or should she try to shoot it from here? This was no ghost; it almost brought the cabin walls down. Or would it leave on it's ow...

Crash!

Amanda was struck from behind by a fast and heavy object that snapped something in her shoulder and brought her down hard. When she opened her eyes, she screamed at the bloodied missile that struck her.

It was her younger hound dog - most of it anyway.

Her shoulder was dislocated, but it was the least of her concerns because the next thrashing sound she heard was The

White Screamer ripping open the kitchen and coming in. Half of it was inside and its demonically contorted Delano head bobbed in and met Amanda face to face. It smiled and spit an undigested part of her hound dog at her.

"Die!" she screamed and shot it point blank in the face. It literally wiped the smile right off its face and the head retreated just as the body broke in and advanced fully.

Pieces of the entire kitchen started flying as the monster burst in. It was blind from the gunshot and thrashing about trying to hit her. It broke a hole through the floor which agitated her shoulder. She dropped her gun down the hole. It was retrievable, but not in this state. It continued to blindly slam its gargantuan hands down on her and break the house down all around her.

The other hound dog seized the opportunity and jumped one of its hands to attack. It tore at the heinous appendage with ravenous energy. Amanda grabbed one of the knives that flew from the kitchen and stabbed at the same hand before she pulled back. She was just in time as the creature reared its wounded hand back with the surviving hound dog on it and slammed it against the fireplace. The dog yelped sharply as it hit the stone hearth.

The knife still in her hand, Amanda tried to go for the other hand, but she wasn't fast enough and demon was able to swipe her and knock her old body across the room. The pain from the collision would've killed any other elderly lady in Tennessee, but mercifully, The White Screamer failed to kill again.

The hound ran behind it to get its leg and while it was distracted, Amanda crawled in excruciating pain towards the hole to retrieve the gun. The creature had reverted to mist and the hound dog chased each end of the unholy cloud; barking wildly as the acidic dew covered and burned its skin. Amanda relished at the small delay in time this gave her to continue, but she remembered the stories of how devious this monster was and still is. The dog played and bit at small tentacles formed from the cloud of the beast that stung and teased it back and forth. It was already planning something. Amanda braved the souring feeling of her enfeebled body as she battled the aches to get her gun and she hated herself for being so weak at her age - a lifetime of hard work and accomplishment as a proud mountain woman about to become a meaningless footnote in a local newspaper.

A new yelp from her sole pup caught her attention and she watched with flaring adrenaline sparks popping in her fractured frame as the poor hound dog was now levitating in the air, ensnared within the mists by the creature that swallowed it whole. It yanked the scared mutt back and forth and tore and stretched it relentlessly. The dog tried to fight back but it was just too stupid an animal to know there was nothing it could do. Amanda broke through her pain and got her bad arm down into the hole; working its way through the darkness to get the gun.

"C'mon, c'mon!" she screamed as she fumbled it.

She opened her eyes and saw something traumatic enough to push her adrenaline to grab it. The monstrous form of the solid gargoyle had returned and wrapped its large, log-like fingers around the hound in its paw and unhinged its jaw for the next main course.

"No!" Amanda screamed and she pulled her gun to fire wildly at the creature. Five shots hit three times. The screecher mimicked her dog and yelped in fiery pain until it finally ground the building behind it in retreat. It was leaving!

Incredibly, the enormous beast left her sight quickly and stomped around to the protected side of the house. First she heard stomping away... then nothing.

She waited and listened... nothing.

Nothing for a whole six minutes.

Silence...

Amanda dropped her rifle, held her bad shoulder and breathed a sigh of relief. "Thank you Jesus... thank you Jesus... thank..."

Crash!

It was impossible, but horrifyingly true. The White Screamer was still there. It just shot one of its ridiculous paws through the window and grabbed the poor hound; ensnaring it again with its long, white skeleton fingers that touch death itself. As it reared the hand back, stalagmites pumped from its knuckles and slowly, mockingly, dragged the hound dog to a grisly demise. Before Amanda could protest in vain, she heard those horrible slurping sounds again. There was a final yelp, and then nothing.

Amanda slowly sank to the ground, utterly destroyed and now indistinguishable from the rest of the wreckage in her cabin. She could hear nothing but ringing in her ears from that screaming. If her battered body could talk it would scream as well.

The gun dropped from her arm. It no longer wanted to hold it.

Her legs stopped aching because they could feel nothing at all.

Her shoulder was no longer broken because as far as the world knew it, it had never been there.

Her back, once strong in youth, melted into the disfigured cabin's wooden floor and prepared to join the rest of her body with the wreckage. It was now an obligation instead of an option.

And hovering above her was the splattered face of Franklin Delano Roosevelt. It did not look happy. As she stared deep into its spiraling eyes and the insane color they produced, the light around her slowly drained from the socket and black was swallowing everything whole - everything including the bobbing, twitching head twisting the last moments of her life into a sad farce.

"I don't understand..." she said.

"We know better than to expect you would." the White Screamer sneered with traces of white noise trailing on its words.

"I know what you are. I've heard of you. I went looking for you when I was a little girl by my father's side. I used to hunt for you. I know you can hear and understand me. What have you come for?"

"The threat of life and death never come for anything else. Every life cut down asks the threat this same question. When this land was corrupted by your people, it was the last thing those who were the rightful heirs of this world asked before you cut them down. Of this truth, the Earth itself has assimilated us for this purpose."

Amanda swallowed hard and thought of her children; holding on to them as she knew what would happen soon.

"We come here because this land is ours, trespasser. Your presence is your fate. You have taken from us what you cannot ever hope to give back. We were there for your hunt, trespasser, in the years before. You took one of ours away from us then, and we watched you take another one from us this day. As you sliced its innocent flesh open, the prayers contained therein flowed out and called out in the darkness. To our people, he was our brother and our friend. To our people, you are the threat and a murderer."

Amanda did not shed a tear. She owed herself more dignity than that as she responded, "I used to teach our children in school. The hardest subject to speak plainly was history. I have been alive long enough to see what happened to what I believe you refer to as 'your people'. I saw the complacency in their eyes as they learned what their fathers did to shape my subject into what it was... and it broke my heart."

The White Screamer hissed an entire river and it became dry with his breath.

"But if you think you've come for justice, your fate has been sealed as well. Maybe I won't be able to show you justice, but my God will. I know what you are. Among that you are thieves. You take our forms and our words but you are not human. You have no right to settle our scores. It is you that do not understand that history has been written and there is nothing anyone can do about it now."

"But there is." The White Screamer whispered, hiding something in his voice. *"With your people gone, history will be erased with it, and life can continue as it was before you were ever here. Our forests will grow back with the rightful life of this land. Our brothers and sisters will repopulate and your God will be crushed just like your cursed race. Everything will be back to the way it was."*

"Nothing ever stays the same. Nothing can last forever. You of all creatures should know that."

The White Screamer's facsimulated head, though unseen, moved closer. *"We also know how to repair things that your people cannot. Such is the blessing of being inhuman. Observe."*

There was a sinister gargling sound and the wet splash of a heavy, clumsy object regurgitated on the floor next to her. With what little light was left, she could see in all her life-shattering horror the sealed fate staring and snorting at her right in the face.

It was the deer she slaughtered only hours before; reanimated and *repaired* for retaliation.

"Do all the reparations you want, we will not pay for the sins of our fathers!"

There was another sickening gargle followed by a heavy thump.

"Yes, you will..." said her father as he stared down at her pathetic frame. Amanda was speechless.

"N.....no... no!" she croaked out at last. "T-t-this is not right! You can't do this! This is not natural!" she babbled as sanity burned from her being like the crisp end of a candlewick.

"You have a very poor grasp of nature."

And there were two more heavy thumps following the unearthly sounds. Joining the group of tainted faces preying around her were her two hound dogs; formerly traitors and now forgiven and siding with nature. Amanda's heart broke and finally died.

"In nature, the strong survive and the weak die. History has proven this time and again. You are a pathetic, ignorant old woman of the mountain. What worth is there in your words? Your God has failed you and you are dust before us. If we cannot convince you to join us..." The White Screamer said with a haunting laugh building in the background. *"We know three people that will..."*

And lo, the zenith of sacrilegious horror had finally been reached as the dead eyes of her three grown children blazed in her sight until she could no longer see. It was really happening. It was all true. No one in this era would be safe from reparations - not her, not her children, not her late father... not even her dogs.

"We welcome you into our congregation. Now that the guest has arrived, we can begin our feast."

And they did. Amanda could not bring herself to even scream as all in this congregation feasted on her and tore her body limb from limb. The deer particularly enjoyed the liver while the hound dogs fought for her fingers. When there was just a husk left, The White Screamer bent low and slurped it up as it always had.

The cabin burned down soon after.

* 1983 *

Dusk was soon to fall over the black leaf branches that curled down from the white ash trees. These trees had grown tall in short years and twisted up their claws to the sky to block the sun from ever warming the cold, subzero Earth below them. It used to be that the evil spirits waited until winter to do their dark bidding - now, in this execrated forest, every day throughout the year was the coldest day of winter. The hollows of this forest, a section of the greater wood area known as *Baron Falls*, were most definitely hollow - devoid of natural life though not without its activity; a fact that even in this day and age repulses the locals who long thought they abandoned their superstitions for reason and sanity.

But what sanity is there when nearly every two weeks, a new corpse is discovered near the falls? More often than anyone would care to know, someone ignores the warning signs posted by locals and local law enforcement and goes over the borders and barriers to do *who-knows-what* in the Baron Falls. People do their research and they find this natural red light district and all the locals, who refuse to say anything about the cursed woods at all so as not to incite excitement, can do is warn people not to go there. Something is out there hiding. Something is watching and waiting for another derelict prostitute or wayward hobo or drug runner to enter its territory and become its prey. Something has bedamned this wood where wood should not have been and has set to kill everything that enters in.

And everyone in White Pine knows what it is.

Dusk was soon to fall, maybe in an hour or so, when Mary Catherine and her husband, Mark Chase, were walking up alongside the river with plenty of fishing equipment and no fish. They had walked about two miles up along the river bank from where their truck was parked; looking for a good spot where the fish were jumping. There was a point where the path had broken off, just before it reached Baron Falls, but the layout of the land, a small opening locals had not considered as they barricaded entrances to this awful place, made it very easy to go down and walk on the rocks over the shallow water to where the path leads up again. Mark went first and hoisted his wife up to continue the path down the water.

"Did it get cold?" Mary asked as she shivered walking along the new path.

"Probably. It's going to be dark soon, but we'll be alright. We just need to stay on the river bank and go straight and we'll get back to the truck without any trouble."

They walked for another ten minutes before Mark found a fat ridge to sit on and cast out a line. His good wife, ever by his side, sat next to him with arms folded so as to cover the goose bumps she was getting from... everything around her.

"Did you see any fish on the way up here?" Mary asked to a husband that was getting somewhat frustrated as he sat there for an hour getting nothing.

"I did not. The man at the tackle shop told me they were all upstream and I thought this was far enough..."

The two sat there as the sun finally laid down and died and cast the shadow of death over the night sky. There was not a fish to be found for miles; neither any other living creature for miles further than that. This fact did not elude Mary as she sat with her husband, so when she heard a howling whooshing and slicing through the trees, her spine froze and spread to her nerves.

"Damn!" Mark screamed. "I got the line all tangled up. How the hell did I do that?"

"No, Mark, please don't go..."

"It's all right, I can get it." Mark stood up and stripped down to his shorts. "I'll be back in just a minute." then he slowly stepped into the freezing waters to chase along the nearly invisible string that had been caught underwater. Any other time in history,

Mary would not have protested, as Mark was a Kentucky state champion swimmer and trainer, but out here...

Out here... it was different.

Mary could feel the icy cold water soaking up her skin and everything inside her... and still she was perfectly dry. Something cold and wet was breathing on her, but what? Her skin was crawling - something was calling it to come near. It wanted to peel off and run to its master...

Five minutes and no sign of Mark. She tried not to panic, maybe he was just out of sight; just out of sight and making no noises whatsoever; just too inconsiderate to shout he was ok or even splash around a little bit. That didn't sound like Mark at all, but certainly it was possible. No reason to panic... no reason to panic. Wait! Maybe he got out of the water and is back on the bank.

Mary turned to the bank above her from where she was watching on the sand and, indeed, there was an outline of a man on the edge of the woods. He was coming towards Mary, but the minute her relief melted to pensive terror is when he stopped, just at the edge, and stared deep into her frightened eyes. She could not look away. She stared back at the man, now joined by two others, with a transfixed stare of glassy eyes and a lazy jaw that fell ever so further to the ground as more and more men and women and children appeared at the edge of the woods. She stared deep into the center of this ashen-face congregation and they stared right back at her - each horrendous immobile figure peering into the depths of her soul looking for things to fondle aggressively and excessively. It was like watching a painting move. Mary's chest began to ache and she realized she hadn't been breathing the whole time. She took in air as fast as she could to combat the queerness of this congregation and found it was dead dark. Whole hours had passed. Mark was still nowhere to be seen. Finally, somehow, she completely broke free of their spell and ran down the riverbed screaming for Mark's name.

As she ran, calling for her husband, she glimpsed at the forest edge where more and more of these people had gathered to watch her. Whereas they saw fresh meat for the master in most of the fools who dared to tread on his land - something was different here and it had gathered all the victims and their remaining, tormented, undying spirits who had to see what this could mean.

Finally, at long last, there was Mark. He was heard choking up water and debris from the river as he struggled to find a voice to call back to her.

"....r....r.......rrr......run!" he screamed as his throat finally opened and he shot past her; too shocked to extend an arm to grab her along.

He screamed for her to run again, but this time it was drowned out. An enormous, soul-splitting, bone-crunching scream blast through the death of the night. It started slow, worked its way up, and finally delivered a stone-solid wall of noise that mutilated one of Mary's lungs and had her coughing up blood.

And then she saw it.

From the parturition of darkness itself, the ghostly mist and people gathered to an apex where the form was seen. The now legendary planetary threat of these cursed woods, *The White Screamer,* strode with earthquake steps towards the living. The form was every bit the icon of sin the locals and family had ever described and Mary closed her eyes from the end of the world before her to run.

Mary caught up to her husband in no time at all. He was hobbled and limping as close to the speed of light as he could, but it still wasn't close to fast enough. She could not witness in this pale moonlight the depth and severity of his wounds from fighting the creature as it took him underwater, but the blood that the creature had literally caused to scorch down Mark's body as it gushed was black even in good light. Mark's leg was either broken or well on its way to it - and it was two more miles to the truck. All of Mary's body was too busy flying down the riverside path to show even the slightest bit of concern for her loved one; as much as she wanted to fight it.

Behind them, slowly creeping up, was a faint white light that somehow made the stygian air they were stumbling through for survival even more sickening. The pale, blasphemous aura of The White Screamer drifted closer trying to suck them in. The monster's thunderous stomping started to shake the ground beneath them. Mary did not dare try to look back to see how close the monster was, but that she could smell its cadaverous redolence to the point where it burned her eyes, made her weak in the knees and give up. When they came to the break in the riverside path, it was do or die. The White Screamer took a swipe at Mary and nearly knocked her down with the force of its swing. In about two seconds it was going to step on her. Something had to give.

With no warning whatsoever, Mark, in great pain and effort, launched off his bad leg to the side, tackling Mary and redirecting their course into the frozen depths of the river below. Mary hit the shallow rocks and nearly shattered a rib, but ignored the crushing pain and scrambled with her husband into the much deeper river ahead. The White Screamer was stunned temporarily and watched its prey try to escape in the water. Mark and Mary dove down into the depths and emerged behind a large rock that protruded from the middle of the river.

Finally alone with her crippled husband, Mary struggled to find the semblance to tend to his injuries and find out what happened, but the shock and weight of this unreal horror finally caught up to her and she found herself babbling and crying incoherently; struggling to stay afloat.

"That thing was waiting for me in the water..." he said as he fiddled with something underwater. "It was already there, but it couldn't move well in the water and that's how I could get out." He put both hands on Mary's face to get her to focus. "Here's what we're going to do. That tree over yonder? I saw an opening down below the water. If you can get in there and hide, stay there and I'll swim upstream to get the truck. I'll lure it away and drive back here. C'mon, keep it together now!"

Just then, the genocide-infusing slash of The White Screamer's high pitched roar soared out like a blade from its frustrated husk of a body; slicing whole flocks of birds flying over and disintegrating them into fractions of dust as they dropped into the fallout waste of its sound. The blasphemous aura the demon wore like a coat of malignant fury slowly went from white to red. It was not used to having its prey evade capture.

"I'm going for it. Get in the tree and wait there, I'll be back soon enough!" He kissed her and swam off; making an enormous noise to cover the sound of Mary diving deep and crawling up into the claustrophobic trunk of the nearly submerged tree. It widened out as she climbed up and found a space with air to breathe.

She could hear nothing. She could see nothing. This position was far worse than anything outside with the danger of the beast and its spectral horde waiting outside - at least then she could understand what was going on around her. Here was the end of time itself; where every moment was an infinite lifetime of desolate zero. Here was the complete absence of being. No awareness - not even the dead are condemned to such a fate; as she recently found out.

"How long have I been in here?" she said in her head. "Where is Mark? Please don't panic. Oh my god, what if he never made it to the truck? What if that thing finds me in here? How do I get out? What if it *doesn't* find me? Am I going to spend the rest of my life stuck in this tree worrying for my husband? Please don't panic. Oh God, what am I going to do!?"

She struggled with these questions for some time still.

Then she felt the waves of the water that numbed her body start to pulse. It was light at first and she couldn't tell if it was her doing it or... no, now she was sure something was coming up from the bottom. Her dreams of a husband safe and sound with a working truck that could take them far from the Baron Falls and the hell it has created were short lived - as the face of the husband she desperately wanted to see faded and was replaced with a different face that was attached to a long, ribbed, tube-like neck.

John F. Kennedy.

"We do not understand..." the creature's head said as it bobbed with a studious look on its stolen baby-face; analyzing and absorbing Mary's figure and essence. *"You... you are not one of them. We find this difficult to believe. You are both of us in one body. We demand an answer. What are you doing with that man?"*

"I... I was just... going fishing with my husband." said the tiny Native American woman who cowered against the tree bark with boiling Cherokee and African-American blood speeding through her veins.

"Disgusting. You who bears the name of countless warriors before you subdued by that pathetic slave-owner? To what do you owe him the bondage of your slavery?"

"He is not my 'master'; he is my *husband*." Mary said with teeth gritted.

"What nonsense do you speak so freely of? You are this man's property by choice? We do not understand how you can be so ignorant."

Mary was stunned, but unusually appalled as well. She was already used to these words from her mother as were the same words from her grandmother and cousins, but to hear it from this obscene hellion was a bizarre dynamic for which she had no conventional response for.

"I know what you are. In fact, a lot of people know what you are now. I didn't think you were real; not just because you are a demon, but because I also find it hard to believe anything capable of social intelligence could still begrudge with these old beliefs."

"We do not understand what you speak of. The man you call a husband dragged you from your safe lands into this pit of unending death to gorge on the lifeblood of our river, did he not?"

"What are you talking about!?" Mary screamed; nearly forgetting what it was she was addressing. "I married him thirteen years ago! He *asked* me and I said *yes*! I am not a slave, nor am I a captive... I am a woman. I am a *wife*."

"Woman, you suffer from grave delusions. You do not belong to that man; you belong to us. You are not a child of the world; you are a child of the planet and its people who the ancestors of this man murdered in the cardinal sin of history."

"What do you know about history?" she asked, trying to distract it as her right hand entered a small pocket of the bark where she found something small and metal. It was a retractable knife of whose origins were largely irrelevant right now. "What do you know about anything for that matter? You're not human; you're just a defiled collection of ancient consciousness given form without context." That was the most complicated sentence Mary had ever said.

"We have no need to return to our primitive roots of humanity to understand how humanity works. We understand history because we are history. Only those who make the ultimate sacrifices down through the ages could ever hope to understand truth as it applies to life and death on this planet, and we have made that sacrifice millions of times over. The white man, from his earliest roots in conquest over the peoples of Rome, the peoples of the Celtic ancestry, the shrines of those who worshipped the nature of the planet and on through the eons, have always been rooted in the purest of evils. And their God, the God who holds its own arbitrary sovereignty over all that is created, has twisted fate to reward them for their evils throughout our history..."

Mary's finger wrapped around the knife; positioning it for a quick retract and stab whenever the moment to strike came up. She could feel an inscription on it. *L. H. O.*

"But even God cannot control fate. Fate is determined by those who wield history as we do. We will destroy the white man and his God and return everything to where it was supposed to be. The planet has spoken and we are the answer. You will join us to bring our destiny back to fruition. You will return to us and twist fate back to where it belongs."

The knife now in her hands, Mary decided she had heard enough. One just quick snap of the shoulder should do it.

"I will never join you. I will not join anyone who threatens my husband and his family. Fate has already decided your destiny, and instead of moving on you sit here, isolated, barricading yourself from the rest of the world and think everyone who has ever lived owes you something." She flipped the blade out, and prepared to thrust. "My father was just like you. I killed him when he threatened my husband, and I'll fuckin' *murder your ass* too."

The face of JFK smiled and shone its evil ruby eyes to illuminate the trunk with hatred. The daggers of its mouth reflected as such. Here it was.

"And how do...."

Mary lunged forward and shot the knife into its mouth. The puncture point sliced through the roof of its mouth and into its brain; if such a thing existed in a creature like this.

For the first time ever, The White Screamer could not scream. Its fracturing vocal chords gurgled as it tasted the blade of true justice. Instead, the hulking body, which was right outside the trunk, grabbed the trunk with its huge paws and lifted it high into the air. It flew like a dart toward the riverbed and splintered as the incredible force crushed it and nearly Mary.

Free from her cage and possibly still alive, Mary emerged from the wreckage with the knife still hand and wasted no time scrambling to her bloodied hands, knees and feet to escape further. She ran and ran and ran until her one surviving lung could take no more. The beast was nowhere in sight, but that made it even more dangerous. She saw a faint light shining a small dot through the forest. It was a different light than The White Screamer's and she heard lighter footsteps from across the distance. It had to be Mark! It was the truck!

Mary forgot the pain in her chest and shot through the dark forest hell-bent on salvation. She waded through the ghostly crowd that now regarded her with a sense of their own fear; a ghostly crowd that refused to descend on her; a warrior of their own who had slashed the master and maimed him. She got closer and closer to the truck. The headlights went from dots to blaring beams of welcome light.

And in the center of that light was her husband, Mark. Battered, bloodied and beaten; swollen with water, he stood about one-tenth of a mile in front of the truck and waited for her to arrive. When Mary finally got there, she dove into his arms and cried into his bloodied shoulder. Again, she found it hard to speak and instead just poured her heart out to him in a whispered frenzy of words.

But she was quickly silenced when my hand moved down his back and found a fault line from his spine to his buttock. There was a gaping hole. Then another.

Mary quickly returned to his eyes and found they were no longer there; replaced with the same red eyes that froze the world with all they could see. Mark held her closer so she could not escape. "Do not cry, Mary. *The Master* said he would forgive my lifetime of sin and the sins of my ancestors if I would serve him and convince you to serve as well. Join us, Mary. We can take back the planet from the people who corrupted fate and then we can live in peace - together forever."

Mary, unable to speak and letting instinct take over, wrestled her way out of his grasp and ran toward the truck before she stumbled and fell. She turned back and in the headlights could see her husband for what he's truly become. A wreck, a traitor, a dead man... a slave.

"The Master said it didn't matter if you were alive or dead. As long as you served, we could begin to make up for our role in history. We have a lot of work, Mary. The night is eternal, but that is no reason to delay. Progress is within our reach!"

And the cadaver jumped forward. Mary rolled out of the way and got to her feet, but was not fast enough to evade him when he grabbed her by the arm. He turned her around and plowed his fist into her face. Her head flew to the right and Mark, in one move, backhanded her sharply and slapped her to bring her back to center. Still holding on to her, he reared back and shot his dead fist into her chest. The rib that has cracked earlier fell away and now Mark was going to try to take her still-beating heart out like the Master commanded.

Mary did not give him that chance. With the knife in her hand, she cut his arm at the wrist and wrestled to get free. She ran towards the truck which was, mercifully, still running. She fell when Mark tackled her at her legs and turned her over on her back. He got on top of her, held her face with the hand she tried to sever and beat her in the face. Again and again.

"Negro woman, you will obey your master!" And he hit her three more times.

He got off of her and, with what little consciousness remained, she watched as he retrieved a collar attached to a chain. It was the same chained collar that belonged to her ancestor from a Kentucky plantation from one hundred and sixty years ago. They shared the same name, "Mary Little", and Mark attached the other end to the back of his truck.

It was almost too late when Mary woke up with the collar around her neck and the truck engine revving.

There was no time to undo the chain; there was only time to hang on.

Mary, with every ounce of strength her ancestors had bestowed upon her at birth, held onto the chain so that even the slightest chance of survival she could fight for. The truck drove over the rough forest land and scraped her torso against the rocks and stones and sticks with waist and legs to receive the cognate damage. Her body took an ungodly thrashing; enough that if fate had not already deemed her important enough to survive the night, she would've died long before now, but she held on; she had to. The minute she let go of this chain, she would be dead and every effort made up to this point would have been made in vain. If she dies tonight, no one in service of the Master would ever be free. More people would die and becomes slaves of an unrighteous crusade and history would continue to corrupt fate forevermore. Everything was riding on her and she held on...

Until she finally collapsed when the truck came to a stop.

"No human can stand against fate, negro-Indian woman. Enjoy your moment of rest - your eternal lifetime of servitude in this land begins now. Come."

As soon as Mark came into reach, Mary turned and thrust the L.H.O. knife deep into his traitorous face. Mark fell back and Mary, with her front end torn to shreds and her body brimming with so much auxiliary life force that she was numb inside and out, got on top of her former husband - the white man who beat and collared her, and tried to deliver her into slavery, and was eviscerated beyond even The White Screamer's capacity to revive. She didn't shed a single tear.

There was a cabin within view. Mary could see its outline even in this desperate and dark time. On the other side was the pale white aura of The White Screamer. It blinked red and Mary could see it was fuming and raging. She could hear its planet-crushing stomping getting extremely close in such a short period of time. In two minutes, it would be here. She couldn't fight it out here in the open. She had to get inside where it would have trouble moving.

As she limped to the cabin, a light from inside shown, and like a miracle, she saw a man at the door. She pleaded with him to let her in and he relented. Once she was inside he closed the door.

"Ok, now... just calm down. Start from the beginning and... good Lord, is that John F. Kennedy?" the owner asked.

To a point, it was. It was the face of JFK leering over the window; shamefully attached to a body that had started to pound on the cabin walls.

"Get down!" the man shouted. "Get behind the couch!"

Mary did as she was told and the man disappeared to his "recreation" room, returning several rifles; one of which he gave to Mary. "Don't you worry ma'am." said the man who identified himself as Lee. "I've done this before."

Crash!

Mary and Lee went for their guns as the maimed face of JFK rocketed through the window and towards the two; hoping to chomp off a head as pull the body back.

Instead, it took one look at Lee and Mary saw it... freeze in terror? What was this?

"Yeah... you remember me, don't you?" said Lee with an exaggerated smile on his face that came from nowhere and he then took aim and fired; puncturing the throat of the tube.

The beast responded by charging through the entrance. It tore open the cabin and ripped the walls out like it was made of paper. The debris flew and crashed against Lee and Mary; battering them with hard wood. The White Screamer slashed its right paw at Mary and threw her across the room. His left paw took

Lee and grounded him against the floor of the cabin. It pressed harder against Lee until Mary came back, gun in hand, and shot up and through its strong arms. The White Screamer reared back and prepared to attack Mary again, but Lee took advantage of its stance and shot multiple times in its chest. It fell back and outside the cabin again. It tried to scream the scream that bore legends and killed scores and armies of innocent men and gave it its vile name for all of White Pine and the surrounding South to fear, but it could not. The bullet that pierced its throat and the knife it took in the mouth had taken away its most forceful weapon. Without its voice, what could the leader of this revolution hope to accomplish? Its slaves and followers, who gathered around the cabin, were now spooked themselves and had begun to disperse among the shadows of the forest; hoping never to be seen again.

The beast even tried to turn back into the mist that bore it, but it was no good. The minute it stood up, Lee and Mary launched another volley of bullets that burrowed through its ancient, mummified skin and bedeviled its malominous insides. The self-proclaimed ruler of this land, just like every other throughout history, had simply grown too old to sustain its immortal empire, and it fell again to the ground.

Fate had dealt it a cruel blow, but such was the way of history. And Mary, knife in hand, stood over the ancient evil - her own eyes burning, and screamed a scream that tore through the forest and echoed through the woods and dissolved rocks in the ground and destroyed the glades in the mountains and froze the waters in the river and the falls. It was the *true* warrior's scream and it hadn't been heard in this region for many, many years.

She dove to her knees and slashed the monster open. She stabbed and stabbed with all the spirits of her ancestors cheering her on and her warrior spirit, like blazing fire, stabbed until the beast finally stopped moving.

Then she stabbed it again.

Lee was inside the cabin, sitting at his chair with a cigarette in his mouth, when a half-crazed, blood-soaked, black-Cherokee woman came inside, the head of John F. Kennedy in her hand.

"You ok?" Lee asked.

"No... I know too much. I've seen too much of what this world can really be like."

"You get used to it." he said as he puffed some smoke. "Can I have my knife back?"

Mary, in her hyper disoriented state, looked down at the knife and studied the inscription again. Suddenly something crept through her skin, and even more suddenly, she found herself holding up the head of John F. Kennedy and staring at it. Something was wrong here. Something was very wrong indeed. A dull throb started in her head and she looked at the man in disbelief.

"You know that's the second time I've had to shoot that guy?"

"You fought that monster before?"

"I wasn't talking about the monster..." That strange, otherworldly smile spread over his face again; twisting it into an evil intention.

Mary dropped the head and lunged forward with the knife. She sliced Lee's throat with the blade he left her in the tree trunk and he died with that same evil smile on his face. It was too hard to tell now if this was justice - either way, there was a level of satisfaction to it that could not be denied.

Mary went outside toward the truck, but the truck was fully dead. The White Screamer burned it on its way over and there was not another one on the property. She was stuck there in this territory; on this land.

She dragged the corpse of *Lee Harvey Oswald* to the corpse of The White Screamer and her former husband. She poured alcohol from Lee's cabinet all over them and stood over them with a match. She took a minute to wonder why she was doing this. What was it for? Fate? Destiny? History? Vengeance? Pride? Conspiracy? God? Love? Honor? Freedom? Family? Justice?

"Forget it. It's all just too fuckin' confusing..." and she dropped the match. Someday this scene would replay itself in a new era, as a new history circled over and wound back, but today is was meaningless as were all these terms that tried to justify that which had no true justice.

As the bonfire outside burned away its cursed history into cursed smoke for the cursed night sky, Mary went inside and made the bed the way she wanted it.

This land belonged to her now, and anyone else who came in it would meet the same fate.

****

This story is based off three stories that were posted on a forum years ago regarding the legend of The White Screamer of White Pine, TN. The first was posted anonymously while the other two were posted mononymously by a woman simply calling herself "Karen".

This forum no longer exists. Like The White Screamer, it has faded into the annals of history and disappeared into the mists.

The Book of the Three Little Pigs

(Bible Version)

1

1In the land of Leid, shortly after the year of Greisth, on the third day of the eleventh month in observance of Ele'ben'thrah, the deliverance of sovereign grace from the Lord, our God, between the mountains of Negeb and Morabah, which were ruled by the King of Og, Fay'shellom'ashis, lived a family of Pigs by the reedsides and the stone gardens, Kyashallom and his three sons, Solomon, the wisest son, Meridikai, the foolish son, and Karrash, the son of no fixed intelligence. 2Shortly after his children came of age, Kyshallom took them to the hills of Setruthuliam, east of the land of Gorohorn where King Zelo'phehad ruled from the city of Ilb, 3and there the Lord spoke to Solomon and Meridikai and Karrash at the foot of the hill.

4"I am the Lord, your God, who delivered you from strife and suffering in the year of Exodus, the fourth month of Fast, from the lands of Slaughter, from Jimmy Dean, the Pharaoh of Sausage. 5Behold, these are the words I command to you that you will keep in reverence all the days of your life.

6"Thou shalt not a burden to your farmhand be."

7"Thou shalt not squeal the Lord's name in vain."

8"Thou shalt not consume food in the lands where thou hast defecated and thou shalt not commit adultery with thy neighbor's ass or spread thy seed to any neighboring mammal of exquisite feathers or girth."

9"Remember the Suckling Day and keep it holy."

10"Thou shalt not boil a kid in its mother's milk."

11"Thou shalt not engage the temptation to frolic in thy own filth or the filth of others. Thou shalt keep thy flesh pure in honor of the Lord. Thus says the Lord, your God."

12The next day, when they returned to their land, Kyashallom said onto his sons, "It is time that you withdrew from the house of Swine to build houses of your own, to which you will then find wives and bear seven children of your own and repopulate the land with our people." And they left the house of their father. 13 Karrash built his house of reeds found next to the river Hezebell in the land of the Gentiles which had no ruler. 14Meridikai built his house of wet sand and mustard seeds 1,600 cubits away from his brother Karrash. 15Solomon, a skilled carpenter, built his house of cement and brick upon the rocks, in a village near the Jewish city of Hahbollah in the province of Magog under the rule of Neirdu, the seventh son of Gilgamith. 16Solomon worked hard every day out of forty weeks to please his father, to please the Lord, and honor the house of Swine. But Karrash and Meridikai did not honor the commandments of the Lord, their God. 17They drank many jars of swine wine every night, gambled in the streets every afternoon and slept with many women every morning. 18Meridikai became very lazy and Karrash became as fat as a hog.

2

1Where upon this time the devil, in the form of a wolf, came to the land of Leid, at the beginning of the year of Rachel, the tenth month of Vapors, to prey upon these swine. 2At this time they were lazy and full of sloth. They stumbled as they walked and fell into much of their own filth, a blasphemy under the Lord. The hungry beast descended upon them. 3He arrived first at the house of Karrash. He knocked upon the door calling, "Little Pig, Little Pig, let me in!"

4Karrash was scared and did not know what to do, and he was filled with much shame as he used God's word in vain, 5"He who rapes this house of its occupants shall find the wrath of God!" He called back.

6The devil called again, "Little pig, little pig, let me in!" 7Karrash became scared again and called upon the honor of his father, "As my father before me, a great leader of the Pig army, said to the invaders of the temple of Pork, 8'Not by the hair of thy chinny-chin-chin!'" 9The devil was angry and warned the piglet,. "If you do not let me in this house, little pig, I will conjure a plague of wind and tear down this haven!" 10And the devil did huff, and the devil did puff, and the devil did blow down the house of Karrash. 11Karrash ran, but his sloth and weight kept him from escaping quickly enough from the devil. 12The Lord took pity on Karrash nevertheless and allowed him to escape his enemy. 13He ran to his brother Meridikai and Meridikai accepted his brother into his house and they spent the night eating, drinking and calling upon a flock of Jewish prostitutes.

3

1At dawn the next day, the devil, in the form of a wolf, approached the house of Meridikai and called to the brothers saying, "Little pigs, Little pigs, let me in!" 2Meridikai then answered, "He who approachth this house in the name of God may enter, but he who opposeth the Lord shalt enter the Lord's judgment quickly!" 3The devil then said unto them, "Little pigs, little pigs, let me in!" The brothers, calling upon the honor of their father, said unto the devil, "Not by the hair of thine chinny-chin-chin!" 4And the devil did huff, and the devil did puff, and the devil did blow their house down as he had done before. 5Being built only of sand and mustard seeds, the haven easily succumbed to the plague of wind and it flew to the valley of Agmeb. 6Karrash and

Meridikai escaped through the brush weeds of the fields of Zeredah, close to the coastline of Beb which was governed by the daughter of Josaphat in the land of Job near the river of Poopalacka and went to the house of their brother Solomon.

4

1At dawn the next day, Meridikai and Karrash came to the house of Solomon, and Solomon accepted his brothers from their strife, and gave them food and swine wine. 2After their supper, they met and prayed to the Lord, "O Lord, protect us pigs, your servants, from our enemy." 3And they spent the night praying around the holy Oink of the Covenant.

4At noon the following day, the Devil in the form of a wolf came to the house of Solomon saying, "Little Pigs, Little Pigs, let me in!" 5Solomon called to the devil, "You will not penetrate this house of Bacon, for it is the will of the Lord thy God that our people will survive and repopulate the land with our people! 6Begone enemy! " 7Without warning, without huffing or puffing, the devil released a horrible storm of breath upon the house, but the walls remained strong. 8Again the devil blew, but the house, protected by the Lord, stayed strong in its foundation. 9The devil did blow for forty days and the devil did blow for forty nights and threatened them with curses of famine and pestilence upon their livestock and frankincense and grains and checkered robes and pigskins, 10but the walls of the house of Bacon did not tremble.

11Then the devil did catch in his eye a chimney large enough to encompass his girth. 12Using the wolf's body, he jumped up to the chimney with great agility. 13The pigs held up the Oink of the Covenant and prayed to the Lord asking for protection against their invader. 14Just as they had prayed, Meridikai did stumble upon a chair leg, and dropped the Oink of the covenant upon the gas lever of the fireplace and flames grew within the fireplace and the devil was consumed by the fire until his ashes laid dormant upon the hearth.

15And the pigs did rejoice and praised the Lord for their protection and the lands became greatly populated with their sons and daughters. From all the lands, the peoples told stories of the brothers who did boldly against the devil and how the Lord blessed them in their strife. 16And the Lord blessed the latter days of Solomon and Meridikai and Karrash until their lives were full of days and each died an old pig. When it was time to bury them, the peoples of the lands all came together and they were feasted upon by those who came to love them in life in a great fire.

17And the Lord said unto the people, "You will call this feast Barbecue, and you will celebrate it each year on this day, the last Sabbath of January, in reverence of me, and you will make pigskins to play games in great congregation and feast upon these ribs and rinds and sandwiches and grilled meat and strips of Bacon to cover leavened hamburgers and keep it holy."

HOPEBLISS

Once there lived a boy who had two heads.
The one on the right was called *HOPE*.
The one of the other right was called *BLISS*.
They shared one body and lived separate lives.
One head spoke only the truth.
The other spoke only lies.
But no one knew which one was which.

One day, the double boy was walking through a wood
when they came across a woman with no head.
The boy on the right offered to share his head with her
so she could go about her life.
She went home that day
and told her son what a horrible mistake he was.
She told her husband she was sleeping with his mom
and selling the videos to pay his disability bills.
She went to work and told the boss she had evidence.
Then she went to Jesus
and told him to fuck off and die.
Then she called the news station
and said she saw a disfigured man
carry a beaten teenage girl inside his shack.
That night the double boy showed up at her door.
"I'm as happy as I've ever been." She said with a smile on his face.
But a deal was a deal
and right there on the porch, she exchanged heads.

The next day, she woke up in her bed.
She told her son how much she loved him
and how proud she was and how strong he is
living in an iron lung.
She told her husband she didn't care
if he ever regained mobility.
She'd still fuck him whenever he wanted her to.
She went to work and praised her boss
and how big his shriveled testicles were.
Then she went to Jesus
and told him to fuck off and die.
Again, she called the news station
and told them to call off the search.
It had been a hoax.
That night the double boy showed up at her door
"I'm miserable." She said frowning. "I cannot live doing this."
She gave back the other head.
The double boy presented her a handmade head
With a smile carved on its face.
"Until you get one of your own." One of them said.
"It's a very bold choice." said the other.

The next morning, the news was on.
The remains of an 18-year-old girl were found in the woods.
She had been beaten
and eaten
and barbecued at the end.
The shack was gone
and so was the man.
The woman had a lot to answer for
but her mouth wouldn't move
It could only smile boldly.

She heard the testimony
of the girl's mother in court
crying her tears and the tears of her suffering little girl.
All she did was smile boldly.

She was shived in prison.
And used for everything under the sun.
The inmates made toilet paper from her skin.
All she did was smile boldly.

Then she heard husband died.
Her son choked, escaping the iron lung
to help his father during heart failure.
He would never be the same.
And all she did was smile boldly.

Elsewhere,
a boy with two heads was walking out of the woods.
One head spoke only the truth.
The other spoke lies.
But they were both eating the same charred remains.

No one should ever talk to Jesus that way.

If you saw him for real, you would be lucky to have words to say
at all.

Ouroboros

On June 26th, 1992, officers from surrounding counties responded to a disturbance at a residential cabin in an unincorporated district of Appalachia (the exact address and location of which is currently protected under law as part of the investigation) six miles from the nearest town. "Something," according to Mrs. Cleo Jones, had forced itself inside the cabin without warning and charged towards the baby's room with some form of conviction. It broke through the door with ease and then there was silence.

The account by Mrs. Cleo Jones has met with skepticism since Mr. Figaro Jones was at work at the time and sources vary what she had actually said since her testimony was given in an understandably hysterical fashion. Her testimony, however, became the least of their problems once responding officers opened the door to the baby's room.

Inside was the aftermath of what could only be described by Sgt. Antonio as an, "epileptic apocalypse of fire and placenta..." for the entire room was razed and soaking and dripping in red waste with enormous veins popping out of everywhere. Where the door was ripped off the hinges and further along the wall were claw marks with deep burn scars scrawled into the drywall. It moved with frightening intensity and somehow made this surreal nightmare canvas over the baby room without a sound and then disappeared.

But the most frightening and disturbing part was when Sgt. Antonio discovered the baby.

Under a flap of tissue that resembled a macabre pair of lips was an infant body, encased, almost mummified, in a wooden "skin" so it had the appearance of a doll. The eyes were hollowed out and yellow. Between the cracks and joints were leaks of blood. The blood was still wet.

If that wasn't confusing and heartbreaking already, DNA confirmed this was not Ezekiel "Dickie" Jones, the child who went missing that night. This was the body of another child who went missing in Appalachia years before and who had no legal persons to be turned over to. Another inexplicable dead end in a case that had no beginning, no middle and no end, so they "adopted" the baby into the precinct.

They named him "Ouroboros", and put him on display in the evidence department, as a constant reminder until the investigation was finished...

****

"...!"

Ezekiel stared into the distant, dead mountainside where he thought he caught it. Somewhere in the deep, dark brown craterous hills that reached high into the sky and sealed off the valley from nearly all of the rest of the world, Ezekiel could feel it pulsating very small waves that reverberated within him. It was a very sudden sensation that vibrated his arm and told him immediately to turn... west! Now!

...nothing.

He searched the skyscraping, brown and gray mountain hill that was dusted with snow leftover a recent storm here in the valley. There were a few cabins and rundown homes in the general vantage point below the jagged white and grayer skyline of the cloudy blanket above, but absolutely nothing in the concentrated spot he was told to look. There was a light mist hanging over head pissing little fragments of snow in silent reverence for the mystic mountains, but there was no other movement or signal of consciousness throughout the makeshift basin; not even from him. This ghostly valley was always akin to little disturbances between the winds, and usually it was surmised that echoes of time before somehow still resounded in the cracks of the ridges of the mountains. It was difficult to define with examples and definitions, but the light curtain that veiled the valley during winter, usually starting with autumn, had the power to bring premonitions of revenants wandering through the trees and the breeze. Even in the great open field out here where Ezekiel was listening for, the curtain would sometimes drop low and create new ethereal walls that shaped new labyrinths with their own haunted valleys and glades.

He stopped and didn't move an inch. He darted his eyes for movement. Silence... silence...

Suddenly, he gasped shortly and started twisting his head around again looking for the *signal* that was being produced. The dull throb almost sounded like a heartbeat inside his head and down to his arm. His arm throbbed deeper now, dancing with the rhythms it was receiving, and reacting naturally as the rhythms evolved beyond normal time. His eyes wandered. His head soon followed. Where was this phantasmal beacon signaling from? His eyes drifted upwards until he came to just slightly up from that same spot where there was a clearing. Nearly invisible before, now he wondered how he could've missed it at all. It was a conspicuous spot of a lighter brown earth that increasingly stood out against the canvas of dark brown Appalachia the more he stared at it. It did not have much snow on it and this was strange as much of the rest of that mountainside was well dusted in white. The spot grew in his mind until he could see a small level square; perhaps a crude foundation of some kind next to a long-dried out hillside farming acre. There was some mild forest growth on it like it was meant to have something there but did not. It looked like the future site of someone's tomb...

What an eerie thing to behold. Ever the *clockwerk knight*, the gears in his mind began to turn as he stared at it; fixated on its empyreal significance. If it is empty, what is the significance of being drawn to it? Why does snow barely touch it at all? There was nothing to it and at all, except the curiosity. It was so slight and yet so... *presuntuoso?* How could an empty space do that?

Ezekiel made up his mind. He had to get there. It was barely a question of want; now it was a matter of need. But how would he get there? It was more than a good walk away - fifteen minutes across field and twenty to thirty minutes to scale the hillside to get there. He was already off school grounds and technically cutting class as it is - trying to alleviate whatever *psionic allure* this one negligent spot in all of Christendom had by going now was simply out of the question, no matter the need. His education at the Clockwerk Academy forbid him from deviating his stone-cold logic to chase a flight of fancy and he would have to answer up for it.

In fact, here came one of the administrators from the academy right now...

"Ezekiel! Ezekiel!"

Over the green hillside came the figure obscured in shadows by the bright white clouds above looking like a scarecrow. It was, in fact, Nurse Gideon trotting up and down the hill in a remarkably surprising fashion for a woman her age sporting a wooden leg and a false arm. As her ancient body with its arguably more ancient attachments came jerking up the road, her false arm was grasped tightly to a set of documents that were waving around in her stride. She did not usually come this far out from school grounds to retrieve wayward students, so this clearly was important...

"Your test results came back..." she said breathlessly; her lightly wired mouth and face dropping slightly... a telltale sign if ever there was one. Ezekiel stared at her - not hard, but with enough intensity to acknowledge the potential gravity of whatever this situation was, and that whatever he was chasing out here in the valley was no longer a matter of need.

Nurse Gideon put her false arm around his shoulder and ushered him back to the academy.

****

Ezekiel waited on the sugar pine bench outside the office of the Headmaster, *David Geppetto*, with the test results in hand. He had studied the documents parallel to the headmaster studying Ezekiel's school records, but as the stars collided on that parallel, neither could make either document out. Both were puzzled by a recent change of things; thus the need to meet immediately.

"Ezekiel, come in." commanded the former commander of some ancient forgotten war no one had ever heard of before and the door opened wide by its own mechanism. Ezekiel straightened up, stiff as a sugar pine board, the way he was taught to address the headmaster, and entered into the highly spacious headmaster's office. Ezekiel stood straight up against the sugar pine desk, the same wood the master of the Clockwerk Academy used to carve his own arm and leg, and prepared for punishment. He made sure to hide his arm from the headmaster...

"...as you were, cadet." said the headmaster calmly as he turned his equally lacquered sugar pine chair with special hidden grooves made just below the knee so occasionally he could perform *richieste* on it away from prying eyes. "Having reviewed your disciplinary record, I don't think a punishment is necessary at this time. However, if you want to retain that privilege, *don't-do it-again*." he gritted his words slowly as they trailed off; as was his authority and method to keep charge over the cadets.

The headmaster started eyeing the documents in Ezekiel's hand for a brief second before he continued on. "What were you doing out there anyway?"

Ezekiel didn't answer at first. Not yet. He had to think of a way to explain his arm which he went to great lengths to keep beneath the headmaster's notice, 'Twas no good; for the headmaster interrupted him again.

"What were you doing out there? You missed a very important test today."

"...I am aware of that, headmaster."

"Ok, then *why* were you out there?"

Ezekiel paused and panicked again, but knew he couldn't keep his headmaster waiting. As David Geppetto glanced towards the medical examination results for his arm, he considered changing the subject to that, but could not find an easy segue into it. He swallowed hard.

"...something was calling me."

"I beg your pardon?"

"...something was calling me... and I responded, sir."

The headmaster's brow furrowed, but before Ezekiel could nervously try to clarify, the headmaster pointed to the test results finally and asked simply, "May I see that?"

Ezekiel sheepishly produced the documents and Headmaster Geppetto almost seemed to snatch it out of his hands. The headmaster took a good look at the readings that Ezekiel found wildly incomprehensible before. But soon it went from typical apprehension to a new form of almost terror as the headmaster's eyes suddenly stopped on the document and his face dropped down low. He started sounding the words out and Ezekiel nearly had a panic attack. He could understand it perfectly, and it didn't look like he liked what he saw. The background and atmosphere just went from a military sterility and now became all too *real*.

"...how old are you, Zeke?"

"Eighteen, sir."

The headmaster did not look up. The look on his face and the whites of his eyes were certainly telling of something, but not clue as to what. Ezekiel wanted to shout something, anything to break this sudden tension. Ezekiel parted his lips to do that, but the headmaster quickly shook his face and all concerning tells from it as he set the document back down.

"...this is a little bit surprising but nothing to worry about. Ahem, umm, anyway, you will need to take a make-up test." The headmaster turned away and started scribbling on a notepad. "Take this to the *Autos Ephe* room and slide it into the *red box*. You will receive your test at any time within the next week. You will be evaluated by a high-ranking senior administrator and your evaluation, once calculated within micrometers of its accuracy, will be sent to me and you and I will have a meeting to discuss the results. Do you have any questions?"

"No, sir."

There was another awkward pause where there really should not have been. The headmaster's face stared right through him in return, as if he were surprised that there was nothing else to ask. Geppetto was not taken to such...

"Alright then. As you were, cadet. Watch for that makeup test."

Ezekiel left the room and found himself alone in the twilit wooden halls of the Clockwerk Academy. His service-issue hard, black boots could not help themselves but boom their nervous footsteps across the almost entirely sugar pine academic complex. During the usual hours when students crowd and jostle through the hallways, the acoustics didn't lend themselves to being so conspicuously foreboding, but alone... it was a different story. The Clockwerk Academy was not a place to be suspicious of, but even a sheltered boy like Ezekiel was aware of the outside world's influence and curiosity to the eremite school which existed wildly out of place and way out of town in this basin and valley.

At the gates is a giant plaque that reads simply,

Clockwerk Academy
"Scientia Verus Universitas"
(The Knowledge of the True World)

Every so often some reporters from network televisions across the globe would show up at the gates looking for answers, but students themselves never managed to see them. Indeed, the students sometimes had questions of their own which they asked themselves privately. Many of the cadets graduate into the world, but to do what? What was it exactly they were learning to do? The school took in students from every walk of life and financial background - so what was the exclusion? The school was not publicly funded; nor did it reach out to collect monies as many of the rich aristocrats of America had never heard of it. The *finanziere riservato* was not known and many cadets whispered about him in the shadows as even mentioning a possible name for this phantom entity in a well-lit, large room with lots of people in it was met with fearful reactions; as though he might suddenly appear and liquidate the entire student body with the mere mention of his name. All sorts of hearsay abounded - it was even rumored that the school was founded by *Pythagoras* himself, but, again, the hyper-logical knights of the faculty administration shot down all such information and reminded the cadets of their diminishing test grades and that such rumors did not reflect the knowledge of *true world*.

Hardly rumors of suspicious intent, certainly, but aberrant all the same...

After delivering his document to the red box of the empty Autos Ephe room, Ezekiel wandered lonely as a cloud back to his dormitory on the east side. It was getting dark, and the biting cold wind of another snowfall greeted him as he passed from the main academic complex to the eastern dorm. His medical document nearly blew away and towards the valley he had wandered off to earlier.

About fifteen minutes after he had changed from his blue academy uniform into regular clothes and sat at his bed in the dormitory, there was a knock at the door. The bland malaise of the day's events in backwash met its sudden contrast with the appearance of the bright-faced *Julie La Fata Dai Capelli Turchini*, a five-foot-eight, eighteen year old nanophysics brunette his age who bounced as she entered with a white *Pass* pinned to her blue school uniform.

"Hello, hello!" she said very brightly as she skipped in; plopping herself on the bed where he was sitting. Ezekiel was quite surprised to see her as female cadets were only allowed in the boys' rooms a strict few number of times. He pointed out the pass on her uniform.

"Where did you get that? I thought you used your last one."

"My instructor gave it to me." she picked it up and stretched it out.

"I thought they weren't issuing new ones until Spring."

"Well, actually..." and she bit her lip and turned her eyes sideways, blushing slightly. "...it's for class. It's part of my course requirement for *Home Sociology*. We're at the part of class where we need to select someone from the student body to have sex with. I need it to complete the course."

Ezekiel was rigid. His eyes widened in a similar fashion to terror and he was nearly afraid to move. He was in no position to escape.

"And *my* name came up? I thought you had to sign up to get your name on that list."

"No! This year they're letting us choose our partners!" Julie's eyes reflected the natural *esuberanza* that radiated from her as she explained it. "And they're actually letting us stay the night too!"

Ezekiel did not share Julie's placid enthusiasm. In fact, it made him freeze further. "And so... w-why did you choose me?"

"Huh?"

"I... I didn't..."

"Well..." she rolled her eyes up and gave a small smirk that lifted her syllable to a slightly flirtatious tone. "I mean, we've been best friends for a long time and I'd get to hang out and stay for the night, I... I didn't think it would be a big deal."

This did not calm Ezekiel's anxiety. Julie took his hand with both of her soft, slender hands covering his and sat him down on the bed next to her. "C'mon, it won't be that awkward. We don't have to do anal or oral; that's all extra credit and icky anyway. We'll just do it real quick and then we can hang out the rest of the night."

Ezekiel cringed when she put her hand on his shoulder, but he braved it to turn to her face. "...you can't get out of it? It's a course requirement?"

"Yeah, I fail the class if I don't lose my virginity." she said, tossing the words off over her shoulder and whipping her bowl cut bangs away from her head. "And if I can't find a student to do it with, I have to complete the requirement with one of the *school administrators*. I *don't* get to choose then."

"...ok... yeah, I'll do it."

"Yay!" Julie giggled and she hopped on the bed a couple times as he started to get undressed. "Thank you, thank you!"

"...no problem."

"Do you want the top or the bottom?"

"I don't know. Let's flip a coin."

"Ok... any requests?"

"No!"

* One Hour Later *

"That was better than I expected!" Julie said, shaping her medium-length, bang-cut hair back into its original format. "See? That wasn't so bad."

"My leg still hurts from you sitting on my lap..."

"Really? I guess I've got kind of a big butt. I'm sorry..." she apologized still with a slight flirtation in her voice. "I've sat on your lap before and it didn't bother you then."

"Well, yeah, you were smaller then and you weren't using it as a trampoline."

"Oh!" Julie said; suddenly remembering something. Then her eyes brightened again and she turned to him quickly. "Hey, how's your arm doing?"

"Honestly? I don't have a clue. The test results are on the table there." he pointed to it and she scanned it over with her thick vocabulary. "I couldn't make any sense of it. Can you understand it?"

There was some expected confusion on Julie's face that twisted the cheery, narrow complexion into wrinkles as she studied the wild "medical" jargon. "...kinda. I know these words because of my engineering classes and nanophysics, but yeah, none of this really makes any sense that I can tell."

Ezekiel's voice dropped as the dormant focus on his arm and what happened earlier slowly crept back in. "It feels like... it wants something... out in the mountains, but it won't tell me what it is..."

"...non-linear alliancing between 800-1000mhz... *multi-theorem compass buffering* over the z-limit... Wave ratios with *uniband compression overclock*..." she read until she finally just tossed it aside. "It looks like a load of crap to me. Do you see the headmaster about it? What did he say?"

"He seemed to understand it, but he just told me I needed to take a makeup test."

"Yeah, I heard you did that! What were you doing out there?"

"...something was calling me, but I couldn't find it."

Julie sat down next to him and started rubbing the arm in question. "If the headmaster couldn't find anything wrong, I'm sure its nothing. C'mon, let's do something fun. Take your mind off that."

The rest of the evening was uneventful. The two best friends, often confused for brother and sister, spent another two hours playing and fooling around like when they were kids, but while Julie had her youthful fun without the slightest care in all the valley, Ezekiel could not shake the trembling from his body that started when she pressed her naked body against his. He put on a brave face when he was looking at her, but when she turned away, his face became frozen again.

His arm did not respond when she rubbed it friendly before, but during sex, it could not stop vibrating...

****

"!"

Ezekiel woke up with a start and threw the covers off his bed. They landed on Julie who was asleep in her uniform facing away from him on the other pillow. He looked outside towards the dark night where snow continued to fall.

There was music - as lonely as the cold, harsh world outside... and it was calling to him. He looked out to the mountain range again... and this time, *he saw it.*

"Julie! Julie wake up!"

Julie woke up with a mumbled start.

"My arm... can you hear it? It's playing music. Take a look outside! There it is! See it!?"

The next thing Julie knew, because she hadn't fully woken up until the cold wind bit her in the face, was that she and Ezekiel were dashing across the snow-covered valley to the mountain range ahead. Inexplicably, and in the back of Ezekiel's mind perhaps from the events of earlier when his actions caused it to vibrate had sent out a message, or even a command of its own, the desolate spot of light brown mountain was no longer there. The white curtain was now hanging much, much lower than before, and it was indeed creating a glistening labyrinth of spectral design for them to navigate.

From the spot where once was a foundation now had the outline of a house.

And inside that outline was a *light.*

And from that light, as they raced across the snow fields that once sustained life, to Ezekiel at least the music emanating from his arm could be heard externally. It got louder as they got closer. The whole thing happened so quickly, Julie still wondered if she was dreaming. Everything was happening so much faster than her sleepy mind could put together. Huge gaps made the scenes wash together, and now they came to the foot of the hill and immediately started climbing. Ezekiel put more effort into climbing and had to help Julie along the way. He had conviction and he wasn't going to stop for anything. No one knew they were out here and there was nothing stopping it from being a matter of need now.

An hour of climbing later, Ezekiel and Julie came to that mystic *terra piana* that had lead them there. The white curtain hanging over head was actually draped down beneath them now down in the valley. The ends of its aurora were far below and the snow picked up and got heavier. The cold winds now were a blessing to the exhausted and overheated teenagers. Julie, now fully awake, could share Ezekiel's foreboding sense of awe and she gazed in wonder at the big, log cabin house that had appeared from nowhere, or the other world that this world was not, with a huge outside stone fireplace.

"This... this wasn't here before..." she whispered.

"We need to find a door and see where that light is coming from..."

"Why? I'm not scared, but, Zeke, I really don't like this place." she said softly as she shivered.

Ezekiel held her from behind and rubbed her to keep her warm. "C'mon, if it gets too weird we'll run back down the mountain, but we need to figure this out. C'mon now."

Both teens in matching blue uniforms traced the outline of the house for a door and its light source, but nothing.

"This is ridiculous..." Julie said.

"Wait... do you hear it?" Ezekiel leaned down to the outside chimney opening. "The music gets louder from here." He motioned for her to come forward. "Let's take a look in here. I can... I can see something."

And the girl bent down and they both peered inside. Their vision seemed to somehow jump up from the black wall they were facing - up through the chimney and to another vantage point like they were looking in from ground level. Like a perverted periscope or something.

Inside, they found an executively decorated log cabin. It was dark inside but it was occasionally lit by an inside fireplace just outside their view. They could see a leather sofa, bear skin rugs and fancy farmhouse nonsense nailed to the walls. It was a far too tasteful scene to fit this illusionary frame. The fireplace from inside had flames that seemed to dance seductively to them as they struggled to make sense of this smoky vision.

Someone was there, but whom?

Suddenly, their view swung to the left where they could see more of the indoor fireplace and more expensive, insanely decadent furniture; some of which Ezekiel could identify and appraise as highly rare, highly valuable pieces of work almost to the point of scholarly interest and study. Absolutely bizarre. The fire was roaring and they could see a leopard print chair, another skin rug... a broken glass of wine... and a used condom. Ezekiel peered further left and found a gramophone hidden in the darkness playing a warbled violin tune - it was the music coming from his arm.

"This is getting scary..." Julie whispered with fear in her throat. "Let's get out of here."

"Wait!" Ezekiel said and the view peered back.

Now there was a man on the couch. A suave looking *signore più anziano* with long, slick black hair tied in a ponytail. Wrapped around his svelte torso was a shiny red robe and fancy pajama bottoms that extended down to his expensive looking gentlemen's shoes. There was a lavender puff of fabric coming from the top of his chest and it was pinned with something small and gold. In his right hand was a smoking cigar, and his left fondled a new wine glass.

This man... this man was the *Impresario*... and it was clear to Ezekiel and Julie, based on the evidence, that this man had just raped someone.

"Come on, we can't stay here! We need to... oh my God!" Julie screamed.

The Impresario was staring right at them.

The teens turned to black ice as they were spotted. A new wave of fear, one neither had ever experienced or even read about, tore out their bronchioles and made them fight for air. The mysterious man rose up, smiling, and gently put his wine glass and cigar down and positioned to move toward them. His eyes turned red and became starbursts in their vision. His smile extended further, and further, until his cheekbones ripped open as it flared back into an unnatural circle.

Suddenly they could hear something like a tea kettle building to whistle and their vision started to quake. Something was building up and preparing to assault them until both the noise and the vision were too much to take.

"*Ha!*"

The Impresario snapped his fingers and a huge flame burst forth out of the empty outdoor fireplace. The flame absorbed Ezekiel and Julie and threw the teens high into the air; straight through the white curtain which bathed them in spectral snow before they plummeted, graced only by the kindness of the revenants watching, back down to the ground. They both crashed into a dilapidated log storage shelter and while their injuries were minor, their spirits were in shambles.

"What... what the hell was that?" Julie said shivering. She was closer to the cabin and she popped her head back up towards the cabin as did Ezekiel when he rolled out of the snow bank he was dropped in to stare at the black box of horrors before them. They both stared hard, unblinking even in the wild winds of winter, and watched for the Impresario to come out and murder them.

He never did.

Slowly, Ezekiel crawled up and toward the cabin. Julie whispered and pleaded for him not to, but Ezekiel did not listen. Faint traces of music were still in his arm and surely the man would've come out again if he wanted to. Very, very carefully he peered inside the fireplace again.

"Julie... c'mere, you gotta come see this. It's ok, c'mere, look at this!"

And Julie did; even slower and more careful than her friend; Julie peered inside too and was shocked at the sight before her.

Nothing. It was all gone. Just some broken shards of things remained. It looked like no one had been inside for years and years...

Now both were eagerly wanting answers. They both scurried around the building to look for clues that that really happened. The snow had stopped falling, probably a warning sign from the heavens above...

"Zeke! I found something!"

Ezekiel came to the other side of the cabin that was facing out to the dead and decrepit, tiny old grain farm towards the cliff edge of the ridge. Now there was a door from this side that was definitely new. There was no chance it had been there before.

"What are you doing? No! You promised me we'd leave if it got too weird. How much weirder can this get? C'mon, let's go!"

Ezekiel didn't listen and tried the doorknob anyway. Fully expecting resistance, he was highly amazed how easily it turned to open - and amazed further at what they saw inside.

As soon as Julie turned on the light next to the door, they found themselves not in a dusky, creepy old cabin, but the inside of a modern *salone* in a ranch-style dwelling. The walls were drywall, punctuated with pictures of any family anywhere, and colored a green robin's egg color. There was a couch with some lazy chairs next to it and a modest coffee table with a crunched up placemat and some magazines. Some pillows were on the floor. If the buildup to this scene hadn't been so inundated with mystery, this room would seem entirely... normal.

"Zeke, this is someone's house; we can't be in here! What if someone finds us here and tries to shoot us?"

Ezekiel went forward; ushering Julie behind him. She held on to his shoulders as he called out for any one in the house. Nothing stirred upon his words.

"...no one's here. I don't think they're coming back." He said as walked further inside and touched a few things and inspected some others. Absolutely nothing seemed out of the ordinary - and that's exactly what bothered Ezekiel. It looked like a family had gone on vacation a month ago and didn't bother to clean or lock up for a trip that long.

Julie reluctantly joined him as he turned on more lights and started looking through the rooms for clues. Clues for what? No one could be sure right now. Ezekiel's arm was still vibrating - very mildly and no longer audible, but still enough to tell him something was going on.

"What did you find?" Ezekiel asked Julie as she came back from the right side of the house.

"I didn't find anything. I couldn't find any entrance to the cabin or any trace of the Impresario." her natural brightness had dipped down to its dimmest in years as she struggled to absorb everything.

"I couldn't find anything either. It's driving me nuts. I'm trying to use logic and everything we've been taught up to now to make a proper hypothesis, but it's just not coming up."

Julie turned her head back up at him and there was a rare *essere indifeso* in her voice. "It's true that something weird happened, but, Zeke, this is a normal house. I don't think we're going to find anything here; y'know, its what we learned in the academy. If it doesn't make logical sense, then it doesn't happen. We can't find anything, so nothing happened."

Ezekiel stared hard at her.

"I know it betrays what we've actually seen and experienced, but that's as close to a real hypothesis as we're going to find here. C'mon, let's go back. I have class really early in the morning."

So they left the conflicting house and trotted back down the mountain and through the snow fields again. Interestingly enough, the snow and the winds had all died down, as did the vibration in Ezekiel's arm. When a fresh new hour began, they snuck back into the dorm and only took their boots off. Ezekiel felt bad that he dragged Julie through that mess and hugged her as a means of a much needed, warming apology. They slipped back under the covers and tried to go to sleep, but Julie could not yet. Her bright eyes shown in the darkness as they were wide awake still. There was something she needed to say first.

"Hey... Zeke..."

"H....huh? What?"

"There's.... there's something I didn't tell you."

"What?"

"Yeah... I did kinda find something... at the cabin."

Ezekiel sat up in the bed and turned towards her. Julie continued.

"We looked at the pictures of the family that was supposed to be staying there. It was a dad, a mom, a grandfather and two kids between the ages of nine to thirteen. The mom was not pregnant and there was no baby... but in the back, in a real dark spot of the hallway, I found a baby room."

Ezekiel stayed quiet, but his arm started to vibrate again.

"It had been used recently and there were signs of someone leaving the room to deliberately make it look nonchalant like nothing happened in there. The closet..." and she stopped to bite her lip. "The closet was open and it was dark inside, but I didn't look in there. When I turned to look at it, something came into my head. It was like a vision of a giant snake, covered in fire, circling around the planet and eating its own tail. It was just for a brief second, but it felt very powerful and very real. I didn't want to say anything then because it just wasn't what we're taught to believe. I just wanted to come back. I don't like being out there. I don't like things happening that we can't explain. Are you mad at me?"

Ezekiel took a second to think before he answered, "No, its fine; really. Let's get some sleep now." and he sunk back down to the mattress facing away from her. Not because he was mad, but because he liked to sleep on his arm.

And tonight, it was playing for him a lullaby.

****

The next day, Julie did not see Ezekiel at all; aside from when she woke up before he did. She took her classes as she was supposed to do and completed her assignment for Home Sociology. The professor gave her high marks but admitted he was slightly disappointed; though he didn't tell her it was because *he* wanted to complete that assignment with her...

It got to be dinner time and she still didn't see or hear of him. He was not in the commissary where he was usually the first to sit down and eat. This happened sometimes but today... for some reason today was different. Something touching her skin made her feel different about it. It was a dull ache in her chest that, slight as it was, made an impact on her generally sunny and energetic demeanor. Several classmates commented that she seemed unusually down today. A couple people hugged her because they thought she needed one. Today was simply strange all-around. Against her better logic, she thought back to some of the folksy commentary her foster parents might've told her, "Well, it was strange last night, so it'll be strange today." She didn't feel quite like eating at dinner. The dull ache in skin turned to her stomach. Maybe this is kind of like what Ezekiel was telling her about his arm.

Finally, as she walked toward the girl's dorm, something from the twilight, snow soaked sky from off the horizon was the outline of a man coming toward her.

Moments later, Ezekiel appeared within that frame and her famously radiant attitude jumpstarted right back up. She felt compelled to run to him and she did; stopping just short of jumping into his arms.

"Where have you been?" she asked hurriedly. "You missed class today! The headmaster was looking for you! The instructor was pissed!"

"I went back up to the cabin."

Julie's smile faded and she looked at him with a sense of disbelief; almost more so than the disbelief she experienced last night.

"You did *what?*"

"I spent the entire day up there. I wanted to go back and check it out with it light outside. I checked out the baby room."

"Well... ok. What did you find? What did you do that took all day?"

Ezekiel ushered her inside and out of the cold. Instead of answer her, he said, "Tomorrow's Saturday; so the instructors and the headmaster won't be looking for us. Bring some of your nanophysics stuff and meet me up at the cabin tomorrow."

He did not stay long after that. Julie tried to talk him out of it, but she knew better than to talk him out of anything. Ezekiel was a stubborn old *bambola*. His head could as thick as swollen wood and his will like a redwood tree when he attaches onto something. The best Julie could hope for is to just go through with it and maybe talk him out of it after a day of failure.

That night, Julie couldn't sleep; she had almost come to it when she heard footsteps going away from the academy. When she looked out her window to see who could be out this late at night, she could've sworn she saw the Impresario before he faded out into the black air over the white land.

****

Julie took extra care not to even walk in front of the outside fireplace on this dull, light late morning. Every nerve of her training as a physicist and a scientist stung at her superstitious assertion, but that didn't make it any easier to tread nearer to it. She did still expected it to volcano the minute her eyes got lined up in sight. Her Clockwerk instructors would've all caned her in turn if they saw her quiver like that.

"Julie? C'mon inside!" Ezekiel called from around the corner. He was arranging certain sticks of wood in a sort of arcane mathematical construct; as he called it. Ezekiel had planned to set it on fire with certain herbs he found inside the house and see what could be conjured. Julie, however, recognized it as a primitive *tetractys* and the herbs as simply oregano and rosemary; though she let him have his fun.

The entire day was much to the same effect. There were lots of esoteric experiments with all of the many devices Julie brought in her school satchel. Typically these were designed for field work and to yield empirical results that could be studied in the lab; not to go ghost-hunting in someone else's private property and turn up nothing. Julie did wish, after hours of wild experimenting well off the top of the head, that she could share Ezekiel's *entusiasmo* for this area of abstruse investigation as it did seem to bring out a shine within him that was rare and just as luminous as her own *splendore*. He became like a child again; interested and invested in everything and everyone around him. It was a side of him she admittedly missed in the last few years of attending the academy, and something she missed in herself as she got older. Day after day as a Clockwerk scientist was so much more demanding than she could ever realized. Seeing how much fun he was having, testing the water, testing the electrical fields, coming up with all these ghostly theories... was there any wonder why he stayed here all day before?

Soon it was sunset. They took a break from their many experiments and investigations on the house to eat some dinner. Ezekiel cooked out of the family's kitchen; eating out of the family's cupboard and using the family's dishes and they ate - both relatively satisfied, for different reasons, with the day's work though it yielded nothing. Somehow the dinner turned into a tickle fight, and somehow the tickle fight turned into a wrestling match where both teens bounced and jumped off the couch and made a little mat on the floor in front of the TV. Julie proved to be a strong contender, but Ezekiel won in the end - just like he used to do when they were kids. He collapsed on top of her crying with laughter just like Julie was.

"Ok....ok..." Julie said, giggling and struggling to settle down. "That was a lot of fun... haaa.... are you ready to go back down now?"

"Down where?"

"To school!" she said laughing, tossing a pillow at him. "We have chore sessions all day tomorrow. I have to wax all the sugar pine floors tomorrow."

"Oh yeah..." Ezekiel said, climbing off of her. "I had forgotten about that. I actually have my stuff here; I was going to spend the night."

Julie's smile twisted into a confused grimace. "Wait, what? You were going to spend the *night* here?"

"Yeah. Because I didn't find much yesterday; just something in the baby's room, and we didn't find anything today. I figured since it was night the first time we got here, I should stay for that and witness anything that happens."

"Well... ok, but what are you going to do about tomorrow?"

"I have some sick days I can use up. You still have your pass, right? Why don't you stay with me?"

"That pass was only good for Thursday." Julie explained. She really didn't want to say no to his offer, but she had an academic career to think about. "I can't stay the night with you, Zeke. I want to, but we had our fun up here. That family could be back any minute."

"No, they won't be." he said and he pulled out some documents they went over earlier. He dumped them in her lap earlier and she just breezed through them. "Remember? These are all the records the county has for this property. There hasn't been any record of anyone living here in over five months."

"Except... you."

Ezekiel was going to say something in response, but he laughed instead. Julie was about to say something, but Ezekiel interrupted her, "Ok, here's what we'll do. I still have some privileges to the messenger system at school. I'll just write you on how my investigation is going up here and have them send the letters to your dorm room. Is that ok?"

"Well..." she really didn't understand what he was saying. "How long do you think you'll be up here?"

"I don't know."

"What about Headmaster Geppetto?"

"*Fuck* Headmaster Geppetto." he said curtly. Julie reacted with acute shock; she had never heard him talk like that before. "I'm not his fucking puppet. I'm doing something up here."

There was an extremely awkward silence after that. Even Ezekiel was rather surprised at his outburst and he did his best not to follow up with it. Julie did her best not to follow up either, because something was clearly sensitive about this little "trip" up here. There was definitely a reason he could curse his headmaster when he had never done so before.

"...what did you find in the baby room?" she asked at last.

"...I tried to go in there last when I was over here yesterday. Honestly, what you told me the other night about the baby room kinda... freaked me out. But at the same time I felt something... release... when you said it. I feel strangely compelled to check it out even though I've mostly stayed away from it."

"...*curiosity?*"

"Is that what it's called?"

"Yeah, I read something about it a long time ago. I'm surprised you still feel that or even *fear*. Most of the other cadets our age almost have it weaned out of them."

"I'm as surprised as you are... I... haven't felt this way since I was really little." he paused for a minute, biting both his tongue and his lips as he struggled to really dive into some of these newfound... feelings... "Anyway, if you want to see what I found in the baby room, c'mere, I'll show it to you."

Ezekiel got up with a start, Julie followed in a similarly hurried fashion to the baby room. Julie failed to admit it, but she also purposefully stayed out of this room unless she had to go in like now. She did not experience any more premonitions - and she didn't have to.

He turned around and showed her what he found. His shoulder shook violently from the immense tremors quaking his arm. It was no longer vibrating - it was flapping like a hummingbird wing. Julie tried to approach but Ezekiel told her to stand back as she likely would get hurt if she came near it. Ezekiel could only stay inside for so long because of the stress his entire body was forcing and he nearly tackled Julie on her way out.

"You have to remember, Julie..." he said on the floor between gasps for air. "Three days ago, there wasn't a cabin here. There wasn't a house here either. Even if these experiments don't produce results, it doesn't change those facts. Something's going on here and it goes beyond what they teach us at Clockwerk Academy. I'm *curious*, and I want to find what I seek."

Julie helped him up and rubbed his arm just as the night before. "Zeke... I can't think that way."

"So let *me*, then. Cover for me any way you have to, but let me stay up here and I'll write you what I find... ok?"

She really wanted to protest. The protest with a thousand words of why it made no logical sense to stay here and perpetuate this delusion was right on the tip of Julie's tongue.

"...ok. Sure. I'll see you later, I need to get up early." she tried to smile genuinely as she hurried to gather up her nanophysics equipment, but she had to fake it. The first time in her life she had to fake a smile and leave before she ruined things for him. "I'll see you soon, ok? Bye!" and she hurried out the door and down the mountain before she does something she might regret.

Crash!

Ezekiel jumped into the air and fell to the ground as the enormity of the sudden crash shook the ground beneath his feet. He turned in haste to find the baby's room had completely fallen apart in a single instant. Clothes and dressers, drawers and toys, and the crib itself had all struck the floor at the same time with unnatural force; completely out of nowhere...

Ezekiel's arm started vibrating violently again, and it wouldn't stop until he closed the door to the room.

****

A great hush fell over the campus of the Clockwerk Academy. An indeterminable near silence had, at some point, washed over every living thing inside the sugar pine walls of the *contradictingly* garish institution. Every student could feel it - inside their breath, inside their heads, inside their hearts and just flowing at will throughout their tiny, wooden bodies. It was as though the mists hanging over the mountains had suddenly gathered in a dome over the campus and became as thick and heavy as *pietra*. None of the students could explain this new stifling atmosphere that had manifested almost over night, and even fewer students wanted to discuss it. There was a block there. Even thinking about it made the rigid little soldiers feel an unearned branding or baptism by fire so as not to perpetuate such sinful ideas and fancies.

This "fear", as it was called back in the days before the academy by children even younger than the kindergarteners now cowering in the shadows for reasons unknown, had multiplied many of the apprehensions the students had before in the loud echoes of the footsteps from the hallways and classrooms. This was the week new cadets were enrolled into the academy and, a result of this new, weird phenomenon, they were the first new class never to even hear of Pythagoras. Even whispering his name to yourself was suddenly too dangerous and inspired many nightmares, hour after hour, day after day, of the cosmic repercussions summoning him might bring to one student or another or the student body at large. Not even a ghost now, just a dark heartbeat pumping ominous *rime* in the back of the head was the phantom figure.

And if the hermetic implications of conjuring this foreboding mirage and have its presence echo back with unimaginable evil were not terrifying enough, then the danger of agitating the academic faculty with hushed rumors of his existence certainly was in spades. Something had changed within them as well. Before, they had been strict but fair monarchs of discipline and wisdom. You had to walk the straight line, but you could go at your own pace. Now the monarchs have been stung by treacherous snakes and replaced by *berating* of hickory. Doppelgangers with their hearts torn out; fragments of grace now swept and discarded like useless glass. Many cadets were being punished for doing things they used to do freely. Some did not have to wait for the crack of the sugar pine stick against their heretical flesh - others had to meet a very lurid headmaster, a man with little *cuore* to begin with, who took to branding the students with his name scarred into their largely innocent backsides. This was not a rumor, this was a fact.

The white curtain that veiled the dome turned a black gray and hung very low. It was like death cradling the world in its arms.

No one knew why.

Several days had passed since Julie last saw Ezekiel. These days soon turned into weeks with only the most fleeting moments of correspondence back from him. With this dynamic and the new ominous veil that hung and clouded the academy like a plague of slow-bubbling madness and the new short-fuse madness sweeping over the faculty, making them both marching marionettes and death knights of authority, it was understandable why her heart would start skipping beats every now and then. Waiting for Ezekiel just to say he was ok under all this pressure coming out of left-field was simply intolerable.

The first note she got from him was pinned to her dormitory door and dated January 18th, three days after she hastily retreated from that queer cabin on that haunted ridge.

Monday, January 18th.

Hi Julie. I apologize for writing you so late. I had not gotten enough to justify what I feel would be an appropriate length of letter to send to you and before I had enough to tell you, three days had passed (or more, depending on when you receive this letter). I continue to experiment and search for clues in this mystery.

After you left the other night, there was a disturbance in the baby room. A great force that I believe is related to this mystery suddenly devastated all the furniture in the room. I do not believe this was natural or coincidental.

Despite how terrifying it was, I have gone back in and fixed everything up as it was and begun investigating that room solely. Unfortunately, I have not yet turned up anything conclusive, though, and this may be a case of nerves, but I have possibly heard voices and other suspicious sounds coming from there.

One night I woke up and I was certain I heard crying. For this reason, I have moved from the couch to the master bedroom for my sleeping needs.

Tomorrow, I'm secretly meeting with some geology students from Clockwerk. Please keep that a secret.

I'm going back into the baby room. As I am writing this, I found myself staring into the room and saying "Something happened in there." and when I looked down at the paper I was writing this on, instead of writing, I found I had drawn the picture of that fire snake you told me about. I thought my arm was simply vibrating again, but this time it had done something.

I will write you later. Good night.

The second note came on January 22nd.

Friday, January 22nd

Hi Julie. I trust you haven't told anyone where I am. I met with some of the geology students and they've been telling me what's going on at school.

Part of me wants to suggest there is a connection between what I'm doing up here and what's going on down in the valley, but I know how you would feel about such a hypothesis.

I found something here with the help of the geology students. As we dug through and examined many of the elements here on the ridge, a lot of what we found were not native to this area and there is evidence that indeed something is manufactured here. Obviously, I could've told them that considering this cabin just appeared out of nowhere, but I digress.

That's just the tip of the iceberg, though. One of the students is a "true world" excavator and you'll never guess what we found underground.

Sugar pine. A whole, I can't believe I'm saying this, "vein" of sugar pine existing underground. I knew all that wood at Clockwerk was coming from somewhere because sugar pine isn't native to this area - yet here it is; underground. Something down here is creating it, but we couldn't get to where it was. It's too dangerous. I suppose you're thinking right now it's dangerous to assume the school has any real connection to whatever's going on here, but where else would they get sugar pine? I have no idea what possible connection this cabin has to Clockwerk, but it's something I hope to explore in the times to come.

I've stayed out of the baby room since then. I'm not prepared to tell you any development there. My arm just... tells me not to go. Sometimes you just have to go with that. I've also boarded up the outside chimney. Apart from that, nothing new has developed. I've actually been taking my time more. I've started to get comfortable staying here. I really like the food here too.

Ok, I'll write you later. See ya.

"Well, I'm glad you're comfortable, Zeke." the snide, annoyed comment ran through Julie's mind and almost came out aloud before she stopped herself. She had never made that tone before even in her head.

Did it even come from her?

Days continued to pass without event, but also without whispers and without actions. It felt like the days were not moving at all. It was like the clock was ticking while the second hands stuck in place. Every day was stabbed in the dark and replaced by the day that disguised itself as the day before. Even the hours started and ended in an ongoing loop while the waves of the ocean itself froze in time. Above it the moon waned and bent over the gelid night sky for it too was no longer strong enough to move the waves of the tide. Conversation among students had virtually stopped too for fear of punishment. Those hard hitting boot steps reverberating down the halls of the main building felt more like funeral bells and still no one could explain it.

When people did talk, they whispered not about Pythagoras, but about Ezekiel. Most of it was rot; some of it was not. Some rumors went that Headmaster Geppetto had discharged him to the military to fight in the *Punchinello Wars* raging in Tuscany. Others went that he tried to escape the academy and got lost in the spectral realm of the outside world. These two were, by far, the most tangible ones Julie had heard, but even when students would come up to her and try to validate it or inundate her with further insane questions, she simply kept her mouth shut and walked on. And while this worked for the cadets, she knew it wouldn't work for the faculty who, sooner or later, would start looking for her too. Headmaster Geppetto, especially, was to be avoided. He made no effort to hide his very foul mood and influence these days. One rumor she heard suggested he had two brands destined for her body if ever she walked out of line; one with her name on it scorching across her backside - the other with Ezekiel's name on it scorching across her front. If he caught Julie, he there was a more decent chance than ever that he might turn them both into *Clockwerk Knights* and send them to fight in Tuscany.

On January the 28th, there was a new note pinned on her door from Ezekiel.

Thursday, January 28.

Hey Julie. Sorry I keep taking more and more time to write you. I hope you're well.

I've been frustrated the last few days as I try to work with the information I told you about last time. Nothing seems to add up. Two and two won't go together.

Every day feels about the same up here. It's like there's a cycle up here that, no matter what I do, keeps determining my actions day after day in a tedious sequence. I eat the same things at the same time, go to sleep at the same time and wake up at the same time every day without fail. I don't know where this is coming from.

But, ironically enough, this is where things get interesting. At lunch, I went into the refrigerator to get some milk as I always had at lunchtime, but when I finally got everything prepared and sat down to eat, I found I had orange juice instead.

I don't know how I made that mistake and I didn't feel like getting up, so I just drank that instead.

And then something occurred to me. My eyes kinda drifted to the family pictures on the wall and I realized we completely forgot to consider their role in this mystery. We had focused on The Impresario, which to this date I've still found nothing, and the baby room and why my arm has been calling back to it, but we still don't know who they are or why they're here on the walls. My immaturity has been impeding this investigation. I've been trying to fix this by wearing the father's clothes which are musty and I need to wash, but oddly enough fit me very well. They're a lot more comfortable than my old Clockwerk uniform for sure. I'm really enjoying my time up here. It's great to be up here.

Oh, forgot to mention something else. When I went back to the refrigerator, I couldn't find the orange juice again. I checked both the cartons, which were unlabeled and with a colored plastic, and both of them were milk. Isn't that weird?

I'll write you again soon.

Julie was glad to get word from him, but conflicted because the message was ever more obnoxious and unhelpful. Still no word on when he would be back. Still no word on how he was going to explain himself to a furious headmaster. Still nothing remotely *premuroso*. Her heart was heavy thinking about him day after day; stuck in a cycle of her own wondering about him, worrying about him, angry with him, sick of being sad about him, and even considering if she was better off without him.

Where was all this coming from?

Three days after that, the snow had started to pick up again. The black-gray curtain had unleashed a fury of flurries straight from *Cocytus* itself. It couldn't have come at a worse time. Every day would get more - it would start blustery in the small, misty morning, slow to a marginal dusting painting the mists that obscured the world, then the sun would be blotted entirely by the black curtain; ushering in an early night which gave the winds all the authority to tear across the densely frigid lands and howl like a wolf at the helpless moon. Then it would dump more and more snow, as if something were trying to bury all evidence of mankind and its ambitions from disapproving eyes. The valley had gotten three or four feet of this awful, blasphemous snow. How much would the mountains get?

The next day at lunch, one of the cadets sat down across from Julie with something new he had heard from a friend of a friend of a friend. She was about to dismiss the new rumor about

Ezekiel and walk away, but the cadet told her something that couldn't be ignored.

"I heard he bought a house somewhere near here." the cadet said between mouthfuls of *polpettone*, "Or maybe not bought it, but I heard he signed some papers and owns a house somewhere in the mountains here."

"Who told you that?" Julie asked; trying and failing to conceal a near panic-attack of concern.

"It's been getting around."

"Well, who's been starting all these rumors? No one even dares breathe a word around here anymore. I can't figure out where they're coming from."

The cadet leaned closer to make sure his words could only be heard by her. "I saw someone last night out in the snow fields. He was dressed in black theatrical clothes - like a costume. He came in through the headmaster's entrance and then left. He disappeared out in the night. I think he's been feeding information to the headmaster and causing some of what's been going on around here."

Julie was numb with terror at this revelation, but couldn't decide which bothered her more - that there was now good empirical evidence that The Impresario was real or that Ezekiel could actually be living up there now and in real danger of just whatever the hell is going on around here.

She considered staying up that night to look for him coming out of the darkness of the mountains, but the fear and anxiety overwhelmed her, and she blocked off her window entirely. The snow continued to fall tyrannically, further separating the true world from the real world...

On the first of February, a new note was posted on her door from Ezekiel. She tore it off the door and ran inside; locking it behind her (which was a serious violation of academic policy).

Monday, February 1st

Great news! I've been focusing my investigation on the absent family now, and I've found some really weird stuff.

The family name is Polendina; or maybe it was. I can conclude now that definitely this family was here at some point and I can conclude that they left a long time ago without packing much, if anything, and without a strong reason as to why they've been gone for so long. Exactly how long I can't be sure, but someone was using this cabin and the cabin underneath this one shortly before we got here that night.

Because I'm writing in ink, I regret that I can't erase what I just wrote and rewrite it to make it more clear (for some reason, I can't find a single pencil anywhere in this house), but what you're probably confused about is true. There is a cabin underneath this one. It sends a chill down my spine, but I first found about it in a dream. It felt so real. I was just sleeping in bed, but I was awake the whole time and the darkness in the room was... shifting (this is the dream, by the way) like water in a current and I could feel something staring at me in the darkness. My heart was pounding faster and faster and I could feel something build slowly until I just couldn't take it anymore. Whatever was building up exploded and I was shocked and paralyzed in my bed. Then I heard the darkness whisper to me and it told me there was another cabin underneath this one.

Of course, I woke up and everything was fine. I looked toward the baby's room and half-expected something to pop out and attack me, but it never did. In fact, my arm didn't respond at all as I looked toward it. I found that even scarier to be honest with you.

The first thing I did the next day was some hiking. I went to some of the other houses on the mountain here. I kind of expected them to be empty too, but no, they were normal houses filled with normal people like we used to see in those films in our sociology and history classes. It didn't, however, stay normal. I went to them to ask them questions about this house. I told them who I was and they reacted with a noticeable change in attitude, but still let me talk. When I told them who I was looking for, I was nearly shut out entirely. One old man, however, stayed to talk and he told me simply, "Buddy, you need to stay away from those people. I haven't seen them in a long time, but I haven't been looking for them either for good reason. We don't discuss them around here. We stay away from them and they stay away from us."

I asked if it was possible the cabin had been remodeled or built on top of, he told me I needed to call the county public records offices because the ones I have don't mention anything about it. I asked if it was possible the family could've had a baby at any point in the last two years or so, he turned back and said simply. "No, that wouldn't have been possible."

Then I made some calls to the county offices and they faxed me records of the history and construction of the cabin. It was true. I have, in my possession, two ancient blueprints of the property here and they are very different constructs, with the construct I've been living in as the newest one.

The oldest one, and brace yourself for this, is the same design as the cabin we saw The Impresario in. I swear to God; if there is one.

The property record lists this house as "two-story", although you've seen as well as I there is no upstairs from here. It has to be downstairs, but where is it? I can't find it anywhere. It had to have been blocked off intentionally and whatever is down there is likely the source of the sugar pine and many answers to these weird mysteries.

I haven't been having a "haunted" feeling lately, but its still getting weird around here and I feel that whatever this "haunting" presence is that shifts the darkness and whispers to me in my dreams is waiting for me to do something. It's hiding. It's letting me do as I please until I stumble onto something, then it's going to come out and do what it's been waiting to do since it called me over here that night.

Don't take that the wrong way. I'm not scared over here. I'm still extremely comfortable living over here. It's a strange conflict, I understand, but apart from the weirdness (of which there is more); I've really liked living over here.

I've noticed something else too earlier today. Apart from the vein of sugar pine I saw underneath here, there is not an ounce of wood inside this house. At all. Even the doors are made of a hard plastic.

And this is where it gets weirder still. The closest thing I've found to wood is a book that was in the nightstand next to the parents' bed I've been sleeping in. It's a book on, brace yourself again, sugar pine wood.

When I opened it up, it was just the same thing over and over, "Hail to the serpent who circles the true world against linear God; the blasphemer who refuses to hail to the serpent who circles the true world against linear God; the blasphemer who refuses to hail..." etc. etc. Seriously, it's just that over and over again.

I still have no idea what any of this is pointing to, but I hope I'm close.

On a lighter note, I fixed the whirlpool Jacuzzi in the bathroom. I knew it was broken, but at some point I was compelled to fix it and I did! I've been using that in my off time here.

I'll write you again soon!

Wow. Julie's mind drew a complete blank trying to absorb all that in. There was absolutely nothing she could get a foothold onto there with her system of logic. She simply let the notepaper drift between her slender, tender fingers and she dropped back on her bed. Her gorgeous white eyes were stuck in a prolonged goggle did not diminish after time lying back in bed. Something stuck out in the note to her that made her suddenly switch like this. She was doing fine reading it along up until...

...wait, what did he say? Did he say he was *living up there?*

Julie quickly turned and grabbed the note, crinkling it at first but nearly tearing it as she expanded it hell-bent.

He did. He said it twice. He's fucking living up there!

Julie wasn't sure what to make of it, and the next thing she knew it was past her curfew and deep into the night as she stayed wild-eyed trying to process what it meant. The rumor was true. Does this mean all rumors are true? How could that be? This and similarly irrational thoughts circled in her head in a clockwise fashion until finally she entered sleep. She was unable remember later what she dreamt about that night - then again, she never does.

The next day Julie woke up feeling far more lucid all over. She couldn't even remember what had really upset her so much for so long.

Instead, she had an idea. Despite the serious crackdown in authority lately, the faculty still gave the cadets their freedoms on this day and Julie's *Advanced Home Economics* class still gave her privilege to use the food pantry as she wished for practice and application. This would be a great idea and she knew it to be true because it made her smile deeply for the first time in a while. Her eyes brightened to their usual luminescence and her radiance grew again back where it was supposed to be.

She made her way to the pantry and returned to her dorm, as she was allowed to do, with two bags full of food and food items. She checked her list, made sure everything was on it, and bundled up to prepare to go outside and do a little hiking.

****

It had been a while since she had been to the site and as the sun set over the mountains to usher in yet another early, bitter night, an old sense of superstitious dread came upon her that she had nearly forgotten about. She took one look at the outside chimney and, as before, avoided direct contact with it. A strange sensation came over her as she had to remind herself there really was a reason Ezekiel had started staying here. Julie hadn't thought about it much herself given her constantly logical mindset and what was going on at the academy, but something really did happen here that night where all of this was put into motion - not to mention she had gotten confirmation The Impresario was not just her imagination.

"No." she told herself. "That's not what this night is about. Stop thinking about it."

She knocked on the door which made a surprisingly loud knock. It made her feel slightly exposed; as though a multitude of unseen eyes were now staring at her.

What she didn't know was that *there were.*

Ezekiel opened the door soon after that and was just as surprised to see Julie standing there.

"Surprise!" she said very blissfully; shining her gorgeous eyes in and through the darkness.

"H... hey there!" and he ushered her in. "Can't leave the door open for too long; heat around here isn't cheap... although I guess I'm not really paying for it; it still seems right to do.

Julie walked to the middle of the living room with her bags of food in hand. "Well, yeah, this is a surprise! I wasn't expecting to see you. What's all that you've got there?"

"I thought I'd cook you dinner."

Ezekiel stopped everything he was doing at that announcement. Most people wouldn't be as somewhat shocked as he was, but, still, given the circumstances and their relationship (with its special dynamic) it still came off quite... shocking.

"You're... going to cook for me?"

"Yes sir!" this was the brightest she had been since the night she stayed over. "It's nearly your dinner time and you haven't eaten yet. Surely the food here can't last forever and, c'mon, guys can't cook!" she giggled and started tearing through her bags to show him what she brought. "I was thinking of making *pasta primavera*. I just learned it in Advanced Home Economics..." she saw the awkward, slightly shocked look on his face hadn't really faded yet, "...is it ok? Can I stay and cook?"

"Oh, sure!" that got Ezekiel moving again. "What do you need? Can I get you anything?"

"Yeah, get me two aprons, one for me and one for you. You're going to be my little kitchen slave. Now get me some water boiling there, slave boy! Yah! Yah!" and she made fun little whipping noises.

Close to an hour later, the *pasta primavera* was made and ready to be eaten. Ezekiel sat his plate down at the coffee table near the TV, but Julie guided him toward the dining room table where they sat across from each other, smiling, but.. not saying much.

"This is really good..." Ezekiel said at long last, awkwardly trying to break the silence.

"I like that polo shirt you're wearing." she said as she sipped some wine. "Is it yours?"

"Yeah. Well, kinda... it was actually hanging in the closet." his eyes drifted timidly downward knowing he was treading on soft ground there.

"I see the baby room is still boarded up." Julie announced as she swirled the wine in her glass in a slow, counterclockwise motion. "Have you been in there lately?"

"Nah, not really. My arm hasn't really responded to it for a while... and... well, as you probably read in the letters, I've been busy focusing on other aspects of the investigation."

"You're scared."

"No, not really." he said between gulps of *pasta primavera* sloshed in wine. "It's creepy alright, but I'm not scared of the boogeyman or whatever's in there."

"No, I mean you don't want to go in there because you're scared the minute you do, your 'investigation' will be over and so will your little vacation."

Julie immediately cupped her hand over her mouth and waited pensively for his reaction. She didn't mean to blurt it out right like that and God knows she didn't want to, but she did. She couldn't hold it in anymore.

"...I'm sorry, I really didn't mean it that way..." she said softly.

"Then why did you say it that way?"

"Zeke, I..."

"You think I've just been fucking around up here? Is that what you think I've been doing?"

"...yes."

There was a prolonged awkward silence that seemed to suck the heat right out of the otherwise exquisite *pasta primavera*. Julie started speaking up again.

"...you said it yourself. You *live* up here now. I didn't come all the way up here just to sneak out of school and cook for you, I... I wanted to see for myself if it was, in fact, what you were doing."

"I didn't mean to give you the wrong impression."

"Well, what did you do mean? Zeke, I couldn't fucking *wait* to get those messages from you and all you talked about how much fun you have up here on top of a bunch of crap I really don't care about. You never tell me how you're doing or if you're running low on food or if you're snowed in... if you need help! My God, what would happen if... if... if something fucking *happened* to you!?"

Ezekiel avoided the questions and went back to something he knew he'd regret talking about, "What do you mean crap? Do I have to remind you how we got here in the first place?"

"No, because I don't care about that, I care about *you*." she leaned back in her chair and stopped short there, trying not to get off-track and lose control of her speech. Her eyes, the only objects in the universe that could outshine the sun, looked sad and angry and dimmed as a result. "Headmaster Geppetto has been looking for you everywhere. He's out for blood these days. The only positive thing I can think of for you being here is that you don't have to face his wrath, but the longer you stay up here, the worse you're making it for you... and for me. You gotta come back *some* time."

There was another lovely little pause in the conversation; where saying nothing can speak volumes of what you're trying to say.

"...you *are* coming back, aren't you?"

"I don't know. I hadn't... really thought about it."

"Well, what *have* you been doing this whole time?"

"I've been investigating..."

"Ok, and what are you going to do after that? If you stay here too much longer, Geppetto won't let you back in. Either way, after a while... I mean, have you thought about what you're going to *do*? Have you thought about the future at all?"

"Sure, I have. I know what I'm doing up here."

Julie sat back and relaxed her eyes as they trained on him for a minute before she said something back.

"Your nose is growing..."

"Well, dammit, I don't know what else I can tell you. I'm sorry I don't live this logically thought out plan everyone wants me to have; I'm sorry I've actually enjoyed myself up here; I'm sorry I'm woefully ignorant of the "true world"; I'm sorry I've been ignoring you this whole time and I'm sorry I'm an awful fucking friend. That's all I can fucking say - I'm sorry."

There wasn't discussion after that. They both simply bowed their heads and ate their food and drank their wine in silence. When the meal was done, they took turns cleaning up and doing the dishes. Once the final dish was clean, Julie did not see a point in staying and made motions to go back. She put back on her regulation issued winter attire to go over her uniform and made steps to return down the mountain to the academy.

"I messed up tonight, didn't I?" she said softly with a slight smile at the end of the left side of her mouth.

"We both did. The food was good, though. Thank you for cooking."

Julie walked back towards him, threw her arms around his neck and placed her cheek against his. She had done this before dozens of times, usually on a birthday or something, but this time she heaved her chest and pressed it further against his. Even during sex that night, he did not touch her modest breast in quite so significant a way. This was different. This was... important.

"I'll stay out of your way. Do what you want to do up here, but please come back and see me. Ok?"

"Yeah... sure thing."

Her delicate cheek moved down to the curve of his neck and her face she lightly buried into his shoulder. She was nearly as tall as Ezekiel so this took a bit of effort to do. Her grip did not loosen and as her body slid down as well, he could very definitely feel her breast slide down as well against his torso. Even if she didn't mean it (and by then it was anyone's guess), it was sending Ezekiel's body a message and he had to break the already awkward exchange before it sent a very rude response.

Julie turned, walked towards the door, crossed the threshold, entered the black shroud of night as the ashen snow fell more and more; and soon she was gone. She did not look back.

Ezekiel looked down at the floor as he heard her footsteps go deeper and deeper into the strange night beneath the curtain that hid the true world from God. There was a moment where his insignificant body felt it would be the last time he would see her. A light filled in his eyes, similar to the light in Julie's eyes which pierced even the thickest murk of evil with her fairy-like glow, and it went in deep into his ocular cavity; saturating the rods and cones with a light that hadn't been there before; coming in from his left like a thief in the night and providing a counterfeit sense of purity and grace that soon gave way to a chilling essence that bore into his soul like a bayonet and filled it with a subtle but surprise grief.

It took Ezekiel a minute, but as this light distracted him and stabbed more and more into the innocence he was still experiencing from dinner tonight, he realized he wasn't imaging it - where did this light suddenly come from?

And he turned quickly, though as he recalled it moments after in the haze of unfocused thought and pure existential chaos, it was more like a full hour and he remembered frame by frame every image he saw, in perfect sequence, until he came to the horrifying conclusion.

The door to the baby's room was open; it had been slashed and mauled until the barriers to the door had given way. This happened just now and he had missed it. The light was on and it made sure Ezekiel could see it. It called to him. His arm vibrated, but this time in reverse. It cowered and wavered like the tides of the dying moon in the sky - the moon that was held captive by the circular logic of the *change*. The arm felt and heard the moon's cries in the dead of the frozen night and it reverberated its cries as it witnessed the horror before them. Ezekiel was drawn to it and even though he told his legs to go away from the light, his authority had been circumvented. The room was calling him and he had to go.

If a nightmare could be dissected in on an operating table, and the doctor could be pumped with steroids and commanded by psychic forces to yank out all the guts and splatter them over the walls until the inner membranes could be feasted on without obstacle in a ravenous banquet to celebrate the unholy one himself, the baby's room would be picture perfect image of what it would look like.

"Oh my God... oh my God..." Ezekiel said as he found himself ankle deep in red mega-tissues that had to have been ripped and teleported to this room from a colossal cyclops in some far off dimension. Blood and who knows weren't just splattered all over the walls, they were caked and burned in among the odd slashes and scratches and marks made in flame along the walls. He heard a sudden sound that could not be reproduced in the English language and he discovered that he had stepped on a giant vein and made that sound himself. The veins were still pumping. Something in this room was still alive though all he could see was himself, but right now he couldn't believe that to be true. Possibly everything in this room was now alive with him. The light flickered above him and surged with more light. His heart was pounding to the rhythm of the veins around him. He had to escape this nightmare and, frozen though he was, a sudden explosion of will power dislodged his feet from the muscle tissue eating at his them from below.

He dove out of the nightmare and tried to shut the door, but the door could not be shut. It was plastic and the plastic had shattered at the hinges. He looked back and nothing had changed; this was not an illusion he had developed at the hands of this congregation of evil, but physical and as real as real gets.

Then he heard it - his arm was no longer vibrating to the tune of the dying moon, but to the sound waves the nightmare was making. It was a baby crying. He was wailing and wailing long and deep into the cursed night. He was crying in pain - not old enough to know what to do, but old enough to know he could not escape.

Fate had long been sealed with this poor, barely alive soul and his cries looped in the same doomed clockwise cycle of the world now. The baby cried and cried and cried - for he knew his fate would repeat.

This soul-shattering shock his body could take no more, Ezekiel dug his face into his arm and the carpet below him and he bawled as well. Though all over the true world everything else had stayed where it was and acted as it had for millions of years, to him his body was announcing loud and clear that world was ending. Everything was breaking up and would soon be incinerated in a galactic fire that would end all of creation in the pyre of its entropy. The sun, once the life-giver of the Earth, was now the great reaper holding dominion over the shrouded planet.

Ezekiel watched the planet as it waited for its turn to die - and when his eyes drifted to the northern curve as the light of the sun disappeared over the horizon, something appeared over the darkness of space - a great serpent of unimaginable size and influence with black iron skin made of fire. It soared over the thick mists of the clouded ozone layer until it made a complete circle. Then, for no reason at all, it bit into its own tail and with his razor-sharp teeth began to drag it inside his mouth and down its throat. It gorged on its own body until the size of its ring became smaller, breaking the planet down with it. The snake did this over and over again, and the life of the Earth suffered for it.

And then the final horror - just before Ezekiel blacked out from systematic shock, the baby's crying was changing. The voice of the baby was starting to modulate from crying and was now speaking words in a baby's voice. The crying faded and was slowly replaced with an infantile tone that chanted, "Hail to the serpent who circles the true world against linear God; the blasphemer who refuses to hail to the serpent who circles the true world against linear God; the blasphemer who refuses to hail to the serpent..."

Then there was laughing - then there was darkness, and Ezekiel finally blacked out.

****

Julie sat in her Introduction to *Aeonic Calculations IV* class, some eighty hours after she had arrived back on campus, trying to pay attention to how Gregorian units of chronological weight could, in theory, be ionized through a sub-letted channel of super-space and used to predict morphing chemical compounds of star systems, but all she could think about Ezekiel. Every once in a while her gaze would drift toward the window, but she could not let it stay there for fear of a public whipping by sugar pine crop. When the instructor called on her to answer a question, her subsequent correct answer could buy her some time to gaze out the window to where he was.

She envied his ability to live without plan or logic - for it was a privilege she could never have for herself.

****

Ezekiel felt like celebrating - for in his hand, walking to the bathroom toward the trash bucket, was the last bloody rag from the baby room. He did not want to chance it so, instead of simply tossing it in the trash; he personally shoved it down deep with all the others and walked toward the sink to wash his hands. It took three long, awful days, but the baby room was as cleaned up as it could get from its previous condition. He was tired, sweaty, bloody and thoroughly drained of feeling and now, at long last, he could get back to normal.

He took his rotten, scarlet clothes and threw them in the wash. He stretched his proud, naked body to release the aches of pains it had received and yawned mightily to augment his triumph over circumstance. He did not change his clothes - instead he decided to cook a late lunch and start a bath in the whirlpool Jacuzzi in the bathroom. It had been a while since he had personally enjoyed a little session in there and this was as good a time as any.

After his lunch, the steamy whirlpool was ready. He took some clothes in with him, folded them and set them near the sink. His foot dipped in first followed by the rest of his body which sunk in very quickly to the warming, soothing, clear lava that his battered, stalactite of a body needed. He released a long sigh of relief that actually materialized and joined in the growing steam cake that hovered over the air; washing each color of the blue and green bathroom into a full, if dull, white.

Ezekiel closed his eyes and breathed the mist into his lungs, full and deep, so he could also taste the comfort and relaxation he had earned. Then his breathing slowed down - way down. It was taking full minutes to absorb, complete and release a breath. His muscles too released everything and there was no tension in his body whatsoever. All he could feel was the orgasmic touch of angel water caressing his aged and stiff ligaments that swelled and splintered as the molecules of elixir filled their hollow holes. All he could feel was breath of life and water of dreams - he could no longer feel his own body or anything inside of it.

When finally he gained the strength to open his eyes, he found himself in a room of cloud. The bathroom, as far as he could see, was gone and the mist was so thick he could eat parts of it. He could only see the edges of the tub; even the blue and green colors of the bathroom were gone completely as the pure white fluffy screen conquered all but his celestial aqueous sanctuary. He tried to swipe the autocratic steam away, but found his arms could not move. He tried to stand up and get out, but his legs could not function either. Only his eyes could see and benefit his oddly comforting conundrum here and they watched as the mists drew closer to the water where a genuine whirlpool had developed within the Jacuzzi. It spun clockwise and sucked the white out of the clouds and the light from the room.

Ezekiel realized he was helpless in this trance and decided his only option was to let the darkness take over. He braced himself as he tranced with as much strength as he could still retain before the black cloud swallowed everything down its drain; until nothing was left.

****

An hour of climbing later, Ezekiel and Julie came to that mystic *terra piana* that had lead them there. The black curtain hanging over head was actually draped down beneath them now down in the valley; setting the land on fire. The ends of its aurora were far below and the flames picked up and got heavier. The cold winds now were an ill omen to the exhausted and frostbitten teenagers. Julie, now fully awake, could share Ezekiel's foreboding sense of awe and she gazed in wonder at the big, log cabin house that had appeared from nowhere, or from the other world that this world was not, with a huge outside stone fireplace.

"This... this wasn't here before..." she whispered.

"We need to find a door; see where this darkness is coming from..."

"Why? I'm not scared, but, Zeke, I really don't like this place." she said silently as she shivered.

Ezekiel held her from behind and rubbed her to keep her warm. "C'mon, if it gets too weird we'll keep going up the mountain, but we need to figure this out. C'mon now."

Both teens in matching blue uniforms traced the outline of the house for a door and its light source, but nothing.

"This is ridiculous..." Julie said.

"Wait... do you hear it?" Ezekiel leaned down to the outside chimney opening. "The music gets louder from here." He motioned for her to come forward. "Let's take a look in here. I can... I can see something."

And the girl bent down and they both peered inside. Their vision seemed to somehow jump up from the black wall they were facing - up through the chimney and to another vantage point like they were looking in from ground level. Like a perverted periscope or something equally convoluted.

Inside, they found an executively decorated log cabin. It was dark inside but it was occasionally lit by an inside fireplace just outside their view. They could see a leather sofa, bear skin rugs and fancy farmhouse nonsense nailed to the walls. It was a far too tasteful scene to fit this illusionary frame. The fireplace from inside had flames that were frozen with ice and carved into seductive figures that called the itch of their bodies to force them forward as they struggled to make sense of this smoky vision.

Someone was there, but whom?

Suddenly, their view swung to the left where they could see more of the indoor fireplace and more expensive, insanely decadent furniture; some of which Ezekiel could identify and appraise as highly rare, highly valuable pieces of work - almost to the point of scholarly interest and study. Absolutely bizarre. The fire was immobilized by the deep ice giving it shape and illuminated a tainted, twisted light from the netherworld. From this twisted light they could see a leopard print chair, another skin rug... a glass of wine... and an unwrapped condom. Ezekiel peered further left and found a gramophone hidden in the darkness playing a warbled violin tune... it was the music coming from his arm.

"This is getting scary..." Julie whispered with fear in her throat. "Let's get out of here."

"Wait!" Ezekiel said and the view peered back.

Now there was a man on the couch. A suave looking *signore più anziano* with long, slick black hair tied in a ponytail. Wrapped around his svelte torso was a shiny red robe and fancy pajama bottoms that extended down to his expensive looking gentlemen's shoes. There was a lavender puff of fabric coming from the top of his chest and it was pinned with something small and gold. In his right hand was a smoking cigar, and his left fondled an empty wine glass.

This man... this man was *the Impresario*... and it was clear to Ezekiel and Julie, based on the evidence, that this man was about to rape someone.

"Come on, we can't stay here! We need to... oh my God!" Julie screamed.

The Impresario was staring right at them.

The teens turned to black ice as they were spotted. A new wave of fear, one neither had ever experienced or even read about, tore out their bronchioles and made them fight for air. The mysterious man rose up, smiling, and gently put his wine glass and cigar down and positioned to move toward them. His eyes turned red and became starbursts in their vision. His smile extended further, and further, until his cheekbones ripped open as it flared back into an unnatural circle.

He opened his palm and it became enigmatically clear that he was controlling the darkness itself as it stretched out from the ends of his fingers. When he closed his hand with a start, the teens were captured by an immense vacuum that neither was strong enough to fight. Ezekiel was sucked into the outside chimney first; Julie held on as long as she could, but against the void of the universe itself, no living thing could hope to outmatch.

The next thing either had known, they were collapsed in a heap on the cabin room floor; memories of being sucked through a winding vein of sable stone fresh in their heads. Ezekiel's breastbone nearly cracked when Julie landed in a sitting position on his chest. She got up first and helped him to his feet; holding his arm close to her as she looked around the barren cabin room which was far more expansive than either had realized. They were in the presence of the fancy, luxury furniture that was clearly set up for an extensive date rape session, but the other sections of the cabin room that they couldn't see from the fireplace were an almost quixotic mess. It was a stage, a sham.

Who was going to be raped?

Around them was a continuous volume of junk from every corner of the true world streaming in a broken marathon around them. They watched as baby toys crawled out from among the mountains of formerly useful debris. The toys came to them, slowly, and begged to be played with; they begged to be saved from their horrid fate and as they begged, small cracks formed along their bodies until they crumbled into pieces. When the pieces were on the floor were firmly rested, they would, after a time, come back up to where they were until the toys were fully formed again. They continued to beg, having been spared their demise, until the cracks formed again and they disintegrated under the weight of their uselessness again only to be brought back to life and continue begging in a downward spiral of never-ending futility.

Julie had opened her mouth to say something but did not get the chance to speak; for at that moment something had lunged at her from behind and knocked her down.

Ezekiel reacted quickly and he pulled the small, wiry figure off of Julie. He did not get a good look at it, but it was humanoid, roughly five and a half feet tall, feminine figure with thin wooden ligaments and a white uniform. Ezekiel jumped back as the creature tried to sucker-swipe him with a claw. It jumped after him and swiped twice more until Julie kicked up and tripped the creature so that Ezekiel could catch the arm and lock it at the shoulder joint. He lifted the creature slightly into the air and went forward for a short distance until Julie could get out. His martial arts training demanded he push down on the shoulder to force the creature to double-over. He kneed it twice in the head while Julie rushed forward and beat down with a two-handed hammer to knock it to the ground. When it hit the ground, Ezekiel and Julie jumped on top of it, unaware it could dislocate its entire lower half, spin it around, and use it kick both off. The creature then jumped on top of Ezekiel, produced its claw, and worked its way to slicing his neck. Julie sidelined with a roundhouse kick to the face and released Ezekiel from its captivity. It jumped immediately after Julie and swiped further with the claw; cutting her bicep. It was going to follow with a hard, wooden punch to the face but Ezekiel popped up in enough time to block the punch and follow with his own. An uppercut soon had the creature back on its back and Ezekiel on top; pinning down both the claw and the legs. Julie came back with a heavy, broken baseball bat and swung down three times hard on the creature's face. Julie prepared for a fourth, but saw it wasn't moving again and had likely died after the second impact.

Ezekiel got off the creature and Julie hurried to examine it. Her face twisted into immortal surprise when she quickly discovered what it was they just killed.

"Oh shit!" she screamed, throwing her hands to her face. "Oh my God! Oh shit! It's Mrs. Signora! Zeke, I just killed my nanophysics instructor!"

"What!?"

Just then, out of the darkness, a booming voice swirled all around them and addressed them promptly.

"Don't be so simple..." said the immaterial voice of eternity. "I have much higher hopes for you children than that. Don't disappoint me by drawing such pedestrian conclusions. We demand far more..."

"It's the Impresario!" Julie screamed and both teens braced themselves.

"Oh, is that you children call me now? Well, I've had many names in my years; enemy, demon, rapist... and that one, I must admit, has an air of regality to it. Wonderful! I accept the title!"

Ezekiel's arm started vibrating again. He could feel a coarse, red energy flowing from it. "What do you want from us?"

"You are the truant boy with the arm. In my day, our arms were used for masturbating. Yours you've made a god! What a strange world we live in."

There was a shutter and a rattle behind them. Ezekiel and Julie both turned and saw from one of the endless, decrepit dark halls shadows coming towards them.

"...and it is *about* to get stranger...!" the Impresario laughed. "Well, go on then! You who choose to run counterclockwise against the currents - let's see how fast you can run!"

There was machinegun fire and both teens were lucky to duck the splatter of bullets. Ezekiel grabbed Julie's hand and both dashed down the opposite direction away from the echoing laughter of the Impresario. They charged through the clogged arteries of this underground log labyrinth. They came to the end of a hallway where there were five doors. Ezekiel checked two doors which were disheveled bedrooms. Julie checked two and found another disheveled bedroom filled with broken doll parts and a closet with broken doll heads. Ezekiel found the fifth door was a way down and both escaped as bullets sailed overhead.

They came to another filthy hallway underground. Ezekiel shut the door behind him and tried to bar it, but Julie screamed for him to duck. Both dropped to the floor as a series of arrows darted the door. When they came back up, a larger figure was running toward them. Mr. Mangifuoco, the physical education instructor, came at them like a hell-bent juggernaut. He crashed into Ezekiel effortlessly and clotheslined Julie. He started with Ezekiel first; putting his bow behind him and punching him with a hard wooden fist. Julie recovered and jumped on Mangifuoco's back to get him to fall over Ezekiel and smash his head on the floor. Julie lifted from the floor Ezekiel and got him to his feet. As Mangifuoco recovered, he launched another hard-fisted blow. Ezekiel blocked it from the inside and returned the punch plus several more. Julie came in from the side with a flying kick to the head which made him hit the door. This was undoubtedly a lucky hit as the mob pursing them had reached the door and mistook this knock for something else. Machinegun fire erupted through the door and Mangifuoco fell dead with bullets piercing his head and neck. He crumpled at the door and made an obstacle for the mob to contend with. Julie picked up the bow and arrows and shot one into the slight opening of the door; hitting one of the figures before they rushed to escape further down the rabbit hole.

"Ha ha! That was very clever, children - very clever indeed! Luck always favors the young, but, being young, you are cursed to believe this luck will follow you forever. Will you do as so many of your peers did and let this downfall be your tombstone?"

The teens dashed haphazardly through more and more hallways and rooms. Some were structured like collegiate hallways with a little break room in the middle while others were like museum and residential corridors still saturated with incredible and incredulous rubbish. They tripped many times and were constantly on the lookout for the horde pursuing them. When they felt they had time, they investigated the many adjoining rooms and still more and more of the same. What the hell kind of a dungeon is this?

"Isn't there *any* way out?" Ezekiel screamed.

They kept running - solely because they didn't know what else to do.

Then they came to a more open room with self-made walls of litter and ancient treasure where they saw two more waiting for them. It was Mr. Raphael, a general administrator, and Ms. Montigo, a chemistry teacher neither had had. They ducked into a room, praying it would further the circuit but it was, in fact, another damn bedroom with broken doll and puppet parts. The two crazed faculty followed them in and attacked. Ezekiel took Mr. Raphael and Julie took Ms. Montigo. This was not a fancy duel because of the lack of space; Ezekiel wrestled with Mr. Raphael and his cold, wooden hands on the bed while Julie tried fighting hand-to-hand in close quarters. Ezekiel kicked Mr. Raphael in such a way that he flipped over the boy and crashed into a bureau. Julie tried two short jabs before Ms. Montigo grabbed one of them and pushed her headfirst into a wall; nearly breaking her nose and jaw. Ezekiel had a sharp stake, for whatever reason it was there, on his foot and he kicked it up to his hand and rolled back from the bed onto Mr. Raphael. He stabbed him in the heart with the stake and got up to help Julie with Ms. Montigo, the two of whom were choking each other. Ezekiel held Ms. Montigo from behind; giving Julie perfect free shots which she delivered in the face three times, twice in the abdomen and a flawless chop to the neck. Ms. Montigo gargled her last breaths and fell to the floor.

"Zeke, look out!" Julie screamed as Mr. Raphael came up behind him with a 2x4. Ezekiel took a heavy shot in the face and, while Mr. Raphael was open, Julie jumped from the bed onto him, but he saw her in time and threw her from midair; landing her headfirst into the corner of the room. Ezekiel came back up and launched a flying kick with both legs, landing on the bed and knocking Mr. Raphael down. He fell next to Julie who immediately rolled over on top of him and hit him in the face five times. He died soon after.

"Are you ok!?" Julie said as she ran up to Ezekiel and tried to wipe the blood from his face.

"I'm fine - c'mon, we gotta go!"

And they continued on their way; barreling through obstacle after obstacle to reach an end that might not even be there. They were hurdling toward a hard-won doom and one man was loving every second of it.

"No respect for your elders, huh? Well, whatever else could be expected of the young? Even in my day, the older generations were never revered; they were just obstacles for foolish children, just like you, who raced as fast as they could to conquer the world. The times change, but the generations stay the same..."

Julie nearly tripped over some exposed cylinder from a heap of something and Ezekiel caught her as they completed nearly a full mile of running through this random, rogue-like mobius strip of insanity. How much more could there be?

"Over and over again the generations repeat themselves on a planet cursed to live and die and never truly change or grow. You are fish in a decaying fishbowl - why then do you dash for freedom?"

They came to a narrow hallway with two doors on either side and one directly in front of them. Suddenly, the door swung open and Nurse Gideon appeared, machinegun in hand, and fired. Ezekiel and Julie had no option but to split up and go down different paths. Luckily, both were alternate paths down and they continued their mad chase out of this hellhole; praying they would meet up again.

Ezekiel found himself in a room that had stairs down and an overlook. Mr. Gambelli, the *Advanced Calculus* instructor, was waiting for him down below. Thinking quickly and without stopping one movement of his rush, he used the inertia and force he had built, grabbed a spear-like object and vaulted from the rail to spike him in the head. Ezekiel pushed off Gambelli's shoulders and took the spear with him as he ran through the door through another dangerous, narrow passage.

"Every year we get someone like you; an ignorant slab of pimpled skin that rises like Jesus from the grave and falls from the sky like Icarus into his. You are a student of the true world - *what the fuck do you know about the world!?*"

"Julie!" Ezekiel screamed as he fought for air to fill his lungs and feed his fire. He didn't dare stop; they were everywhere. Every second he stood still was a chance for them to destroy everything. He refused to stop; even if his legs were ground to shavings, he would never stop running. He searched further and further for a way out. Dozens of misshapen bedrooms - hundreds even! Corridor after corridor of filth and degenerate darkness crawling with these creeps. "*Julieeeeeee!*" he called as he begged God not to let his best friend in the world get caught.

At the end of what had to be the fifteenth hallway in a long, bent, series of surreal passages through offices and apartments and miscellaneous rooms, there was yet another basement staircase; but this one was different. It was filled up to the brim with doll parts and carved wooden anatomy. There were sounds coming from wherever it lead and a certain smell that demanded to be scrutinized; even in this state of emergency.

The darkness was the darkest down here and the air was molten lead and charcoal burning smelts; the clanging was so loud that it would've been softer to just bang whatever it was directly into his brain. Yet even through all these hazy cloaks breaking up the senses in his head, he could clearly see and understand what was going on down here.

What his blurry eyes attested to seeing now, in awe, was a processing factory. It was not huge, but it was big enough to demand his attention as he watched, stunned, as multiple former (or current?) faculty creeps were working along the conveyor belt lines - and on those conveyor belts were the cadets of the Clockwerk Academy. There were faces he recognized and faces he did not, but it barely mattered even the slightest as they all wore the same plastic expressions as the puppets locked them into place and loaded them into the machine. He watched, as if nothing else in the world mattered, while they were fed into a small semi-circle hole with white-hot flames shooting out as if they were being cremated. The bodies came out a different hole covered in a gleam that could bring down empires - they were primed and shellacked and locked into place again as they traveled up another conveyor belt and were dumped into a vat of unknown acid-based chemicals. The vat was connected to a larger machine at ground-level which dispersed the matter in a great, hard sheet of something and it traveled to the last major conveyor belt where the largest machine press in the world stamped down on it like a megaton cookie-cutter and divided the sheets into 2x4 rectangles to disappear into a final hole.

Ezekiel knew exactly where it was going - underground... with all the rest of the sugar pine.

And Ezekiel watched as this realization set his half-soul so ablaze that he wasn't even aware he had jumped over the railing to the ground to personally dispatch all four of these creeps himself until he held the crumpled puppet of the first one in his hands and discarded it. The second one came from the side and tried to jump onto him. Ezekiel was able to grab the puppet by the sides as he jumped and held it over his head until he slammed it onto the conveyor built where the press did the rest until he was nothing but a pile of smithereens. The third and fourth hit him at the same time; one coming from the front and the other coming from the side. The one upfront swung a blunt object and Zeke rolled to the side where he met the one from the side. It was too dark to see who was who, but not dark enough that Ezekiel couldn't see her arm as it came in for an attack. He locked the arm and positioned himself to push the puppet into the line of swing where her head was smacked by the blunt object. Ezekiel then jumped back out and kicked the male faculty puppet in the chest hard to knock it away.

Still holding on to the female, he bent her down where he kneed her in the stomach at a rapid-fire speed before driving his elbow deep enough to puncture her thinly walled, wooden back. He then picked up the puppet (who were all much lighter than people) and threw it at the quickly approaching male. In another fit of luck, both went flying to the press just as it had come down again.

"Such violence in your manners... is life in a fishbowl really that hard? Is the desire to rise above eternity really that strong?"

Ezekiel struggled to undo the locks keeping the other students held strongly to the conveyor belts, but they would not budge even the slightest.

"You waste your time, child. The locks are purely for show. These cadets are here by their will and their will alone. They have long understood their place in life as was dictated to them since birth."

"Why..." Ezekiel said back, fighting tears as he knelt to the floor. "Why me? Why am I not among them?"

"That was *your* choice, boy. You refuse to accept that which you cannot ever hope to change. Even with our immense strength, there is a limit to how much we can truly control you. All we can do is watch you try to defy the true world and laugh when you get crushed by your own obstinacy."

"You won't be laughing when I get my hands on you..." Ezekiel seethed: letting his tears flow.

"Well now! Here's a child who just put on his big boy pants! Don't you see yet; even now? Every child who was unlucky enough to survive his own birth has stood against the true world as you have! *What do you stand for, boy!?*"

Ezekiel stood up and ran toward the opposite end of the factory where there was a door up from a small staircase. He had not expected to see what he did, but his heart was renewed when he looked through the window to find the black of night contrasted with a parallel line of white rising up from beneath and lithe snow falling from the heavens.

It was the way out.

"Aren't you forgetting someone?" The Impresario asked.

Ezekiel stopped short of opening the door. "Julie..." he said aloud by accident; too tired to think only in his head. He was going to remember this place and how to get here - he needed to go back and find Julie.

He ran up the stairs and headed to the left corridor this time. He called her name over and over again as he ran to find her. Ezekiel didn't care if it attracted the faculty - he could take care of them fine - his biggest problem was getting lost. He ran nearly half the entire length he had ran through this maze in total in sidetrack as he searched for his beloved friend; calling her name more and more. He dashed through more of the same identical corridors of this insane convolution of the ages. He scaled two more floors and even backtracked to find her. Then, from the right, he heard shots fired and the sound of fighting. Ezekiel's heart sank as he rushed toward this new center of chaos with every ounce of strength had left in him.

He passed through another nameless hallway and actually had to jump over the bodies of two former faculty administrators to get to the doorway where another one had slumped in its death against the frame. He could hear the machinegun firing and Julie screaming.

When he arrived though, he found it was Julie with the gun. She was backed into a corner but stood straight and tall with the gun in her hands as she boldly fought off the last three of what looked like an army of faculty puppets that had cornered her in here. The last one fell and so did Julie to her knees. He could see her clearly now - her bowl-cut hair drooped low as she doubled over; holding her side dramatically as it was deeply wounded. Ezekiel could see many other cuts and rips along her uniform which were crowned with cake-layers of blood drifting slowly down to the floor. There were visible bruises, even in this dark room, and when she looked at him, he could see a large gash where blood was dripping down half her face from her forehead. He made a valiant effort to step over the dead in the room, of which there had to be at least fifteen, and held her up.

"I went the wrong way..." she explained with what was left of her voice. "I went so far down; deeper than I thought Hell could get. I hit a dead end and they caught me..." she started crying. "I fought so hard, but I could only save myself... I c-c-couldn't save h-h-h-h-himmm..." and she fell into his arms and needed to be supported by his embrace.

"Who? Save who?"

"Wouldn't you like to know..."

"*Shut up!*" Ezekiel shouted back. "*Shut the fuck up!* We're getting out of here right now! C'mon Julie, I found the way out! Let's go!"

And with that he carried half of her as she struggled to stay on her feet. Ezekiel still knew the way back - it was going to take some time to get there. Julie reasoned that there couldn't possibly be any of the faculty puppets left, but they still needed to hurry. Who knows what the Impresario had planned if they stayed?

By all means of incredible fortune, they were able to get back to the factory floor without incident. Ezekiel's bones were breaking from the constant stress he was putting on his body and Julie nearly fainted twice from blood loss, but he wasn't above slapping her to keep her awake so they could live to see tomorrow. He explained what this place was on the way and Julie kept her eyes closed the entire time until they passed through to the outside.

But there was no outside. Ezekiel opened the door expecting a blast of winter wind to cool his overheated body and the whistle of the crystal air to pierce his eardrums, but no such thing happened. The snow scene was painted on the door - in fact, it was yet another hallway filled with trash and debris the likes of which he had never seen so amalgamated in such an atrocious, ghastly design.

Ezekiel let Julie down from his possession near an open door and proceeded inside. It was *insane*; it was *unbelievable* but it was *true*. It was all too true.

They were right back where they started.

Ezekiel turned around to where he left Julie, but she was gone. Dark hands that could not be seen in this blackness had reached for her from the inside of that room and covered her mouth so she could not scream. Her body, being weak, could not begin to fight back or even scream for his name, and now she was in their dominion. He had failed her, twice, in roughly an hour; right to her untimely demise.

He was just about to let it all go once and for all - to let his failure and anguish wash over him a final time before he laid down and died so she could not suffer alone - when his arm began to vibrate. This held sovereignty over every other neurotransmission and spark of feeling in his body and he gravitated toward the room so he could complete one of life's many, many, diseased cycles.

As he approached, he heard a distinct clicking sound coming from the table. When he came just to the edge, the cycle was complete and the fire burst forth from the ice that held it hostage. The sudden burst of light brought a welcome return to color - and as color filled his sights again, he saw the macabre core of the clicking sound and, possibly, the end of the road for him.

It was a baby. It was the body of a baby - encased in a complicated carving of a sugar pine death cask - its arms and legs bolted and the halves glued together with blood coming from each puncture and sliver contained therein. As the fire roared higher, he could see the eyes or what was meant to represent them. There were two yellow thumb-sized cut-outs which were the gates to its captive soul. They were as sickly and pale as any other cadaverous lens, but Ezekiel knew it could still see and it could still see him. The clicking got louder as he got closer. He could see this child died in pain for its cask captured the last moment of its life before its fate became corrupted and it was trying, in the most heartbreaking vain imaginable, to crawl away from what its now frozen and phlegmatic yellow eyes could behold would be its cruel series of futures; one just like the other, over and over again, without the slightest prayer of an end.

"You two have so much in common." said the Impresario, who now appeared in the flesh before him. He walked over and gazed with Ezekiel over the greatest unfortunate soul ever to live and breathe. "It's like looking into the past... or maybe the future? At this point of the cycle, it's pretty hard to tell with you two."

Ezekiel did not look away; his heart was fixated on the child to whom life and death were no longer within its grasp. "...who are you?"

"I have many names," he stated calmly, "but the one I used to be called... was *Pythagoras*."

Just then, the baby disappeared along with the table.

"It is far too early to save him, I'm afraid - and therefore far too late." He turned Ezekiel to face him head on. "Well - here I am, boy, and here you are. I am within grasp of you getting your hands on me and guess what? I'm still laughing at you. Where are your big boy pants now?"

Ezekiel's rage had returned quickly and he swung his fist with a low growl, hitting only the thick, musty air in front of him. Pythagoras appeared next near the fireplace; wine glass in hand.

"You have much, *much* to learn, boy. You are only a student after all..." then he faded slowly in the darkness after sipping his wine. "But what if there is no true world?" the vapors carried his venereal voice among the ribbons of smoke from his tell-tale cigar, "What have you been a student of this whole time? How did you get so far being so ignorant?"

He appeared again on the couch behind him. He drank another sip and held his cigar aloft.

"Tell me truly... are you the boy who will break the cycle of the true world?"

"Yes!" and Pythagoras erupted in laughter.

"*You!?* The boy who listens to his arm instead of his heart or head? The boy who left his woman behind when she was with child? The boy who tried to fulfill his own selfish ambitions and left her to fight on her own?"

"I only split up with her!"

"Yes you did. You split up with her like so many deadbeat, useless teenage fathers who have come before you. What makes..."

"What do you mean 'father'? What are you talking about?"

"Do not interrupt me. What makes you worthy of a girl like that? What makes you so significant a man that you can simply use her and toss her aside as you did, not once, but *twice* in my sight? Did you not see those bright shining eyes that dispel the darkness even in my soul? That gorgeous radiant skin that only the vessel of an angel could wear? That lissome, athletic body? No? I'm afraid you're not good enough for a girl like that. She won't be due for another... eight months or so, but that's plenty of time to manage I suspect."

"Due for *what!?* What are you talking about!?" Ezekiel screamed until his head was sore.

"Oh, you truly do not know anything do you?"

And Pythagoras snapped his fingers; turning on all the lights electronically until the cabin and its thousands of corridors and bedrooms and offices and apartments and cafeterias and gymnasiums were all fully illuminated so Ezekiel could see each and every one of the mechanical faculty members that had gathered around him; wielding clubs and claws and swords and guns and axes the likes of which had never been seen before.

"Such an ignorant boy. You have so much to learn and so precious little time to be able to learn it in." Then he snapped his fingers again and all of creation went black. *"We'd better get started!"*

From the darkness came light and Ezekiel emerged from the now near-icy waters as he continued to splash and fight off his cannibal nemesis mob. Even as he opened his eyes and took in the air he so desperately needed, he still believed he was being torn limb from limb and burned alive in the acid vat in a factory that turned children into utility wood. The mists parted, and suddenly visions of blue and green entered back into his frame. His breathing picked up and the cognition that had been missing for who knows how long now was just as quickly coming back to him.

He was back in the whirlpool. Further evidence suggested he never left. The wounds on his body were gone; having never been bruised in the first place. Ezekiel breathed a prodigious sigh of relief and sunk back into the waters that even in their extremely low temperatures now brought him comfort. Everything was ok now, he told himself, everything was ok...

"Excuse me, what are you doing in here?"

Ezekiel popped his head and sat back up in the water. At first he thought he imagined it, but as he still felt the hairs in his ears twitching from the surprise sound, he had to wonder how an imaginary voice could do that.

"Hey, I'm talking to you! Who the hell are you and what are you doing in here!?"

Then the final mists parted, and Ezekiel found, standing before him, an angry man who looked familiar. He was then followed by a bewildered set of faces that also looked familiar. He still wasn't completely lucid, but Ezekiel wasn't willing to chance this was illusionary residue from his episode earlier.

"Who are you?" Ezekiel asked with a timorous blush appearing on his face as he started to finally realize what was going on here.

"We're the *Polendina* family!" said the father, "And you, my young friend, are trespassing on our property! What is your name?"

"I'm... I'm..."

"*Yes?*"

"...I'm in big trouble."

"Oh, that doesn't begin to describe it. Come with me!" and he reached into the water and proceeded to drag him by his testicles out of the bathroom. The children averted their eyes. The mother did not.

****

The gray was no longer present in the ever-thickening veil that separated man from the beautiful blue sky that used to guide them to their destinations at night and fill their hearts with hope for tomorrow - it was now an unrestrained negative of all color and light that blacked out all but the sun for only a few hours of the day. Trying to isolate and ascertain a definite cause for this new omen was a worthless effort for all in the valley who have suffered more than their share of this vile, outrageous and melancholy winter. It simply required too much energy with no discernable point. It was better to just accept it, lay back, and wait for the next step in this atmospheric campaign to make this post-existence period obsolete.

The timing could not have been a coincidence, Ezekiel figured one day as he watched the sky's precious little bit of heavenly luster give way to the negative night long before he could finish his wildly imprudent chores out in the field. For two weeks straight, Ezekiel had been charged at this time of the day to till the fields and work until something started growing. When the father of the household told him this, Ezekiel immediately balked out; not out of youthful insolence but out of pure and solid reason that crops don't grow in four and a half feet of snow. At the end of his sentence, the father thought hard, rubbing his chin and occasionally looking skyward for wisdom, until he just decided it was easier to shock the insolent boy with his remote-control electric dog collar and sent him outside naked to till the fields.

Endlessly toiling in sub-arctic temperatures while your brand new pubic hairs froze and cracked off over the seeds you planted was, in hindsight, a considerable upgrade from then having to work inside the house at night. He would typically come back inside when he was allowed to, 7:00 PM, and shortly after dinner had been served to immediately be charged with the chores of the household as well. Most days he would come back to a porcelain massif of dishes to be washed followed by routine dusting, wiping, vacuuming, manually removing the waste that had collected in the toilet that was purposefully broken because Ezekiel was found eating some of the crumbs off the used dinner dish before washing it. Other menial chores regularly existed cyclically in-between and ranged from the random to the downright anti-edificatious. These chores lasted three hours and were present and accounted for every night without fail. After these tasks were done, he was allowed a meal of microwaved carpet or something and then he was to tend to whatever bedside nursing assistance he could offer their grandfather, the grandfather's many corroding digestive elements, and their subsequent consequences.

The collar fitted to Ezekiel's neck, which was just a size too small for the electric halo to comfortably fit upon, was not a negotiation. The moment Papa Polendina got his hands on Ezekiel's still swollen testes, he was taken to the kitchen where it was strapped on in seconds and immediately programmed to disrupt the electrolytes and balances of Ezekiel's system anytime he came the slightest bit out of line. It was at that moment Papa Polendina announced that he was to work off his debt for using their house and everything inside it with a supreme residual interest. No mention of police, release or escape was ever offered - not to mention whatever possible equity could be attained with a slave houseboy - it, like the indomitably black, solid iron curtain in the sky, just became something to simply accept as part of fate.

Then one day, exactly one day ago from the present, as Ezekiel had somehow finished some chores early, he had been assigned to straighten up the baby's room. This presented itself a strange quandary for Ezekiel; whose history with that room his tyrannical family was unaware of, and he cautiously entered to do his master's bidding. He cleaned while the lord of the manor watched over him with glaring lumps of coals for eyes; possibly for fun but with these people it was hard to tell.

"Umm... sir?"

"What."

"Where... where is the baby?"

"What baby?"

"Well... sir, this is a baby's room."

"I'm aware of that. We don't have a baby."

"But sir, why is there baby stuff in here if there is no baby? There's evidence that one has been here in the last..."

Papa Polendina shocked the collar and Ezekiel fell to the floor screaming the rest of his words out.

"That will teach you to talk back to me, boy. You need to learn *respect* for your elders! There ain't no baby in here! Never was - never will be! That will be the last time you ask me that, is that understood?"

"Y-yes sir..." Ezekiel said meekly as he bowed to his master's feet as he was instructed to do.

"...oh, fuck it." and Papa held the shock button again for a sustained period of time so that Ezekiel and his body both knew who was in charge around here.

Ezekiel convulsed on the ground like the worm he was reduced to until slowly the shocks left his body. It was an hour later before the pain and numbness gave way to feeling again. The first he felt, regrettably, were the soiled undergarments wrapped tightly around his waist; then cognition came back slowly and he could think clearly again.

Then came the arm. It was vibrating again and not as a result of the constant shocking. The implications this sudden contingency could have for his effetic state of current affairs meant thousands of unique and possibly dangerous cogitations - it could mean anything.

Yet only one was clear as daybreak used to be in this scourged valley at the bottom of Hell - and it was the only thing he could do to possibly resolve this once and for all.

When the latest of the late nightfall, only a few short hours before morning, came to the Polendina household, Ezekiel got up from the laundry basket he was expect to sleep in every other night and quietly crept toward the baby room so as not to wake up any of the foul creatures that disguised themselves as people and a perverted parody of a family. The plastic door, which inexplicably was brand new and had never been broken or ripped from the hinges, gave way easily and quietly and he closed it behind him just as softly. He grabbed a blanket from the crib and stuffed it under the doorway so the light could not be seen on from the outside.

He carefully adjusted the knob for the light so he could see without making too much for others to see. The room was clean and cheery as it had ever been. The bright white walls and green tables with the equally green dresser and diaper bin could not fool him. The smiling stuffed animals lining the bars of the crib with the little Easter egg wallpapering bordering the tops of the walls did not erase the memories of the nightmares that were burned into his brain so long as he lived. Other nightmares he was aware of floated in an advanced state of decayed lethargy in the air and mixed with his own to create exponentially insane signals that his arm was receiving. It was in here somewhere. The answer was in here somewhere.

Then he heard it. He had swatted these other nightmares and figments away so he could hear for the sound that changed the rhythms of his heart with its spectral aural presence.

There was the clicking sound.

It was coming from the closet.

Caution be damned - Ezekiel jumped to the closet doors and tore them open. Inside were thousands of baby clothes and broken baby toys. He clawed at the mound; throwing them wherever they could not get in his way. The clicking sound could be heard audibly now. More and more discarded memories of precious blessings were tossed aside just as they had been tossed aside in her; events that marked important days in the life of the youngest of the young. They were garbage now. The clicking sound got louder. More toys, larger ones this time, were slammed against the wall by the force of Ezekiel's furied excavation. It was very loud now and any minute he would see it; he would see what's been calling him and calling his soul to respond this entire ti...

"Oh my god..." Ezekiel said in so low a tone as to betray to all celestial and damnated audiences who might be watching intently his true reactions as he found within the short end of the pile of clothes, toys, pictures, diapers and memories long forgotten - a finger. He pulled another shirt away and found a tiny little hand attached to that finger and three more. He pulled a set of little boy pants off and found the arm that held the desperate hand high in the air and, finally, one last blanket discarded, he found the tiny wooden body of a baby.

No, not a baby - *the* baby. The one that called him that night, and every night since, in this world and the one beyond where he lost Julie. His arm nearly shook the entire house with it as the strength of their signal was at the paramount of their clairvoyant link. It had called to him, as it had called to everyone for who knows how many years, until at long last Ezekiel came to save him from his perpetual cycle of immortal torment.

"I've come... I've come at long last, *Ouroboros*. I'm so sorry it took this long for me to find you. There is so much... too much I want to ask you." Ezekiel held the baby close to him and cradled him in his arms.

"I don't know what to do with you. I honestly don't... but we'll find a way. Julie knows the way. We'll find her and everything will be ok. Let's just take it one step at a time. First, we need to get out of here. I'm going to get up now, Ouroboros. I'm going to turn to the door and just walk out until we get outside..."

But as he turned to do what he had promised, Ezekiel became completely immobilized by the collective glare of the Polendina family who were all looking down on him with eyes that were glowing red and burning holes in him with ardent rage that had climbed to the top of the mountain and just plummeted *over the edge*. Their limbs transformed and produced weapons that were hidden in their wooden cavities for just such an occasion. Ezekiel swallowed hard, and as the unrighteous embers ignited sparks within the frames of their sugar pine skulls, Ezekiel squeaked out what may as well have been his last words; a small address to himself thematically designed to express how little he could truly grasp the gravity of this situation.

"I'm... I'm..."

The scowls on their faces sharpened as the red drowning lights dimmed the lit room and fed their bloody avatars until they could be seen blighting Earth from space.

"...I'm in big trouble..."

"Diiiiiiiiiiiieeeeeeeeeeeeeeeeeeee!"

****

Ezekiel stumbled and fell down the ridge that looked safe for his weight until the last second. He tucked Ouroboros deep into his chest and tried to protect him as he rolled down a length of the hill over broken branches and sharp, broken tree stumps. A few jagged shards of ancient boulder helped to slow the daredevil hurdle, but at the great cost of precious oxygen and chunks of flesh he would need to improve his chances of surviving. At great length, his tenderized torso came to an abrupt stop at a well-placed rotten tree that fell from the speed of his weight hitting it. It gave him a small bridge and ladder to climb down to more solid ground and continue diving to the valley floor.

He was used to struggling by now, but nothing could compare to how he fought just to stay collected and awake. Whatever memory he might've had that could explain how he got out of the house was bashed out from the mother's heavy mace-head some two or three times before he got out the door. He was able to escape, but barely able to escape unscathed. The family reached with their claw-like puppet hands and scratched him as he fled their continuous clutching and grappling. One, possibly the grandfather, was able to stab him with a blade concealed in his palm. The children, boy and girl facsimiles, produced claws and a small flamethrower respectively. There was a sister-in-law who, previous to this new struggle, had harassed him sexually every night and once he got a good look at what was waiting for him between her legs, which was now, he could only count his blessings that his temptation only went so far.

"There he is!" cried one of the children who produced a hillbilly-action rifle and shot him in the foot from a great distance. A portent of things to come, Ezekiel realized as he stumbled down the last hundred feet of the ridge with Ouroboros held closely again.

"He's headed to the valley!" cried the sister-in-law who failed to pluck him with her own rifle. "Get the truck!"

The pain in Ezekiel's foot was irrelevant to all matters except running, the boy felt as he limped as fast as he could through the snow covered flat farmland. Everything would be for nothing if he couldn't get Ouroboros to safety. He trotted like a lame horse across the nondescript white stretch until he came upon his intended target - a stump with wood nearby where some farmer carelessly and thankfully left the axe out overnight.

In front of Ezekiel was a field full of heavy cows - each one more frozen than the last from hoof to shoulder. There were close to fifty scattered around the multi-acre flatland. Above, he could hear the whistlin' and hollarin' of a hillbilly truck full of hillbilly marionettes with guns blazing and engines roaring down the narrow road of the mountain to meet him.

This was going to be tricky, but it was his only option.

Once the truck entered the flatland had Ezekiel in its sights, the boy ran zig-zaggidly through the dark field; dodging lazy bullets as best he could until he ran straight into one of the heaviest bovines on the farm and subsequently slid under it. The old hillbilly truck swerved in time not to crash completely, but the rear right side clashed and threw one of the puppets off the truck. Ezekiel quickly returned and vaulted onto the cow which he used as a ramp for a flying chop with the axe. He was able to cut one of the Grandfather's arms off, but it wasn't the one with the blade he needed to cut off first.

The Grandfather stood low and threw a straight stab in Ezekiel's face. Ezekiel flung the heavy axe blade upward as fast as he could to sway the blade elsewhere and he followed by swinging his back leg to a heavy roundhouse which missed. From his crouched position, the Grandfather charged with a stab again and nicked Ezekiel in the leg. Ezekiel dropped the axe and when the Grandfather charged again, Ezekiel spun to throw off his aim and caught the arm with both hands. He continued the spin, which plastered the facsimile of an old man hard into frozen cow buttocks. Ezekiel proceeded to bend the old dummy over and drive his knee four times into his cheap, splintered excuse for a stomach before he did the simultaneously unbelievable and inevitable by inserting the old dummy's head into the cow's rump. The next move was to grab the axe again, swing from high up and sever the head most unceremoniously; which he did without hesitation.

One down, five to go.

The truck had recovered and was circling around the outside; firing at the whites of his frightened rabbit's eyes. Ezekiel ducked under a frozen cow for a period of minutes while he heard the truck circling and guns firing. Then he heard hurried footsteps layered into the engine and firearm ambience of the night and scrambled to dodge the pounding of the mace that could've cost him his throat.

The Mom was much faster than Ezekiel had anticipated and she was much better with a heavy-ended weapon than he was with the axe. She swooped high and low to trip him to the ground and leak the rest of his brain through his nose. He ran from this cow to another one some fifty feet away (which, with the gunfire that followed and the extreme duress of the general atmosphere, may as well have been a mile) and vaulted clear over it; barely escaping her mace. She did not have time to guard as he slid under with a ground kick that took her balance away. As she fought to stay on her feet, he had a clear shot and cracked her evil body with the axe. This brought her to her knees where he chopped again freely, but before he could bring a deathblow from above, the mother aimed the mace and it launched, rocket propelled, into the equivalent of getting punched in the stomach by Hercules. Air, blood and vomit shot from Ezekiel's mouth, also rocket propelled, and the Mom grabbed him by the throat and held him high against the ice-blue behemoth until his final words could not even be choked out.

The truck appeared again, and launched another side-swiping assault. The Mom, in the line of fire, dropped Ezekiel and ducked low to avoid being hit herself. As she crouched, her spindly twig legs locked into place and she could not get up. The last thing she saw was the boy she came so close to eliminating for her master push with all his might until the metric ton of future cube steak came crashing down onto her.

Two down, four to go.

Ezekiel dodged more gunfire as the truck decided to drive within the field again, and he picked up both the Mom and the Grandfather's discarded rifles and hid behind a cow that was frozen on its knees as a barrier. The chips of ice clipped off the baby bull as bullets failed to push through and Ezekiel returned fire to no great effect. The truck turned and went over a small, rickety bridge over a man-made ditch as it made its efforts to chase him down again personally. Gunfire continued. Ezekiel returned fire until the rifle clicked empty. As he stalled once he heard the final click, one of the bullets finally found his shoulder and sent him screaming in pain to the snowy floor.

"Hey!" screamed an unfamiliar voice attached to an old man who appeared near the barn. "What the hell is going on out here?"

The old man ducked his own gunfire and went to retrieve a shotgun he kept in the bales of hay at the barn door.

The truck was turned around and needed to go over the bridge again. Ezekiel, running low on health, willpower and functioning organs, began to get desperate and in his desperation he shot the remaining ammo of the other rifle at the bridge until he miraculously shot away one of the support beams and sent the truck crashing into the small ravine. This threw the older nemesis of the puppet brood off the truck and running toward Ezekiel for a suicide attack. The old man across the field found his shotgun and fired back at the attackers and the truck that was locked into the unnamed tributary.

His combat training failed, for better or worse, to address children as adversaries on the battlefield so Ezekiel, who could not swing the axe at full power with his injured shoulder, had to play it by ear from the waist down. This was the child with the claws that were exceptionally fast. Ezekiel had to attack with and defend his groin at the same time. It was a dwarf-sized street fight for some time as both youths traded blows back and forth. Ezekiel took many cuts to the leg and one to the scrotum before he grabbed him and threw him like a baseball into the fattest frozen cow he could find. The old man was a godsend as he could take the pressure of the truck off Ezekiel and let him concentrate on the tiny terror ahead of him; which was now climbing the taller cows with his claws and running toward him for a jump. The Boy dug his heels into Ezekiel's good and bad shoulders as he landed. He raised a clawed hand ready to make some new eyebrows and Ezekiel caught it. The Boy decided to kick his face instead. With the fifth instep pound, Ezekiel fell over, half-intentionally, and pile-drove his enemy into the ground. With that, he limped, gushing blood into his socks, until he got on the other side of the kneeling baby calf. As expected, the Boy dug his claws into the frozen side of beef and jumped onto the kneeling cow; giving Ezekiel all he needed to fight the midget marionette properly.

The truck was now out of the ditch. The old man foolishly tried to run after it, but was very soon being chased. More gunfire was exchanged and now he was running and gunning for his life in, around and behind frigid livestock himself.

Ezekiel's fists flew furiously as he blocked and locked all the Boy's claw attacks. Fighting now was considerably easier and the Boy clearly had no experience where he could be on equal footing. Ezekiel locked his puppet arm behind him and punched him viciously. He feigned the fifth punch and instead broke the wooden arm altogether and followed with a dislodging sweep kick. As the Boy fell to his back, Ezekiel, with a burst of strength, sent the axe high and, with a meteor smash, the blade hit and broke through the puppet and the frozen cow until all three were in two pieces. That was the end of the axe.

Another vain shotgun blast to the side of the truck was quickly depleting the old man of his ammo. He was too old to run and too old to slide underneath the cows as Ezekiel had done. He had suffered two piercing bullets and already his former wife was calling him from beyond the grave. However, his knees were still under warranty from Cedar Sinai and this meant he could fight and run as long it needed to take. Cataracts be damned as well; he was going to dart through the legions of cows until they thawed and came home!

Of no small coincidence, a sudden warming sensation gripped Ezekiel's gushing leg as he looked down and realized he just barely missed a flaming enema courtesy of the Girl who had bailed from the truck to take him down. When she fired again, Ezekiel popped his kneecap as he dove behind a great-sized cow that he hoped would offer him enough protection to get a new strategy in place. What he learned was that frozen livestock dissolve into water when someone pumps thirty pounds of pressured flame per second at it for three seconds at a time.

Ezekiel raced to the next bovine barrier until it too melted into nothing from the far-extending snake of fire behind him. This was not a problem he could run from. He perpetuated the inevitable with a third cow that, thankfully, took a full five seconds to melt; giving him time to come up with a plan.

The old man dug into his pockets for more ammo - only five shells left. He had to make these count.

The kerosene container was behind some brush that Ezekiel had to make a courageous rush to get. He brashly threw some at the brush mound right as a new line of fire shot towards him and the mound exploded with superheat. Although it burned the pimples off his face, it was a blessing in disguise to Ezekiel who could now get started on his plan. He jumped out to the Girl's right and ran in a circle; dumping the kerosene as he went until the circle was complete. Naturally, the Girl inadvertently ignited the ring they were both forced to share until one of them quit kicking; and the duel was on.

One of the tires went as the old man's gun blasted its only successful shot at the treacherous truck; causing it to slow down and stumble permanently now. The sister-in-law could no longer aim a successful shot to his head from her gun.

Unfortunately for Ezekiel, the Girl still had her gun, and the flamethrower burst from out of her chest; meaning she could easily shoot and fire at the same time while Ezekiel could only barely escape. Sparks licked the blood from his legs and shoulder as he spun the air and lunged to any temporary safety he could find. The Girl was a terrible shot as she had to avoid her own fire and could not aim right. The flamethrower spun like a slow helicopter blade around the ring. When it went low, Ezekiel found his means to be able to jump and attack her. His descending foot was the one she had shot earlier and its vengeance was sweet. He had to move quickly as it re-calibrated the flaming path.

The old man, knocking on death's door, moved with all the strength of his one good side to the inside of the barn. He held the shotgun pathetically; six bullets in his body - two in the arm he was holding it with - and fired at the truck that was aiming straight for him. His stratagem, as the old man would soon learn, would fail as the puppets didn't mind ramming his barn with their truck; considering the size of the vehicle and their complete lack of conscious thought.

The Girl swooped low again hoping to burn his legs off and Ezekiel leapt into the air for another flying kick - except he landed right in the Girl's line of rifle fire and took one to the chest as he tumbled back to Earth.

"Forgive me, *Doloressssssssss!*" screamed the old man as the truck struck him and the frame of the barn with all the collateral force of a satellite missile. The barn exploded on contact and, with additional kerosene stored inside, it was quite a fireworks show. The sister-in-law became black sawdust and the smoke that rose from the barn.

Ezekiel's last move would be a costly one. His only real option would have to mean splitting the hurricane of fire with his body as he charged. The spiraling blaze covered the aura of his body as he ran as fast as he could straight through the fire and bubbled his skin; peeling it off like a reptile shedding a new baby brother. It seemed like an eternity, but Ezekiel made it to his destination and, instead of stopping, he drove through the Girl and punted her not high into the air, but at a safe enough angle that when she exploded like the barn on contact with the flame, the burst would not harm him any further (as far as he knew, anyway, since he couldn't feel anything but soldering pain outside all but the last layer of skin on his body).

But just as he sat down to rest, the horrendous roar of the engine loomed forth and just as sure as he was born and dying of third degree burns, the tall spires of conflagration split as the barreling truck jumped over and nearly killed Ezekiel as it crashed to the ground; missing him by a hair.

Before he knew it, he was running again. Five were down; there was only Papa Polendina left. He did as before and sprinted erratically through the maze of frozen cows that likely had no idea what a prominent role they played in the fate of the planet. Ezekiel slid under another cow and got on top of it. From here, he jumped onto the back of the flaming truck hoping, in his last few moments of sanity before succumbing and becoming one with the madness around him, to decommission Papa Polendina with a neck-snap and be done with it.

The cardinal mistake that he made here was forgetting, somehow, that his mortal disputant was already insane - having jumped through the roof of the truck to meet Ezekiel while the truck was still driving.

Covered in flames that would reduce his body to the same ashes of that burned his sister-in-law, Papa Polendina stood like the last golem on Earth protecting its ideal from the threat of the youth. The embers rolling around in his head destroyed the night sky with their scarlet, glaring hue over-spilling and assassinating the order of reason and color throughout the great macrocosm of man. They spoke no words to each other - slave and master - youth in rebellion and the man who did not understand anything but control; of whom lived the penultimate irony of being controlled himself by this still unknown figure. They spoke no words because there was nothing to say - they just went at it.

Ezekiel dashed inside with several fierce jabs cloaking Papa's body. Papa accepted the blows and returned each one right back. Ezekiel twisted his body and fired a roundhouse kick which cracked Papa's jaw. The leg fell dormant on his shoulder and Papa grabbed the leg and elbowed it at the knee; breaking it. Ezekiel had no time to scream in the extreme numbing agony coursing through his blood and killing blood cells along the way as he had to immediately block a volley of beatings from the old man. Papa kicked mercilessly at the dying young man until Ezekiel grabbed and twisted his foot so both were at ground level. He snapped his knee back together for just long enough so he could win this fight. Papa stood up as well and threw more punches. He carelessly went for the sides on the last two and Ezekiel trapped both; setting up a massively disorienting head-butt which cracked the rest of Papa's wooden face. Still in position, he forced Papa to his knees, stepped on his groin, and broke off the rest of his jaw with a sudden knee upwards. Incensed beyond one's wildest dreams, Papa immediately rose back up and reversed the double lock. He particularly dug at Ezekiel's shoulder wound and lifted him high in the air to crunch his upper torso like a taco. These were the last moments of the boy's life - so at what cost would it mean to re-break his leg, use it as an airborne whip and beat Papa about the head with it? He was distracted just long enough for Ezekiel to deliver a strong kick with his good leg to set his release and re-balance the playing field.

What neither had counted on as they drove far off from the field was the fact that one of the cows had escaped earlier and was a large, frozen roadblock directly on their path.

As Ezekiel went forward to strike, the truck had collided with the brumal land mammoth and sent both flying into the air.

And lo and behold - like the wrath of God being delivered to the enemies of the Hebrews in ages of antiquity - like the angel of death - Ezekiel Dickie Jones rained on his assailant with arms spread wide open; legs perched for a righteous lancing; his own eyes sucking the color out of the night sky and replacing it with the glow of the light that used to be. Only those who were not old enough to know slavery of the true world could ever reach this potential and overcome that which was impossible. Papa Polendina was just a puppet after all and such concepts would forever elude him in this world and the next. Ezekiel's body decimated the harrowing harlequin upon landing and his pieces were buried in the snow where they were destined to rot into the earth and be reborn as nutrients for beings that actually knew how to live.

His adversity overcome, Ezekiel retreated in his great, crippling pain back to the log where he found the axe previously - it was where he left Ouroboros for safety. A new irony was delivered onto Ezekiel as he took a second to reflect on his choice to leave the baby, the child of wood, on what was literally a chopping block. It reminded him of the biblical Abraham.

And all he wanted now was God to come down and tell him this was all just a big goof.

****

Dawn was just breaking as Ezekiel, the wounded *holy warrior*, the prodigious *prodigal son*, the limping *limit breaker*, the last fleeting ounce of humanity in all the world full of truths and the all true worlds that lie falsely and lie caustically beneath the layers of awareness no living being should ever be expected to question and second guess, broke through the gates and the doors; back to the only true world he had ever known.

His heavy steps thumped eternal echoes along the hallways. The sugar pine was cold wood that rang funeral bells with each thud of his bleeding, shredded cadet boots. With each gallon of air he sucked in to move inches closer, he asked himself why he was here. Why here when there was help all over or across the mountains? Maybe into town? The answer, dawned on him from some unknown source, was that there was no one else out there. The neighbors were all gone. The nearest town was hidden far away by the mists under the negative curtain. This was all that was left. There was the sound of heavy crying and at first Ezekiel thought it was the baby he pushed his near-corpse to keep walking simply to help somehow, someway - but it was coming from his mouth. His eyes were the ones dehydrated with salt water evacuating - jumping ship. It was the pain of his dying body, but it was more.

Would the headmaster help him? Was there room in his paper sack heart to forgive the one who left and came back with one of his own? Ezekiel once cursed the man who was closer to a father than anything else he had ever been privileged to have. Would Geppetto look down on the adopted son who carried an adopted son of his own? Would he be proud?

Ezekiel could take no more. He fell when one of the sugar pine boards lifted slightly by means unknown and upset his balance. Ouroboros fell onto his shattered shoulder.

A shadow came over him and took pity; if only for the moment. It was Nurse Gideon who lifted the boy with his boy and carried them to where Ezekiel wanted to go.

"Send him in..." Geppetto replied from behind the door. Nurse Gideon opened the door and set Ezekiel on the chair - paying no attention to Ouroboros. She left and closed the door behind her.

"I've been waiting for you, cadet." The headmaster said softly without turning to face him.

"Sir, this is an emergency..." the boy sobbed.

"It can wait."

"No, sir, it can't. I need your help. Something has happened and..."

"It can wait, cadet." the headmaster said callously, developing a snake-like hiss that had never slipped from his tongue before. "We have far more pressing issues to discuss - very pressing issues."

A sudden tremble in Ezekiel's unstable body form drew well-earned ominous suspicions that, even now, after all he had seen, he still hadn't seen anything yet.

"I'm very disappointed in you, Zeke. Among the most disappointed I have ever been."

"...sir?"

And the figurehead swirled around in his sugar pine sex chair to meet Ezekiel's gaze with his own medusa stare. Had he blinked, Ezekiel might've missed it and would've ended up petrified instead of simply paralyzed with fear.

"Your *test results* came back last night." Geppetto snarled as he waved a series of documents before slamming them hard on the sugar pine desk. "We received the evaluations of your make-up exam from Pythagoras and the results are appalling. Appalling, Zeke! I was actually appalled! I have been expressing extreme displeasure in the conduct and academic performance of my students for years and years and somehow you *still* managed to shock me!"

Now the thunder dropped; the ground split open by the shock of its quake.

"...I... I don't understand..."

"Neither do we. I, myself, had high hopes for you, Ezekiel, and you've let me *and* this institution down greatly."

The room started spinning in Ezekiel's eyes. "I don't... I don't understand what I did wrong, sir." he sobbed further; new tears streaming down his face.

"Yes, that would be too much to ask for, wouldn't it, cadet? Or maybe not - considering how you would have to explain to me and the academic probation council just what exactly you were doing up in the cabin for weeks on end - I would trade nothing to be in your shoes."

Ezekiel was about to speak, and then vomit, before Geppetto cut him off further.

"First of all, you were not cleared to have Miss Julie perform your exam alongside you. You would've needed no less than my *explicit* permission for her to join you and I have never given it in my tenure at this school. Secondly, you didn't show an ounce of logic in your actions during the examination. As Pythagoras writes, and I quote, 'Student missed very obvious clues and elements. Student failed to examine the outdoor fireplace beyond initial curiosity and seemingly failed to recognize that no such thing needs to exist in a regular home. Student's methods of intuition very weak; relying on arcane, random experiments to draw a hypothesis. Student lacks competency in arranging resources to lead to scientific conclusions whereas a more creative student would've found the outdoor fireplace is actually a *periscope* below the house, not inside, and could've deduced its existence much earlier in the course of events. Both students exhibited near comical cretinism as both had failed to find a common house door leading inside. Student relied on superstitious mythology to draw up the conclusion that the house had appeared from nowhere when, in fact, the signal had not yet been properly aligned. Subliminal and even *superliminal* clues did not lead student to the discovery of the whirlpool's function until weeks after initial entrance. Student exhibits singular prowess in hand-to-hand combat, but also exhibits poor skills in teamwork; leading partner to nearly die from careless injuries..."

The headmaster, sighing heavily, dropped the documents from his hands and stared coldly into Ezekiel's fractured soul.

"And what about the *rape victim*, cadet? Did anything ever come about with that? No. You completely overlooked that part of the exam entirely. This should have taken you a day at the most, instead you piddled for weeks and made yourself at home like a lazy, good-for-nothing teenager and Miss Julie nearly died from it. What do you have to say for that?"

"Sir... please..."

"That house, Ezekiel, *belongs to me*. That was *my summer house* you freeloaded in for over a month! Those puppets you destroyed? They were *my family*. Their job was to keep up my house and protect my interests."

"You mean your *base of operations...*" Ezekiel hissed, an ember of his own appearing from nowhere and starting to smoke from within.

"Damn right." answered the twisting headmaster as he slammed his wooden fist of iron on the desk that was made of his friends and predecessors. "I had high hopes for you, Ezekiel, and they extend over a decade and a half. The other babies we took were failures and I was sure you weren't like them; instead, you're even more of a puppet than they were *and the cycle continues!*"

Ezekiel clutched Ouroboros closer and twisted his leg while he leaned slightly to one side; preparing to run.

"You've exposed the true world and this cannot be overlooked. Pythagoras recommends immediate expulsion from the academic sector of this institution, immediate transfer to the military sector and that you are moved to the front lines in Tuscany. I second this recommendation," and he did so by stamping it with the official imprint on his palm, "and your fate, my friend, is sealed."

Headmaster Geppetto leaned forward, his menacing aura continuing to build.

"Now give us Ouroboros..."

Ezekial turned 1/16th of an inch to left before he stopped. Through the sugar pine door, he could see the other murderous marionettes that have disguised themselves as faculty for years just waiting to pounce on him. Nurse Gideon was scratching the glass on the door with an enormous scythe coming out of her left forearm. What part of the glass she wasn't slicing she was licking in anticipating.

"Don't even think about running. You are not capable enough to resist us; you're just a puppet for God's sakes. Put Ouroboros on the table and walk away. There is nothing you can do to break the cycle. Your energy is better spent in Tuscany as another of our Clockwerk Knights."

Ezekiel held Ouroboros so close that no fiendish doll hands could ever rip him away, and slowly he stepped back from the desk; prompting Geppetto to stand up on his specially designed sugar pine legs with special joints and hydraulic lifts to allow him to capture significant delinquents like him. Ezekiel crossed in circle strafe until his back met the window overlooking the wide vista of the fields and the mountains.

"Son, I can chase down a jaguar with these." he snarled as steam shot from his knees. "Get away from the window."

Ezekiel kissed the dead baby in his arms and pressed his back against the glass of the window. He produced a blunt object, a rock that had landed in there from his fall off the ridge, and threatened to break and jump.

"A fool right to the very end. Here I come, puppet!"

Geppetto needed little to build up speed to an incredible sixty miles per hour; just one pump from his lifts and he shot like a rocket towards Ezekiel.

This would've been all he needed to catch the boy and retrieve Ouroboros except Ezekiel purposefully lead him to the window, prompted him to jump and ducked down as the mechanical madman tripped and flew over him through the window. Glass shards struck Ezekiel in the head while Geppetto flew like a javelin; screaming all the fury of hell on his way out. With his speed, the force had caused him to dive face-first into the solid, frozen ground with the same impact as a small airplane. He too exploded on contact.

Blood poured from Ezekiel's mouth as the wooden leg broke his hip and punctured through the bone, but he got up anyway. The mannequin maraud outside were now tearing the door apart trying to get in. Ezekiel raced to the former headmaster's desk for his set of administrator keys and then back to the window to jump through as the door finally gave way.

Ezekiel rolled out of the way so he wouldn't be crushed by the pursuing horde jumping after him. Luckily, their legs did not have special attachments for speed and he could marginally outrun them as he circled the enormous main building for the outdoor entrance to the basement. His arm had secretly been throbbing again; moved to pulse by nothing other than the fact that there was quite simply where he had to go next. Some of the puppets had the same rifles and firearms the Polendina family had and he tried to zigzag as best he could as he ran forward into the ice and snow, but he couldn't avoid all of them. One bullet shot straight through his other shoulder and he nearly dropped Ouroboros. Sucking up the pain, he took two more in the back and severed his spine. This only slowed him down temporarily and he continued to run for all he was worth.

God would not let him stop now. Nothing could stop him now!

He burst through the basement door and had to press his splattered back against the door to keep them out. Nurse Gideon's arm was not made of flesh and slamming the door against it as it poked through would not deter her from stabbing him. She was able to plunge her knife into his chest. Ezekiel screamed but thought quickly; he grabbed her arm from there, pulled her through up to the shoulder, and then hit the wooden joints until it came off. He pushed through the pain again and slammed his back against the door until the lock clicked. He hit the lock, grabbed the knife from the derelict arm and prayed he had enough blood left to survive.

His arm pulsated with response. It made audible throbbing noises as he came closer. Pythagoras was down here. He just knew it.

And this was confirmed much earlier than he had anticipated; a bloodied version of his body broke through a door as he hurried down the hall to find him and Julie.

Then Julie herself came after him. She got on top of him with a kukri in her hand (where she got it could be anyone's guess). Her formerly neat bowl-cut hair was smeared with blood and in every direction known to man. Her tattered uniform reflected the wounds on her body; many of which dated back weeks to the last time he saw her while others were new and had torn the one piece regimental that used to mean everything to her into three loose sections; one for her neck, one for something to wrap around most of her ruptured, mangled innocent torso that went beyond violated, and one for her pants that needed to be held up with a makeshift belt so that no one could see the damage it had incurred for the last few weeks. This and the Kukri were all she had left to her name and she made sure both would take down the beast once and for all. She lifted high the weapon and slashed three times - then three upon three more times - until all numbers and logic were lost... and her assailant was finally dead.

She turned to Ezekiel; tears in her eyes; blood in her eyes; both sluicing down her once bright, rosy cheeks and the proud blue vestment that she formerly and formally wore like the battle armor of the *valkyrie*. The suit that she connected with and made her identity now drew a new parallel with her as both were sundered and pulverized well beyond repair. She limped into Ezekiel's arms and made herself truly vulnerable for the first time in her guarded, logical life.

"He raped me." she said softly. "He chained me to the wall... he put on that music... He scraped my face and body with the wine glass. He used a condom just to *amuse himself*..." then she collapsed in his chest and bawled.

"Was that his plan from the beginning? Was that part of the cycle?"

"*No, Zeke, I think he just wanted to rape me.*" she sneered and growled at the same time. Ezekiel knelt down and tried to hold her up without getting his own blood over her. Collateral damage... that's what she was. She was violated purely on a whim; no plan, no reason, no logic for it and, more than the physical damage, he knew it was tearing her up inside because none of it this made even the slightest bit of sense. The blood pouring out of her arms and legs and chest and eyes were all physical, empirical proof, that everything she had ever been taught and believed in her heart was a lie.

And it was all his fault.

"Will you ever forgive me?" he asked.

She reached up and buried her face in his cheek. Her arms went around his neck and she held on for dear life.

"...always."

The outside entrance came crashing down moments later. It was time to run. Ezekiel picked Julie up and dashed with her to the last room of the hallway. They speared into what appeared to an archive and supply room. They took as many of both as they could and blocked off the door. The puppet horde would get in sooner or later, and they only had one shot at this.

They knew what they had to do.

"There's no going back. Are you ready for this?"

Julie didn't even have time to think. She just tore off her pants and everything underneath and laid flat on the floor with her legs spread. She took the pants into her mouth and bit down hard so she wouldn't lose her tongue. She closed her eyes so her life wouldn't flash before them.

Ezekiel took Ouroboros in his cradled hands and knelt down where the legs parted the red sea for yet another exodus to freedom. He kissed the child whose wretched fate was damned for all of eternity in a cursed repeating lapse throughout the recurrence of the universe; a child whom no mother has ever born or loved and whose real name had long been forgotten into the mists; a child that could neither be dead nor alive; forever trapped in a false world full of veils and curtains and clockwork logic and spiraling, horrible cycles that made hope for a better life to come a thought that would have never even occurred throughout the evolution of life.

"Today, we give birth to tomorrow." he whispered softly as the last fragments of water in his body formed tears and splashed Ouroboros. "Carry these tears into the next life... and cry them for us when you take your first life-giving breath... in the real world..."

Then he took the child by the head and pushed it against Julie's narrow vulva until it broke through the anterior wall. Julie bit down hard and nearly cracked her teeth as she screamed in muffled pain. She forced the lower half of her body to expand as far as it could, but as conventional birthing standards and arousal were completely out of the question under this duress, it would not expand. It would not even provide a reason for the *bartholin's glands* to lubricate the path.

The door was starting to crack behind them and the throng was getting louder. Ezekiel was forced to force it in faster. Again, Julie screamed for all she lived for as the entire head has passed through the posterior wall. Ezekiel had to brave Julie's pain and continue to push. Julie screamed again as muscles and flaps snapped to accommodate the child. The shoulders had broken through the vaginal *rugae*. The cracked wood splintered the epithelial ridges that were currently freezing under the shock the body was receiving.

"Zeke, hurry!" she screamed as loud as she could. Nearly every orifice that belonged to her was leaking or bleeding something as the torment sent rivers of paralyzing shock through every one her fried nerves. Her shrieks of anguish signaled another break through the impenetrable female fortress. The arms, immobile, were tearing through the already shredded early entrance of the vulva. One of the fingers had caught on the *mons pubis* and Ezekiel had to fix that himself.

Another sickening crack from behind; this time an arm came through swinging a hand axe. Time was running out. Ezekiel had to swallow hard and accept that he was killing his best friend by pushing faster - as if failure were an option - otherwise all they had suffered already would be for nothing.

Julie moaned for a full minute as the midsection of the baby was now inside her. Ezekiel doubled over and nearly blacked out on top of them from his own blood loss. She kicked him in the face to wake him up and force him to keep pushing. He pushed harder and Julie whined and wheezed, too exhausted and in too much pain to scream, as the head passed through the cervix. Julie couldn't control her legs any further and they nearly closed up on Ouroboros. Ezekiel had to hold her legs down with his knees before she bisected the abominable anti-baby.

"Just little further, Julie! Hang on!" he screamed at her as the knees disappeared under the hymen. The previous near-death experience that had removed her will to scream before did nothing to hold her back now; as a seismic shriek rattled the books in the shelves and cracked the rock of the foundation.

A huge piece of the door flew over Ezekiel and Julie and now growling, psychotic puppet heads could be seen. Ezekiel pushed again to get the ankles through. The insane amount of blood was actually helping lubricate the body through the mangled passage. Julie held on for dear life because her slight body was not built to sustain this much contra-banded mass. She couldn't breathe because her lungs were compacting. Her heart was seconds away from stopping altogether and her amateur uterus was more than filled to capacity.

Any second it would be all over.

Another huge chunk of door was laid to waste and more arms popped through shrieking for blood. Their weapons were knocking at the hinges of the door and loosening them for immediate entry.

"It's in!" Ezekiel cried as the feet finally were the last to enter. He jumped over Julie and held her head in his lap as she worked to process it through what's left of her fallopian tube and everything around it.

"Pull! Pull!" he commanded. "You're doing fine, darling, c'mon! Pull!"

"It's going in... it's going in! It's working!"

An enormous chunk of door flew off and now the malevolent moppets could crawl through the top broken part if they wanted. Ezekiel jumped and held them back, knocking over a bookshelf onto the garbage heap that blocked them entry.

He returned to Julie and held her head again. Her stomach, once swollen full, was starting to go down. As Julie took his hand, new tears, not of pain but of relief, formed in her eyes as she looked into Ezekiel's eyes and squeezed his hand harder and harder...

...until finally...

...at long last...

Ouroboros was gone.

By all conventional logic, all three should have been dead by now, but each held on just long enough to perform a miracle and rewrite the determined fates.

Far, far above them, in the heavens, a blue bolt of electricity shot forth from the center of the universe. It travelled light years in seconds and it had travelled for weeks and weeks until, finally, it met its target at the back of the iron-fire snake that ruled the world. As the energy that once created the spark of life on the dead rock known as Earth spread and choked every molecule of the unholy serpent, its mouth was forced to give up the tail end of its body and burn its dying breath in a screech that announced the triumphant return of God. Its shriek was the trumpet; its carcass was the feast and there was nothing more of the mist that separated them for so long.

The last piece of the door was broken.

There was nothing the puppet horde could do about the girl who was already out the window when they got in. There was nothing the puppet horde could do about the baby who was already on his way to whatever path the risen God had for him. All that was left was the boy who was on the floor, near-death, and removed from all his fake wooden ligaments. The legs he took off with both arms - and the wooden arm he took off with some difficulty with the flesh fingers from the other one.

All that was left was a single arm, his last ounce of humanity, that swung proudly in his last moments - the rare last moments of life that would be his first moments of true freedom.

"You little son of a bitch..." sneered the head of Geppetto that one of the faithful carried down.

"I wouldn't know." Ezekiel said back.

The horde produced their weapons and leered over the boy who had accepted his fate and did nothing to impede its natural progress at the appointed time.

"Do what you want to me." Ezekiel smiled. "The chains that held Ouroboros are gone. The cycle has been broken. Ouroboros is free for all time and there is nothing you can do about it... That means you will come to an end soon. Our children will parade on your graves in Tuscany in the years to come... so do as you will to me! It means *nothing* in the end!"

"Bold words, boy." the final words Ezekiel would ever hear seething out of Geppetto's hateful teeth. "Fine. I accept defeat. It's all over. We're done for. You've won. Puppy dog kisses and gumdrop sunshine. Kum-bay-fucking-ya. *Is that what you want to hear!?* Does that satisfy your precious little faggot ass!? I didn't get what *I* want! What makes *you* so damn special!? The whole fucking world revolves around you! It's not *fair!*

"Baby want his bottle?" Ezekiel laughed.

"*Fuck you!* If I'm going down, I'm using you as a *sled*. My one regret is that I can only kill you once. If that's all I'm going to get out of this, I better take my time and *make it last!*"

And everything went black for Ezekiel as the horde descended on him, but unfortunately for Geppetto, the darkness would not last long at all. Ezekiel was only seconds away from being free from the bondage of his flesh and as soon as they put their hands on him to tear him apart, he was already gone. His eyes closed forever, but he could see again only moments after.

He said goodbye to his arm, thanking it for all the service and humanity it brought to him in his short lifetime, and he ascended to the warm embrace of the father he had never had - the true father of all.

****

Above the basement, in the main halls that were empty and only minutes away from the day's first period classes, only one student was present throughout the whole of the building - and she was flooding it with kerosene that had been stored in the agricultural wing.

Julie struck a match and, for a minute, hesitated to drop it. She regretted that she didn't have time to say goodbye; or thank him for all the years they were together; or the fun they used to have; or the one time they got to be intimate. She regretted there wasn't even enough time to cry one last time as she knew she would be ending his life as well; if he wasn't already dead. The souls that were trapped in the sugar pine screamed for her to drop the match. She regretted much of her life before now and knew she would regret this forever after, and regretted especially how little time she truly had to grasp all she wanted to grasp at this unforgettable moment and apologize to God for what she had to do now.

But there wasn't time for that, so she dropped the match and ran for her life.

The students who witnessed that morning on their way to first period classes would never forget the image they saw that day as long as they lived; the image of the school burning up and burning down while a lone girl cadet ran out in the snowy fields never to be seen again. They watched as the only home they've ever known, and the womb that bore all their slavery and insecurity, reduced to sugar pine ash that excreted white smoke into the air. The white smoke burned the black, negative curtain hanging over the valley and it, too, vanished from sight and memory - now and forever.

Now and forever.

Seven months later, after Julie had made it across the Appalachians and settled down into a nice town, she gave birth a little *girl*. This was the child she had conceived that night with Ezekiel. Julie named her *Domani*. She would be a child of God, a child of logic and a child of magic. She would have the logical brain of her mother and the spiritual strength of the father she would only get to know and admire through the stories of the mountains. She would live, she would grow, and she would die the way all children eventually do.

But these people are tired now. They have earned today and tomorrow. Let's let them enjoy that for themselves.

The Feast of 1000 Famines

Tonight was going to be a special night.

Every year on July the 20th, the Lyndon LaRouche Amphitheater on Highway 48 would open wide its doors for a benefit performance. At 7:00 PM, scores and scores of children with their respective parents would flood through the turnstiles. Before the auditorium were the standard food courts and snack stands where not even the sky had limits to the corns that could be popped; the beans that could be jellied; the Raisins that could be Netted; the Kits that could be Katted; the Reese's that could be Piece'd and the chocolate that could shake, shake, shake! No beer for sale on this special 16th annual evening; though parents and supporting adults were, for a certain level of contribution, served wine and cocktails that were lower in the alcohol content than others might have been. The prices, naturally, were exponentially exorbitant, but few were willing to keep their wallets hidden from pimply, prickly skinned post-teenagers wearing wiener hats because every penny, every red cent, from any revenue aggregated on the premises went to the *Children's Center for Cancer Rehabilitation*. At least one-third of the patrons this night had a son, daughter, brother or sister inside the good Children's Center, so few were willing to deny them the chance for quick and high-quality recovery.

It was 7:20 PM and, by now, most of the rowdy children had taken their seats; bursting with excitement to return for *Roscoe the Clown* and see him dazzle with magic tricks and buffoonery that even caught the attention of the Queen who made him a generous offer for the position of the contemporary royal court jester of England. He turned it down; believing his place was not in the rich old money of the British monarchy, but in the richer hearts of the children the world over. It was a great delight for the parents; some of which were old enough now to be exhausted and cynical of life's dimming pleasures. Here was a great man who opened his heart and influence to the even greater needs of the children and everyone could benefit from his presence in our community.

Then, at 7:30 PM, right at the curtain was set to open, that dream took a sharp U-turn and drove right into oncoming traffic.

"Ladies and gentlemen, boys and girls... we regret to inform you... that Roscoe the Clown... has died of *syphilis*..."

The mute button suddenly swept across the inverted bowl of the amphitheatre main arena as the air got sucked right out of the sky above them.

"And now, ladies and gentlemen, turn your attention forward to the main stage as Free/Mendrix Entertainment, in conjunction with the William S. Burroughs foundation, is sorry to present tonight's entertainment - a man who holds the title of the longest running frontrunner on *America's Least Wanted*; a man whose faulty quarter-helix farted into the primordial soup, made us mortal and capable of death and sadness; a man whose prestige has been shouted from the rooftops of every sanitarium in the world; a man who has inspired volumes of banned literature burning in great piles of fire outside every library in the country; a man whose eccentric electromagnetic ejaculations will one day usher in the next ice age - please put your hands together, but for God's sakes do not clap, for the one, the only, *Meteo Xavier the clown!*"

From the hot boiling lights melting the gels above came a concentrated spot of a pale yellow circle for which a fool had tumbled upon like most clowns (though intentionally) and ended his acrobatic folly with the all-too-unforgivable "Ta-da!"

"Oh my God, we're all gonna die!" someone shouted from far off in the back. The rest of the audience was all too stunned by the sudden shift in circumstance to disagree.

"Good evening, ladies and germs!" said the bellowing Meteo Xavier who, under his twenty pounds of make-up, forty pounds of frilly-ass clown costume, thirty pound clown hat and walking in clown shoes so big he had to walk spread eagle, was still immediately recognizable although now he couldn't perform any of the acrobatics and tricks the children had all come to see. "I just flew in from Ohio and boy are my legs tired!"

Even the crickets refused to acknowledge Meteo's poor grasp of contemporary humor and there was dead, dead, *dead* silence.

"So, anyone hear of that new Apple computer?" Meteo said as he swallowed the microphone. "It's a great new invention, but trust me, you don't want to take a bite out of it!"

The mute button that previously swept the audience was replaced with a slow-evolving moan of despair that sounded a lot like "*gluhhhhhhhhhh...*"

"Umm... a priest, a rabbi and Joan of Arc walk into a bear bar..."

The stage manager off to the left was striking his finger across his throat which told Meteo to ditch the act and move on (although the stage manager was actually threatening to decapitate him) and so Meteo reached deep into his frilly clown pants and produced his magic mystery bag. The magic mystery didn't last long as Meteo had accidentally dumped all the items on stage, but proceeded anyway with the next act. He travelled down onstage into the audience and went to the nearest child he could find.

"And what's your name, little boy?" The child was, in fact, a girl.

"Don't answer him - it's a trick!" screamed the mother.

"What kind of animal do you like?" Meteo pressed.

"*Cryptobranchus alleganiensis.*"

"Oh... ok..." Meteo struggled as he wasn't prepared for an answer like that. "Alright, that's easy to make; easy as cake!" And the poor dumb animal took his special balloons out and blew them up and wrapped them around with world-class incompetence and tied it all together until the child had the world's biggest erection crowning her head. The mother was literally beside herself with rage and both conspired to take him out right here, right now.

"And how about you, sir?" Meteo said to the morbidly obese man sitting across and next to and behind the previous victim. "May I guess your weight for the amusement of the audience?"

"May I bust your dopey ass up and down the state of Virginia for the amusement of the audience?"

"Wonderful!" Meteo said quickly and moved on to the next person. For this person he attempted to pull a dime from the next man's ear - and when he pulled the man's brain out instead and failed to get it all back in, Meteo had started to wonder if perhaps he made a mistake taking this job for the former Roscoe the clown.

And it leaned closer to that after the segment where he played the theme music to *Rad Gravity* on the kazoo with an orchestra of untrained circus monkeys.

And it got hinted far more strongly at when he tried to tight-robe walk over an open septic tank that he fell safely into as it leaked its swimming pool sized contents into the good people who just wanted to benefit a children's hospital.

And by the time Meteo's burning man performance piece came in contact with the septic fluid in the audience, it was extremely obvious that this was, indeed, a mistake. The wild phlogiston destroyed most of the stage and melted the supporting elements of the band-shell and it, too, came crashing down, effectively destroying the proud legacy of the Lyndon LaRouche amphitheatre. Luckily, no one was hurt - until the collective audience saw Meteo Xavier was still alive.

At 7:42 PM, the police arrived on scene to control the crowd until they too descended on Meteo Xavier. As he laid flat on his back absorbing blow after blow after blow from angry fathers, despondent mothers, tiny children with big feet, armed enforcement officers, perturbed pickle-eaters, box-office bullies and the *Shriners*, Meteo Xavier thought back to how he got here and how this all got started and became such an enormous, egregious mistake.

He remembered it like it was yesterday.

* Four Days Earlier *

Tonight was going to be a special night.

On July the 16th, shortly before 8:00 PM, Meteo Xavier, in his smartest suit, had waited under the canopy of the famous *L'infection de levure surestimée* restaurant where he was waiting for his date; a lovely and sharp young lady by the name of Zelda Melysia Chere. It had been drizzling throughout the evening and he had hoped, with the all the effort he made to look handsome and presentable for such an exquisite lady, that she wasn't the kind of girl to back out on a little wearisome weather. Meteo was most definitely a handsome creature, but built more for his constant meta-heroics and anti-adventures. He had long light blue hair tied tonight into a mildly presentable ponytail and all of his thick muscles were hidden in an expertly tailored suit that cost him every last quarter in his bank account.

He still wasn't quite sure how he was going to pay for dinner.

Just then, a lithe figure with long blonde hair in a light, tan coat came dashing through the light rain on the pavement. Once she reached the canopy next to Meteo, she pulled back her soaking blonde hair to reveal the thinly pointed and snowflake skinned Zelda Chere. She smiled and asked how long he had been waiting there. Meteo blushed and said he hadn't waited too long before opening the door for her to enter.

They were seated at the center of the restaurant in a cross matrix bleed of surrounding lights so that they got enough light for themselves without being pestered by its brightness. Meteo's continued blushing also helped to keep the table from getting too dark as he struggled for words to start with.

"It's ok; you don't have to be nervous around me." Zelda said as she sipped her wine. "I know your name; you don't need to tell me that. You're famous I hear - tell me why you're famous."

"Oh, it's nothing much." Meteo lied and continued to bloom his cheeks like a rose garden. "I'm something of an adventurer."

"Go on..."

And did he! Meteo was not one to brag incessantly, but the stories he told were numerous in number and purely unbelievable bullshit in content. He told the story of how the Vicar of Essley stole his tiddlywinks and he had to fly across a planet of volcanoes to get it back. He depicted to her the story of how he was imprisoned by a medieval guerilla group that tried to take over southern Austria and how he single handedly fought the *Tea Cup Army* who was funding them. He recounted his days as a World War V fighter pilot for Zimbabwe and how he, with the help of his trusty sidekick, Bungie, the pecker-headed wood-tit (God rest his soul) took down the psychic Hitler youth cult that had resurrected King Kong to run in the 2004 election against George Washington. And whereas the other paying advocates of this absolutely putrid French cuisine found his stories to be long, rambling chains of random words and name-dropping, Zelda chuckled at the end;

lifting Meteo's nervous spirits and possibly giving Meteo some time to figure out how to keep his date from running out the door as so many times before.

"You're a wonderful storyteller." she said as she stirred her drink sweetly.

"I'm not joking - I really did all that."

"Oh, I know. I can hear it in your voice that you mean it. You have honest eyes and honest movements. Most guys don't have that." she sipped her wine as she looked for a waiter to offer a refill. "And with that, I want to know what you think of me."

"Excuse me?" Meteo said nearly choking on his wine as he sipped it down the wrong pipe.

"Go on. Are you enjoying yourself tonight? What do you think of me?"

"Well," Meteo said with a shaky voice that broadcast his skittishness very clearly. "I mean, I've done all the talking so far... I... don't know that much about you."

"You don't need to. I want to know if we're connecting on another level. What are you thinking right now?"

Meteo blushed some more; a very predictable move and quite a tell. He hesitated in his speech, but eventually tried to deliver.

"I... I kinda like you."

"Oh?" she smiled and stared brightly into his cowering eyes. "Tell me more..."

"Well..."

And just then, Meteo and Zelda were both sidelined by the emergence of an incredulous presence from the stupidest circle of Hell that stormed on over from whereabouts unknown. His eyes were fractals of pure, hedonistic madness twisting into a conundrum of subsistence. Clearly some maximum security penitentiary nearby was missing its star crack-head and decided, of all the rotten luck in the world, to come to Meteo Xavier on his big date.

"Hello, crotch-stain!" he addressed Meteo. "My name is Brad Sandley Donihe, Mr. Fuckface to you, *Toilet Insurance Salesman and Professional Sumbitch* by trade! How are you, sir?"

"I'm fine. What do you..."

"Oh!" He squealed as he took one hell of a good look at Zelda. "Now there's a nice pair of giant honkin' hooters!" he came dangerously close to burying his head into her cheery bosom before he spun his face into her hears and screamed, "What's your name!?"

"Zelda."

"Zelda... I love your mouth." and he went for it. Zelda grabbed his face and pushed for a full minute before he went to the ground.

"What do you want, Mr. Donihe-Fuckface?"

"Well sir," he jumped up with an amazing start. "I couldn't help but overhear your conversation through my parabolic microphone and I heard you were looking for someone to double-date with..."

"We didn't say..."

"And here I am! In the flesh!" he leered over to Zelda, "And maybe in yours, my sweet little vaginal flower... overflowing with excitement at the very mention of my name... the throbbing manhood from which it springs proudly like *God walking over the face of the water!*" he grabbed her slender arm and licked it from wrist to shoulder blade before she smacked him.

"Mr. Fuckface." Zelda said in a very matter-o'-fact tone, "To double date implies the presence of *four* people. You can't just crash someone's dinner; you need to bring a date as well."

"No problem!" He snapped his fingers and called to the back. "*Bonerita!* Get the fuck over here!"

Meteo dropped the spoon into his soap (yes, soap) and both he and Zelda bent their heads high, high up as they witnessed the advent of Andre the Giant as the world's largest and hairiest ginger hooker. Neither one could find a single bone in her body.

"This is the biggest woman I'm ever seen." Zelda scrawled out.

"*She's french as the day is long!*" he reached up and slapped the top of her thigh. "Bonerita, open your mouth and say something."

"Heeeeehh..." she sucked in.

"*TrololololololoLOLOLOLOLOLOLOLOLOLOLO...!*"

Meteo nearly fell out of his chair as the nuclear sonic boom tore at his face and the beautiful face of his date. The vulgar sound waves rocked the restaurant with each explosive syllable repeating over and over and over again. The windows shook and broke; severing fingers and eyeballs for the poor fools who dared to sit near them. Heads detonated like cerebral TNT and at one point the turkey waiting for them jumped up and ran out the door to impregnate a poodle until finally she closed her mouth and a fraction of balance was restored again.

Some time passed over that. Any pleasure the hot meals could have offered Meteo and his date where quickly balanced in atmospheric mediocrity by the vexatious nature of this cruel new man and his barbarian prostitute.

"So, Meteo, what do you do for a living?" he would ask.

"Well, I'm... something of an adventurer?"

"Fuck you!" he screamed and pounded his fist right into Meteo's *boeuf bourguignon*. "You will work for me! I'm starting you first thing in the morning come Monday!"

"That is eight hours from now."

"The toilet industry moves fast, jizz-face!" he stopped a waiter to steal the bottle of wine from his hands. Brad uncorked it, drank the entire contents and promptly spit it back out all over the waiter. "We have a saying in our market, 'We get our shit together so you can take yours!' I didn't put Jesus on the cross so that I could pussyfoot my company into the ground. Fuck no! Human feces are gold! Gold! The economy is the in the sewer; so that's where you need to look for your next fortune! Let me ask you this, Meteo, have you ever dragged a homeless man out of his wheelchair to throw him face first into the fecal sludge below?"

"No."

"It's like backpacking through Italy; you should really do it sometime! God, I'm horny!" and Brad got up out of his chair, knocking both waiters away from the cart with the large tin of rump roast on it, and proceeded to have his way with it. Meteo exchanged sorrowful looks at Zelda, of whom he'd sat only across the table from the entire time and was still completely barred off from thanks to these two blackguard caricatures.

"You see, what people don't understand about the commode industry," he said as he sat back down without bothering to wipe himself off, "is that it thrives on innovation. You can't just build an outhouse and expect people to just walk on in and deposit! Fuck no! Fuck you! You have to keep up with demand and people demand more when they wake up in the morning and they have to take the biggest shit they've had!"

"Could we please move the conversation to something else?" Zelda asked.

"You got it, sugar cunt!" Mr. Fuckface exclaimed loud for everyone on the street to hear and ate the last bit of Meteo's dinner before he ever got to taste it - forcing Meteo to head towards the appetizer - whatever the hell it was. "Right now we've got a new division of business out - it's called 'core foods', right? You listening to me, cuntwad? It's a new, state-of-the-art toilet we've developed that hooks up to a machine outside and then to your refrigerator..."

"Oh my God..." Zelda moaned.

"...and it takes the waste and processes the unprocessed nutrients your body expelled by accident and turns into a packaged block of 'core food'. It's something you cook to create food, like flour, or, fuck, you could just eat it straight out of the can."

"That's horrible." Meteo said as he chowed-down to battle his hunger. "Do people really eat that shit?"

"You're eating it right now."

Meteo spit the offending revelatory substances out on the floor right before an unlucky waiter placed his foot on it and slid far across the entirety of the restaurant (which was impressive for carpet) right into the kitchen where a symphony of crashes and sounds ignited visions of chaotic chain reactions many were thankful they could not see.

"Are you uncomfortable, Bonerita?" Zelda said as she chose to dismiss the last few minutes.

"I got *firecrotch* up my ass." she growled from under her mustache.

"Pretty much sums up the evening..." she said and looked towards Meteo with slightly sad and frustrated eyes.

It was clear to him, at that moment, that, indeed, she wanted something more out of the evening than a free meal with a famous freak who was now, by comparison, Mr. Rogers to Mr. Fuckface. In any other situation, Meteo would dusted this guy and released his captive back to the wild, but tonight he resolved to be on his best behavior for her sake. Meteo was an idiot, but even he saw better than to wear his heart out on his sleeve and the truth was, even with this hyper, nihilistic malefactor ruining the evening and the concept of evening altogether, he still stole glances at Zelda that filled his heart with a joy he would not have expected to get on the first date alone.

"Would you excuse me, please?" Meteo said as he neatly laid his napkin, probably the last known one to exist on the premises right now, on the table, promised Zelda through a whisper that he was coming back, and made his way to the restroom.

Inside, he quickly found a stall for which to freshen up and hopefully come up with an idea to re-rail this evening back into something at least halfway socially acceptable.

After many minutes of stalling for time, Meteo finally put his nice, Italian shoes up on the toilet seat to tie and could only draw one collected thought about where this evening was going.

"Well, it can't get any worse from here." he said as he looked out the window.

Plop.

That was the sound of Meteo's foot getting lodged into the toilet.

Even worse, as he looked up from above his knee - he saw he wasn't alone.

"What the fuck are you doing?" the wild-eyed man on the toilet asked Meteo who had now locked both them to the porcelain throne.

Outside, the remarkably restrained insanity continued as abashed as anyone could ever hope for.

"*I wanna fuck the both of you right here!*" Brad Sandley declared with a fist pounding resolve. He grabbed a beer from another table, took a swig and just as promptly as before sprayed it back on the innocent. "Jiminy fucking Cricket! Why is this fucking beer lukewarm? What planet are you fuckers from!? If there's anything I can't stand, it's lukewarm fucking beer and *your* fucking face! Come here, fucker!"

And with that, the professional sumbitch pounced on the first person he set eyes on and wailed on him with extreme prejudice.

Just then, a cold wind blew in from the humid summer night and the mysterious stranger, while everyone else focused on an obnoxious center of attention, moved in and through the restaurant completely unnoticed; carrying an enormous katana and wearing the demon samurai armor that had been cursed for centuries.

"Ok, if we're going to do this, we need to work together." Meteo said to the perplexed man staring at him with fantasies of murder flowing through his synapses. "Let's get to know each other to build camaraderie. What's your name? Where are you from?"

"Man, get the fuck out of here!"

Suddenly, a laser-hot white blade broke through the thin stall door and swiped a disastrous line across the section from Meteo's shoulders up. Meteo's reflexes allowed him to dodge in him, but the man, sadly, no longer had to worry about his plight as he lost his head.

Meteo fell to the ground; foot still lodged *occupado*, and slapped the blade that tried to strike him. He wrestled with it and tore it away but could not take it. It came down again even more forcefully and Meteo caught it, but it pushed him down into the ground and made swiping it aside more difficult. He was able to push it up slightly and aim the pull so the blade would sail past his legs and he could get a better control of it. He was able to pull it down, but taking it for himself did not work. The blade fell out and was quickly snatched up from the unknown assassin behind the walls. Meteo took this opportunity to get up on his foot and get ready.

"Has anyone seen Meteo?" Zelda asked as the fight was finished finally. "He went to the men's room and never came back."

"Doesn't surprise me." Brad said as he lit a cigar with a match he stroke off the beaten man's nose hairs. "I've sold a lot of toilets to this restaurant and we built ones you can literally get lost in; like the old saying goes. I'll go check in on him. If you two start *lezzing out* without me, I'm going to kick your fucking asses." and with that he headed towards the men's room.

Zelda turned to the leering Bonerita where she shrieked simply, sharply, "No!"

The assassin in red samurai armor and demon mask charged through the stall frame and tore it up like the toilet paper Meteo threw in his face to distract him. He jumped up and launched a massive back kick with his good leg and knocked the samurai back a bit. Fazed, he readied a giant slash from above which Meteo was able to step back from. A horizontal slash came next and this was harder to dodge. He got scratched across the stomach. When the samurai approached again for a strong downward slash, Meteo was able to intercept and pull down. He let his grip off for a strong punch to the Samurai's face before regaining it. The samurai twisted the blade and used an avenue Meteo had not forced down upon and slashed upwards. Meteo dodged only slightly and had to be ready to dance around the next attacks without moving at all.

"Meteo, what the fuck is going on in here?" Mr. Fuckface said as he became aware and unmoved at the sight of a demonic Japanese warrior fighting a man trapped with a corpse in a toilet.

"I'm stuck! I need some help! Get me out of here!" Meteo said as he struggled thoroughly with the assassin and attacked.

"Oh, you're not going to be able to get your foot out of our model 26A0 Masterson... that's what we designed it for."

"Well, then get help!"

"What, and miss this show? Who died and made you everyone Sean Young has ever worked with?"

Meteo held onto the blade for dear life the last time he could catch it. He needed to hold it there for a few minutes as he tried his latest daring move.

The bolts from the floor were uplifted with Meteo's great concentrated strength. The body of the unnamed man fell over as Meteo lifted the toilet high into the air, turned sharply as he let go of the blade, and cracked it down on the samurai. The helmet split and so did the toilet as Meteo was released from two major conflicts in one fantastic move.

"Now that's what I call innovation!" Mr. Fuckface vociferated.

But as Meteo turned to walk away and call the authorities, a final decree of adrenaline got the samurai assassin to impale Meteo's leg with a hypodermic needle holding a green content.

Meteo's vision went first; the last image he saw of Zelda's sweet face twisting in concern. His feeling went second as he fell in her arms. His hearing went next as he heard her call his name in great distress and his smell went last as her perfume would likely be the last ion of her being to be recognized by his system as everything else was soon lost to the ocean of black he dove headfirst into.

* Three days later, but still one day earlier from previous events way at the top *

"Wake up, Meteo X."

A groggy shell of a fool stirred in his sleep atop the chair that bound him by the wrists and ankles. It was formerly an execution chair that had been converted to keep prisoners and read their thoughts via engineering creativity. What this villain found as he researched Meteo Xavier was an appalling lack of signals and presence; hell, they got better reception from the Formica table. It was decided then to go with more generic forms of torture. The delicious irony of using Meteo's fears and memories against him would be lost, but there was nothing that could be done about that.

"...get up, you *piiiiiiiiggggggggg!*" swelled the deranged voice of the conductor who had precious little patience as he beheld the vision of the knightly knave. Meteo's eyes opened with a start and he slowly began to take in whatever in the darkness that could produce form.

"Wha... what? Zelda? Where did you go?"

"She's long gone, Meteo. The dinner is long over. You've been asleep for three days."

"Three days?" Meteo absorbed with some difficulty. "Shit, I missed a job interview."

"Shut the fuck up!" screamed the vicarious virago from what was now a speaker-box in the ceiling. "Time and place have no meaning for you now. This is my world and you are the invading parasite that must be squashed!"

"Umm... I didn't come here myself; you brought me here."

"Shut the fuck up!" the voice cried with the essence of trying to save face. "Do you know who I am, Meteo?"

"I would assume if you wanted me to know your identity, you would just talk to me in person."

"Fuck the shut up! I mean... dammit!" there was a brief and frustrated pause before the shrill microphone scratched feedback and he returned. "I am the son of *Rhotharg the Zaramite*! The only child of the former reigning monarch of the former Republic of Diphtheria! The scared and sniveling child who watched in the freezing rain and storm as you dispatched the only family he had ever had in cold, brutal blood!"

"Wait... Rhotharg..." Meteo pondered, "Was that during the invasion of the Pale Crusaders? Yeah, I remember doing that; that was one of my first missions."

"Oh, how your God must bless you to love you... for if I had found you'd forgotten the day my life ceased to have meaning and all came crashing down by your sword, no description, no matter how great, could truly depict what I would do to end your trivial life once and for all."

"You were still going to torture me and kill me like you're going to do now, weren't you?"

"*Stop talking, you cheese-faced motherfucker!* Today, years and years later, I get the revenge I had savored for many, long, unpleasant years!"

"What is your name?" Meteo asked as he wiggled in the chair trying to get out.

"Hahaha. Do not be so impatient, it would prove boring to torture you in a chair. My name is *Fido.*"

"Fido!?" Meteo laughed. "L-like the dog? Fido!?"

"Laugh now, you inbred ingrate, for soon your throat will be so squelched with the burning sores of your screams that laughter will be but a far and distant memory..."

"Here boy! *Ruff Ruff!*" Meteo mocked. "Ooh, good doggy! *Bark, bark! Ruff!*"

"Shut the fuck up!"

"Ooh, does this bother you?" Meteo set his jaw line down. "*Meow? Me-yowwwwwwwwww... Meow!*"

"*Plug your gob, you degenerate demagogue!*" the voice left the microphone and a sound was heard. The iron shackles held around Meteo's arms and legs unsnapped and gave him free to access to the white rectangle opening before him.

"Step forward, Meteo X. This is the *Feast of 1000 Famines*! A festival of fear to saturate your weak soul before you die! Come! The dinner bell to Hell has rung!"

Meteo shrugged, rolled his eyes, plucked a few nose hairs and did exactly as he was told.

From the entrance to the room to the center of light where he was guided, Meteo walked until Fido instructed him to stop.

"Hey Fido, I was just wondering something." Meteo said casually. "If I beat your games here and take you out, is there any chance you could give me a ride back to my place? I need to make a call and maybe straighten something out..."

"You have far worse things to worry about than your temporary woman, Meteo X! Today, you will learn shame - the shame that I have felt every day since you felled my father in combat. Being a sickly boy, I could not even grasp the hilt of the blade I've wanted to stab your back with every waking moment of my life. My childhood is all I see when I think back, Meteo. The day you killed my father was the day I quit developing as a male heir to the throne and as an adult in the eyes of God. I am shame, Meteo. Shame made sickly flesh that has never stopped being sick because of you!"

Meteo gulped down hard on the exclamation point of that last sentence. What could be waiting for him in this dark?

"And now I want to make you sick, Meteo. Sick with shame! I want you to step back and literally *fuck your own face!*"

A light cut through the darkness to the shape before Meteo - a boxy frame of what genuinely was a box. On this box was the poorly scribbled and colored effigy of Meteo Xavier; a well sized hole cut into his mouth.

"Go on, then! Take that cock you keep strutting around the world out and start fucking yourself! Do it! Do it!"

Meteo sighed and shortly after dropped his pants. He was absolutely sure Tom Cruise and his armada of lawyers were waiting around the corner to pounce, but none such figure ever emerged from the darkness. Meteo inserted his member awkwardly into the effigy - the exact details of which will not be referenced here.

"Well, Meteo?" cried Fido as Meteo pulled his pants back up. "Do you feel shame? Is the taste of your own diseased cock tearing your soul apart? Do you yearn for the better days you used to have before now?"

"What was that you put in the box? Was that a pillow?"

"Indeed - it was the pillow I've spent many nights crying my eyes out into."

"It wasn't too bad." Meteo reviewed. "Not the best pillow I've ever had sex with, but it got the job done. I don't know... I don't feel shame; just kinda confused. I was expecting like a trap with hidden jaws that were going to cut or bite my testicles off."

"...shit, that would've been a great idea." he pouted. "Next!"

And another door to a similarly dark room in this underground lair inspired by however many psycho-slasher movies of yore opened wide to accept Meteo the same way women the world over accept the common gynecologist into their lives. Meteo entered and walked to another circle of light where the next trial was awaiting him.

"Fido, before we go any further, I just need you to know that I didn't kill your father out of cold blood, I did it because it was my job. Your father was a tyrannical maniac and hundreds of thousands of lives depended on me. There was nothing that could be done."

"...you're very bold, aren't you, Meteo?"

"Hell yes. I'm Meteo Xavier - I wear bold like a condom. That's what I do." Meteo said as he dipped his head down in reverence. "That's my job."

"Yes, and you wear that bold hat well, but it changes nothing. The last innumerate years where I struggled as a sickly man in arrested development do not change. The promise I made to myself that I would do anything to eradicate you will not change. My resolve to do everything in my power to make sure no sick child ever has to go through what I did *will-not-change!*"

Meteo could only barely hide his anxiety at what might come from the darkness next. His left leg started shaking a bit.

"Now feast your eyes on the next famine! Today you will learn humiliation! The same humiliation I feel every moment my eyes open to another empty day of harrow and heartache! My people, whatever is left of them, look upon me with heaviness and regret for my very birth! Their mighty King slain by a vulgar vagrant and the successor to the throne too weak from innate illness to grab even the smallest sword! The throne is no longer! I am naked in front of my people and I refuse to let your humiliation upon me continue unabated!"

The darkness was shut off and the room became white with light; filling Meteo's vision with a vanilla emptiness that was only obscured by the presence of himself and a cardboard box with a small puppy inside.

"You are going to breast-feed this dog on national television!"

From the ceiling come a small robotic arm that stopped at shoulder height and produced a small camera that broadcast Meteo to the world. Millions of sloppy, wet-seated individuals from every country in the world were tuned into the gaggling gallant as he held the puppy in his arms and were expecting a pretty good show.

"Well, Meteo? Where is your boldness now!?" cackled Fido.

"I don't understand what the point of this is." Meteo said as he held the twitching little puppy that demanded to be back on the ground.

"Stop your squabbling and put those milk-monsters to work, you great shitwart of Bethlehem!"

"Fido... no, not you..." he said as he brushed the puppy off of his legs. "Fido, first of all, contrary to surprisingly popular belief, I do not produce white substances with enough nutritional value to advance this puppy into its adulthood from my nipples," he lied, "and secondly, even if I could, what would be the point? I do things like this for a *living*. I do things people do not have the guts to do themselves for a price. I pay bills breast-feeding dogs and assassinating world leaders and ghostwriting biographies and licking doorknobs and so on. I've been on TV for years. None of this works on me."

There was a deep silence from Fido and indeed from the world at large as televisions sets clicked off and the camera reset itself back up to the ceiling.

The door to the next room where the next trial was lying in wait opened wide.

"Proceed..." Fido slurred as he clearly could only barely contain his shaking anger at Meteo Xavier's impetuous impudence. Meteo did as he was told and slowly advanced from one dark cube to another. His thoughts, much less bothered by dread now that the trials seem to be poorly thought out and hardly dangerous to anyone, much less a superman like Meteo Xavier, turned to Zelda. If there was any pain to be felt in this scheme, it was that he had to envision Zelda's pretty face drooping in disappointment that Meteo could not deliver the proper date she deserved. Once he had arrived, Meteo's heart inspired him to try again.

"Ok, Fido, if there is no way I can talk you into dropping me back off near civilization, is there anyway I could get you to maybe send someone something from me? I have this friend, you see..."

"Zelda is beyond your means, Meteo X!" Fido screamed from atop, "I already know this woman you covet. I have known her for many years and when I saw you with her in the restaurant that night, I was both vexed with your existence for coming into my world again and blessed with how open you made yourself to my long-awaited revenge."

"Fido, I'm beginning to believe that that assassin you sent after me was your best shot at revenge and I took him out quickly."

"Yes; you would know, wouldn't you? You are an assassin as well; you would certainly be prime to judge that quality of others... but what about yourself?"

Another robotic arm extended from the ceiling - this one a mechanical hand that, when opened up fully, contained a composite amount of $20,000.

"Go on. Take it."

Meteo stayed his arm at first; looking around in the same darkness that imbued every other room like this one for a possible weapon or double cross - none could be found. Wanting to desperately move this along already, Meteo took the money and pocketed it.

"Good. Today you will learn sadness! The sadness of every second of my waking life as I resign myself trapped in a nightmare from which no man-child can ever awake! The sadness of a boy missing his father - infinite tears filling an ocean of emotion that drowns the sick boy who just wanted to be a man like the man who came before him! The sadness of knowing that even if he succeeds at removing the thorn, his paw will still bleed; a little less maybe, but still bleed his childish tears from his childish heart."

"Fido, really now..."

The robotic arm returned, this time with a small revolver pistol in its hand. Meteo ducked and covered himself habitually - until he found that the gun, not the bullets, were for him.

"Go on. Take it."

Meteo took the revolver; steadying his shaky grip that came from a sudden intense need to take Fido seriously.

"Now then. I gave you the money and I gave you the weapon. You have all the tools you need to complete your next mission."

"*Mission?*"

Then the lights came on, but instead of a box or a puppy or a box with a puppy in it or a puppy with a box in it - it was a child. A lone little boy stood the circle of light; chained with tiny chains to the floor.

"You are going to shoot this child *in the face!*"

Meteo's eyes lifted in horror. Fido was serious this time. Meteo made the rookie mistake of underestimating his enemy and now it was either going to cost him his life, the life of a child, or both.

"Why do you hesitate, assassin? I paid you for a job and I expect results!"

"Fido, I understand it's a silly question right now, but are you fucking crazy? I'm not going to kill a *child!*"

"Oh, is that right? Where is your boldness now, heathen marksman!?"

"It doesn't work that way!" Meteo screamed; the first time fully emotionally defiant of this shadow man. "You don't just do crazy shit no one else would do and expect that to work. It's a matter of life and death! The wise men live and the fools die."

"Yet you are still alive, yes? You must be the exception that proves the rule. Either way, you're not leaving this room until you aim that pistol at that child's face and fire!"

Meteo's dilemma had grown. Had he taken a little more caution, he might not have been caught in this mess. Firing the plastic pistol was not an option, that much was certain, but what would Fido do if he didn't? What other traps lie in wait for Meteo to tread upon if he didn't shoot this child hostage smoking a cigar and coughing up a lung while a playboy magazine fell out from under his wig?

"What a minute..." Meteo inspected as he got a closer look at the "hostage". "The hell? You're not a child; you're a midget!"

"We're called *little people*, motherfucker."

Meteo's gripped tightened on the plastic pistol which squeezed in a way most pistols would not be able to do. He tugged at the trigger lightly until the little plastic flag popped out. Meteo rolled his eyes faster than the wheels on a bus and the worrisome look on his face disappeared under it.

"What the hell, Fido?"

"Does your soul sting with the sludge of sadness? Shall I fetch yon soiled pillow to drown out your tears as this day lives in infamy for as long as you walk the Earth?"

"Fido, I'm a dumbass and even I know this is stupid. I'm annoyed more than anything. Why didn't you have this famine as the humiliation one?"

"...excuse me?" Fido said in a rather obeisant tone that did not fit him well.

"Yeah, this could've easily been the part where you humiliate me in front of millions of people. I admit I bought it until the last second; so why didn't you think that far ahead? I mean, if it's obvious to a fool like me, why wouldn't it be obvious to you?"

"...shit, that would've been a great idea!"

"Fido, can I assume very simply that you're not actually a villain of any kind?"

"*What!?*" he screamed back in his despotic tone. "Who do you dare think you are to match words with me? I am death to you and my name is Fido! I am the son of the tyrant and like my father before me I will..."

"Fall at my hands!" Meteo shouted. "Let me out, Fido! The feast is over!"

"Very well!" Fido shouted and a door from the side lifted from the black wall. "Let us brush aside the other nine hundred, ninety-seven famines and go straight for the main course!"

Meteo laughed and, ignoring the pleas by the starving midget, he walked gracefully towards the door and inside the final cubic room with the overly predictable beam of light where the biggest of the big reveals was to take place.

"Fido, I don't know what you're planning," Meteo said with a swagger about his words, "But so far, you have demonstrated nothing short of a wildly amateur performance as a calculated villain. Usually the only people I fight as piss-poor as you are at this game are people who are doing this for the first time."

"Go on..." hissed the real thing as he hid in the shadows.

"Fido, I'm sorry for what happened to you over the loss of your father. You are clearly a man who was never meant to take up the sword and come after good people like me; yet you do it anyway. Evil men are not strong men, but weak men are not evil. I understand you now and I think we have no more business to discuss. You were bold to come after me like that and you even got me once. Very good. Now please accept my apology and let me on my way."

"What makes you think you're getting out of here alive?" Fido asked as some gears pushed against others from somewhere very close.

"The... fact that I'm leaving?"

"Sorry, I meant to turn on the lights as I asked that, I pushed the wrong button. Let's try it again." he cleared his throat. "What makes you think you're getting out of here alive?"

And as Fido had originally planned, the bright lights came on all at once, and before Meteo stood a bipedal suit of red mechanized armor some fifty feet tall with missile hangars and laser cannons every foot or so down. It stood just ten feet in front of Meteo Xavier and he could see a massive abdominal compartment where a large battery bomb, usually reserved for mechanical suicide missions, was *prairie-dogging it* out of the giant. Across its arms and legs were giant spikes; clean as a whistle. There were four arms on this slightly amphibious design; each holding a macroscopic replica of a famous sword or weapon throughout history. In its upper right was *Caladbolg*, the incisor of Satan; beneath it was *Muramasa*, the bleeding bastard's thief knife; opposite of it was *Thor's Hammer*; the concussion from Heaven and finally the *Ginsu* knife; which was alleged to be able to cut through magical objects like lead pipes and butter. On his shoulders were the barracks of two army platoons and the head was a giant chainsaw.

"Fido, I take back everything I've said up to now." said Meteo as he thought it best to relieve himself right then instead of waiting another five minutes when victory was hopeless.

"You're taking back the apology then?" said Fido as he trained all of his laser sights on Meteo X.

"You're never going to get away with this..." Meteo said as he looked for any weaknesses or chinks within the armor and set up.

"And why is that?"

"Because all I need to do is sever your power supply and you're done."

"Impossible."

"No, really, I can see it. Your armor is so big and bulky I could get under and behind easily and damage the supply without breaking a sweat."

"Shut the fuck up, you fuck-faced, shit-headed, cock-gobbling, *cum quasar!*"

"Watch your language, *cuntwart*." said the indomitable Mr. Fuckface from atop the rafters overlooking the giant. How he got up there with a toilet on his foot would drive a man insane to wonder, but it didn't matter because he jumped from the rafter, sailed down like an arrow, and broke the toilet into the power supply; immediately short circuiting all the programming from inside and detonating one or several explosive devices.

Both Meteo and Brad retreated to the room where the midget was still chained and starving. He did not have to suffer long for the resulting explosion concentrated the fire away from the bomb-proof walls of the underground and straight into the path of the doorway for which he stood. All was dust in its path. Meteo and his savior of the utmost surprising nature remained unharmed.

"That was incredible. Brad, what are doing here?"

"Fuck you. Am I not an angel? Do I not watch over you with my rainbow wings fluttering fast as I come to your aid?"

"I... I guess..."

"Well, quit thinking that faggot shit. I came here because I want to fuck you in the ass. Now bend the fuck over." Brad's wings covered Meteo only briefly as he was able to slip out.

"Maybe another time... I need to go see him."

"Why? He just tried to kill you!"

Meteo thought hard about that question; it was a question he asked himself many times as he got older and more accustomed to these situations. "Its part of the job." was always his answer.

Inside the smoky wreckage of the room, Meteo pulled off scorching hot iron after iron until he came across the beaten and disfigured image of a small, frail, and weak man who, it seems, hasn't grown or developed much since his late childhood. Meteo recognized the face now; except it was much older, smeared with soot, and crying different tears than before.

"Meteo..." the strained Fido said with his dying breaths. "Who... was that man?"

"Umm... that's Brad Sandley Donihe or Mr. Fuckface; I don't know. I guess he's an angel or something..."

"An angel... ha, how funny..." Fido spit up a mass of blood between his teeth. "I turned my back on God... so he sends one of his own down to teach me a lesson."

"I really don't think that's what was going on here, but think about it now, Fido. You went to all this trouble now and I didn't even move an inch for you to lose to me. This was not a path you were supposed to go down. Was your hatred really that strong for me? You know so much about me, but you could never past your rage to see me as I truly am?"

"Meteo... for most of what I can remember now, I chased you and you didn't even know it... I tailed you; I tried to kill you so many times, but life... or whatever you want to call this... would not let me finish the deed. I could not even get close enough for you to notice. I was never meant to be powerful like you or my father used to be. I cannot wield the sword that cuts down lives. I tried to be bold like you and wield the power of life and death for once... and I failed."

Fido coughed up a sizable chunk of something and choked pathetically on his own decompositional fluids. Soon he would be dead.

"My illness, the thing which robs me of my strength, only provided me one outlet to be a great man... to be powerful and use my weaknesses as a means for power. If I can not reclaim my honor by finishing you off, will you at least honor me by fulfilling my final obligation?"

"...yes, I will do this."

"In my office, just behind here, is a letter on my desk. Everything you need to know of what to do is in there. If anyone asks, just tell them I died of syphilis. Farewell, Meteo. I shall be privileged to see my father again. Farewell, *Meteo Xavierrrrrrrrrrrrrrrrrrr...*"

Minutes later, Meteo went back to the room he fended off a sexual assault by what was arguably one of God's representatives on Earth to thank him for saving him. In the room was a new toilet with a big pink ribbon on it and a shoe lodged inside with a note card saying "For Meteo." He turned his eyes back forward to what was without a doubt the most disturbing image he had ever seen as Brad climbed the mountain of flab and saddled Bonerita.

"That's for you, Meteo Xavier." cried Mr. Fuckface from on high. "It had never occurred to me that the future of the human waste management industry could be found on a man's foot. That's just the kind of innovation our industry needs. I'm proud I hired you. You are like the son I didn't eat for recreational purposes all throughout the 60's."

"Wow... I'm... I'm touched," Meteo stuttered out, certain it was another form of bad touching this freak was a prolific expert in. "For a second there, I thought you came back to rob me."

"You know, the thought had occurred, but then again I took your wallet from back at the restaurant so I figured we were even already."

Before Meteo could say anything, Mr. Fuckface spoke up again; in a new tone that wasn't brash, offensive, or anything having to do with bestiality.

"She's looking for you, by the way." He said smiling, "You should call her up tonight and meet with her tomorrow to finish the date."

"I can't actually..." Meteo said as he held up the opened letter in his hand. "I have plans tonight and tomorrow..."

"Well, I always knew you were a faggot. You're fired, faggot. Ride, Bonerita, ride! Yeehaw!" and he struck the back of her back with a crop. Bonerita reared back on her hind legs and launched forward; breaking through the ceiling to soar up into the stars.

Propelled by the gas that leaked from Bonerita at high jet speeds, it would be the last time Meteo would ever see them as they faded across the distance into the night sky; twinkling right under the northern star just before a mighty Djinn took aim and struck them down with a well-deserved catastrophic lighting strike igniting her fart path and spreading their excremental ashes over the ocean.

Meteo had no time for tearful goodbyes; it was time to rehearse for the big show!

* Present Day - Ruins *

The big show was an enormous disaster; so much so that real life disaster relief workers had to be called in to tend to the scores of helpless and lame peoples who needed to be rescued.

Meteo sat alone in the back dressing room and wiped the makeup off of his face. He tried not to feel too heavy-hearted as his entire life was one bold exercise after another - some that worked - others that didn't. This was another one of Meteo's failures that made him as famous as his successes.

Still, he hung his head low as he thought of the promise he made to Fido; the former Roscoe the Clown. Meteo felt shame, humiliation and sadness as he sat in that chair; the wreckage all around him, and only the image of his sad clown makeup staring back at him his own source of illumination.

"Knock, knock. Can I come in?" asked a sweet voice from nowhere.

"Who is it?" Meteo asked as he turned to see... Zelda...

She was standing in the doorway wearing a typical black coat with her shiny blonde hair drooping over it. Her eyes narrowed down slightly as she was aware of the slightly awkward reunion, but there was a smile on her face anyway and it gave Meteo great relief to see her.

"Hi. I've been looking for you." she said; her voice soft as cotton.

"Yeah, something came up and I... ummm..."

"I saw the show."

"Oh, did you?" Meteo asked; his sudden happiness now drowned down by overwhelming mortification as he turned back to the mirror.

"Yeah, I work with children. I don't think I ever got a chance to tell you that." She walked closer until she could put her hands on his shoulder. "I know what happened with Fido. Is that why you did this?"

"How did you know him?"

She settled her hands down over his chest and draped her arms around him as she slid. "He was my ex." she said softly and carefully. "I met him through my connections with this charity show. He had a lot of problems. He was very sick and self-abusive and had major inferiority issues. He used to blame everyone on this person who I find out, now, was you."

"Do you hate me now?"

"I would have..." she said as she dipped slightly to kiss his cheek, "But then I saw you on stage and I knew you were an honorable man. Roscoe was the one thing he felt he could do right, do it for the other sick children in the world, and give his life some meaning; away from the shame he thought he had in his other life."

"And I ruined it..."

"You were bold. It doesn't always work, but it always means something to stand up and do it."

Meteo smiled upon those words. It made him remember who he is and why he does what he does. When her hand crossed his chest, he took it into his and got up to walk her out to her car.

"By the way, have you seen Brad Donihe lately?"

"Nope."

"He sent me something the other day to 'thank me' for something. It was a brand new toilet with a red heeled shoe inside it. He called it a *ladies size four*..."

"Funny," Meteo said as he wrote down Zelda's phone number. "He sent me the same thing."

Also available from

www.BurningBulbPublishing.com

THE
BIG
BOOK
OF
BIZARRO

JAM PACKED
OVER
50
WEIRD TALES

EDITED BY
RICH BOTTLES JR. AND GARY LEE VINCENT

WARNING:
The book you now hold in your hands may be one
of the most controversial and dangerous books you'll
ever read.

The Big Book of Bizarro brings together the
peculiar prose of an international cast of
the most grotesquely-gonzo, genre-grinding
modern writers who ever put pen to paper
(or mouse to pad), including:

NIGHT OF THE LIVING DEAD horror writers
John Russo & George Kosana

HUSTLER MAGAZINE erotica contributors
Eva Hore & Andrée Lachapelle, and

Established Bizarro genre authors
D. Harlan Wilson, William Pauley III,
Laird Long, Richard Godwin and
so many more!

From Alien abductions to Zombie sex,
The Big Book of Bizarro contains
OVER FIFTY STORIES of the
most outrélandish transgressive fiction
that you'll ever lay your capricious
and curious hands upon!

Burning Bulb
PUBLISHING

www.BurningBulbPublishing.com

www.ingramcontent.com/pod-product-compliance
Lightning Source LLC
Chambersburg PA
CBHW070601130626
46556CB00001B/239